YELLOW FEVER

YELLOW FEVER

Ted Neachtain

RavensYard Publishing, Ltd.

ISBN 0-9667883-1-1

Library of Congress Catalogue Card Number:
99-074499

This book is a work of fiction. The persons and events depicted here
are drawn from the imagination of the author. Any similiarity
between the characters in this work and actual persons is unintended
and purely coincidental.

Dedicated to the women in my life who put up with the time it took.

_____

CHAPTER ONE

New York, March 1896

T he first time I saw Richard Harding Davis was at 4:30 p.m. on a rainy Tuesday in March 1896. He was sitting in my chair. Well, it wasn't really my chair. It was the chair and desk that Mr. Chapin, the assistant city editor of The World, had told me to use when I returned from my assignment. Desks and chairs were sparse in those days for freelancers working on space rates for New York City newspapers.

I had waited for two days for an assignment from Chapin, and now, as I stood dripping rain behind the chair, it looked like I would have to do battle for the chance to write it before deadline.

The story was simple enough. About 11 that morning a body had been pulled from the lower East River. They called them "floaters" in those days. For all I know they still call them that. But it's been some time since I was last near the East

River. At my age I don't pay attention to such things, though I do read the New York papers, and they still do devote much coverage to what we called "police news." Some things never change.

The police news assignment was my chance to get a position on the staff of The World. New York newspapers in those days worked with permanent staff, and a floating staff of freelancers who worked on space rates. The freelancers were generally men who could not latch onto a permanent job because they drank too much, or otherwise were unreliable. Some were young men like myself who had come into Manhattan from other towns, other newspapers, looking for a chance. It wasn't difficult to get an assignment as a freelancer, but it was tough to shine at it. The permanent staff got the best assignments, and a freelance needed luck. It was with me that day.

Mr. Chapin had called me over that afternoon and told me to chase the floater. His regular police beat reporters were busy with other work. It seemed a simple two-paragraph item, at best. I thanked Mr. Chapin and walked rapidly out of the third-floor cityroom. I didn't wait for the slow elevator. I bolted for the stairs. This was my chance to show my stuff.

I ran down Park Row to South Street in a light rain. I wasted precious minutes hunting for the pier where some longshoremen had found a body tangled in the pilings. By the time I arrived the police and dock workers had fished the corpse out of the dirty river. They hadn't covered it, and no one seemed to be looking around for a blanket. They just stood there and nervously stared at the body.

I introduced myself. Two policemen, beefy fellows in tight uniforms, grunted. Then they looked down at the girl. She was about 20, I guessed. Pretty, very pretty, though her hair was all tangled. She wore a brown dress, but no coat. Rain sprinkled her face. Her arms were out-flung, as if she were reaching for something. Nothing in this life.

"Do you know who she is?" I asked, looking from face to face. One of the policemen grumbled, "Ah, them coroners men can look through her pockets. I've not the heart for it." His brogue matched his red face. I knelt and searched for pockets in the twisted, soaked dress. There were none. The girl looked like she would awaken at any moment, and scream at my impertinence.

"She doesn't seem to have any wounds. No bullet or knife holes," I said.

"No," the second cop agreed. His helmet was too small for his large head. "From the looks of her, I would say she was a jumper. From the bridge." He looked upriver in the mist, toward the Brooklyn Bridge.

I stood there nervously wondering how I was going to turn an anonymous death as this one was, into a job on The World. To tell the truth, until that point the only other corpse I had ever seen was my grandmother, who had died three years earlier, when I still lived in Pittsfield.

I had been a newspaper reporter in Pittsfield, but I had left there a month before, deciding that I must work on The World. It was the newspaper, the one all news-papermen worth their salt read, and wanted to work for. They considered it to be the stuff, in a term of the day. That meant that it was the most important rag in the United States. Joe Pulitzer had made The World the single most influential paper anywhere. "Well, she ain't goin' anywhere," said one cop. He walked to the end of the pier. I looked at the dock workers. "Do you have anything we could cover her with. We can't leave her like this." A man nearly black with coal dust returned with a dirty oil cloth.

Within the hour the body was taken away by the coroner's in a battered ambulance. I walked down to the coroner's office, where I waited for an hour until a note brought a distracted doctor to my side.

"Are you a relative?" he asked. I mumbled something which he didn't hear.

"She died by drowning. She has a broken arm. Probably happened when she hit the water." He sighed.

"She was also pregnant."

He asked me to wait, to sign some papers. I told him I would return. He shrugged and went back into his workroom.

I trudged through the wet streets to police headquarters near Mulberry. The sergeant at the main desk had no more information than the original telegraph report of a floater. I went up to the second floor detectives' office. There, with his fat legs up on a wicker waste basket pulled close to his swivel chair, a red-face detective sat smoking a long cigar. He had just come from a saloon, I discovered soon enough when he breathed in my direction.

"What in hell you want?" he barked, as I looked nervously around the room.

The desks were in disarray, papers everywhere. Nothing seemed in order. I told him about the girl. He snorted, and then shifted the cigar in his mouth. "Another goddam leaper. We get two, three a day in here. Don't pay much attention to them. Somebody comes by and gives us an identity, we'll go over to the morgue. Girls killing themselves everyday in this town, fella.

"You'd be surprised how fast folks forget ya." I left him to his cigar and inertia. At this stage I was worried that this assignment was not going to turn out as I had planned. In fact, I doubted that I had more than a few brief paragraphs about the girl's death. Nothing much to recommend me to Mr. Chapin, let alone Joe Pulitzer.

I stood out in the rain for some time, depressed and wondering if I shouldn't just buy a ticket back to Pittsfield while I still had the the funds. I didn't have a hat and the rain trickled down my neck. For no important reason, I returned to the coroner's office. I was in luck, if you could call it that.

I arrived, shaking rain from my tweed coat, to see a distraught woman questioning the doctor with whom I had spoken. She said she was looking for her niece. She gave a description, and it fitted the dead girl. The doctor nodded, and took her into his workroom. I followed. There, on a large metal tray, lay the girl. The doctor had not sewn her back up. The woman took one look, and fainted. We carried her outside. The doctor helped me bring her around. Despite the shock, the woman began to speak. Between sobs, she told me the story. The dead girl's name was Jeanne Armiter, from Peekskill, where her parents lived. She was 21, and she had come to Manhattan the year before, to work. Her parents let her go, the aunt said, on the proviso that she live with the aunt. Miss Armiter had worked in a small department store on East 15th Street. In the hat department.

When I asked if Jeanne had a beau, the aunt nearly fainted again. She mumbled a name, that of a fellow who was a clerk in the same shop. I had enough at that point. I rudely looked at my pocket watch. It read: 4:05 p.m. I hadn't much time. I bolted from the coroner's office. It has bothered me since that I didn't properly apologize to the aunt. But, it's too late for that now.

After running back to Park Row, and up the grimy staircase to the third floor, was also worried that I would be out of luck because I wouldn't have time to pull it together for Mr. Chapin. Fortunately, he was not in sight when I headed for the desk and chair he had told me earlier I could use. It was near one of the dirty, smudged windows, but I was glad it had some milky light.

It also had an occupant. It was easy enough to recognize Richard Harding Davis sitting lazily in the chair I wanted to be in. He wore a light gray suit, high collar and tightly knitted tie of small red and white stripes. He smoked a cigarette, a novelty in that room of cigar smokers and chewers. Davis was recognizable from the Gibson pen and ink portraits of him in all the leading magazines. Davis was the epitome of the New York man-about-town. He was a man's man, and also crushing with the ladies.

He must have felt my sweaty presence behind him, because he turned in his chair, and said, "Oh, hello. You must be a new fellow. My name is Davis," he said, smiling. "Say hello to Steve Crane." He nodded to a sallow-looking young fellow slumped in the next chair. Crane nodded. I barely nodded in return.

"You should really carry an umbrella," Davis said. "The fellows here will laugh at you, but, you'd keep dry."

I shot a nervous look at the big wall clock which ran the lives of all in that building. It was getting late, and I decided that, star reporter or not, Mr. Davis would have to be dislodged. "Mr. Davis, I"m sorry, but Mr. Chapin told me to sit here when I returned from assignment. I don't have much time." Davis immediately popped out of the chair.

"Sorry, fellow. Didn't realize you were working here. C'mon Steve, let's go get a drink." With a nod, Davis walked away, followed by the barely awake-looking Crane. He, I noticed before grabbing paper and pencil, was more poorly dressed than I was. Crane was never much of a dresser, and this failing caused many to think he was a lazy Bohemian, instead of a serious journalist and writer. Crane was serious about many things, but not the ones that counted for first impressions.

I bent to my writing. I had composed a lead paragraph in my head while trotting back to Park Row, and it flowed easily, but the second and third pages were difficult. After that I had no trouble writing. I stopped at six pages, and walked nervously to Mr. Chapin's desk.

He sat at a desk on a raised platform. We later came to call it "The Pulpit." Chapin looked at my pages, then said, without looking up at me, "Didn't think you'd come back." I mumbled something and wandered back to my chair. Within minutes a copyboy, a youth with a large nose, named Rosenbloom, came by and said, "Mr. Chapin said to keep it coming." He wanted more. I was surprised. I had enough color notes to describe the dead girl in detail, her clothing, and the look on the policemen's faces. I put everything I had into the story. Naturally, I didn't write anything about the doctor telling me she had been in the family way. We did not refer to such things in those days. I gave Chapin the extra pages. He was busy reading through a pile of copy before him, snapping orders to a squad of copyboys, and occasionally laughing at something only he saw as funny. Before I left the World building that night I stopped at his desk and asked if there was anything he wanted me to handle the next day.

He looked up, startled. "See me tomorrow," he grunted in his sour way. I left, and to save carfare, walked to 23rd St. and Seventh Avenue, where I had a small room in a cheap boardinghouse.

I was in the cityroom by noon the next day. I grabbed a paper, scanned the front page, and was surprised to see my story on it, under a double-column headline which read:

Woman Drowned
Aunt Identifies Niece
Tells How

Girl Lived
And Died

I was in such shock that I could not make out the words I had written only the day before. I sat numbly at a desk. The copy editors had shortened my story. It was not quite as florid as I had written it, but essentially it was the same. I felt a pat on my back as I reread it. I turned to see Richard Harding Davis standing behind my chair. "Nice job, that," he said, smiling. "Had a nice feel to it. Most of them, you know, they aren't as neat. I've had my share of floaters." He nervously readjusted his derby. "Keep that up and you'll soon be on staff." He laughed. "They'll probably have to put you on staff to keep you from making too much money doing freelance. Say, what are you doing for lunch? I'm to meet Crane. He won't mind if you come along. But first I think you ought to tell me who you are. I already know your name, of course, but it would be polite of you to introduce yourself." He laughed again, an easy laugh. I stood. "My name is James Comming Botwright, and I'm from Pittsfield, Massachusetts. I graduated from Yale, and I've worked on a paper in Pittsfield." I also bowed. A minutes later we were walking on Park Row, heading for a German beer hall Davis said served the best wurst in town. The phrase made him laugh, so he repeated it a few times for his own enjoyment.

Davis was in excellent spirits that day, but then RHD always seemed to grasp life by both handles. I didn't know it at the time, but Dick Davis did not take up with every tramp reporter he came across. In fact, he snubbed most of the breed.

Crane was waiting for us when we got to the beer hall in Chambers Street. He looked the same, sallow, unshaven, and wearing what seemed like the same suit of dusty black coat and unpressed trousers.

"Steve, meet Jim Botwright of Yale and Pittsfield, Mass.

He wants to be a reporter." Crane smiled. Dick called for beers and platters.

"Of course, gentlemen, you're my guests." He said it forcefully, to quash any possible protest. There was none. In truth, I was nearly flat broke.

The beer arrived and we raised our steins in toast. "To adventure, and to report it," Dick said. Crane grunted. When the food was before us, Crane and I dug in, while Dick talked, and only picked at his plate. The wurst, I recall, was as good as Davis had promised. That was the day of the good 25-cent lunch, including a large slice of apple pie for dessert. I had been making do for weeks on free lunches in saloons. I had quickly tired of day-old boiled eggs and older cold cuts. I can remember that meal as if it were yesterday. Funny, I can't remember right off what I ate yesterday. The memory plays tricks.

Davis turned to me and asked what I wanted to do. I rubbed the wet stein on the wood bench before answering.

"Well, I'd like to get a chair on The World. I haven't done any writing outside of newspapers."

"I think you'll get your wish," Dick said. "But, for me, I'd rather work for Mr. Hearst. He's more liberal with his pocketbook. Mr. Pulitzer (he pronounced it Pew-litzer') is too cranky for me. I'm doing specials for Hearst. Want to keep my hand in, y'know. Sort of miss the run. I had a fine time on The Evening Sun. Jolly fine pals, there.

"I don't quite understand why you continue to write for newspapers when you can get $500 from Scribner's?" I said,

"It's the excitement, of course," Davis said. After Davis paid the bill we stood for a moment on the pavement, enjoying the sun which had broke through the clouds which had covered the city for days. Crane smiled and marched off down the street. Davis watched him go.

"That fellow has a wonderful future, if he lasts," he said in a low, serious voice.

We walked back to The World, chatting about New York. Chapin greeted us in the cityroom with a scream, "Goddamit. Where in hell have you been? Anyone who wants to work for The World had better be in this newsroom when an editor needs him." Chapin had a whining bark, a snarl one never got used to. It terrified most of the staff. Strangely, it didn't bother me that day.

"He was my guest at lunch, Mr. Chapin," Davis said easily. Chapin looked at Davis and walked away stiffly.

"Sit down. He'll forget it," Dick said. Davis treated Chapin as he would any other person, despite Chapin's rank and personality. Much has been said in jest about Richard Harding Davis, but the truth was he was a gentleman, even when he was dealing with the rude and nasty individuals we met in high and low places in our work. He went to war repeatedly, but Dick never lowered his standards, not even when he was on a dirty battlefield one thousand miles due east from civilization.

Many blackguards learned to their dismay that Davis brooked no scorn for his manner, or dress. Davis left a trail of broken noses, and among the ladies, broken hearts. He never sought fisticuffs, but many times he defended his own, or a friend's honor. Many fools miscalculated and saw only the Brooks Brothers finery, and not the heavyweight's muscle underneath it. Davis was not intimidated by princes, kings or queens. Or even newspaper publishers. Or even such fearsome creatures as city editors like Chapin. He treated them with the same respect he showed to waiters. A man like Chapin must have realized that he was unable to terrorize Davis and that realization made Chapin nervous around Davis.

I often think today about my awareness in those days what I knew, and what I thought I knew. I knew that I could make it, with the right breaks. I was nothing if not optimistic.

What I didn't know would fill books, perhaps one like this. I didn't know that the war going on between Mr. Hearst and Mr. Pulitzer had wider application than how many papers each sold in the dirty-opulent, rich-poor city. Or, that I would become one of the active participants in this war. Or that I would help push the United States into war, a war as simple and short as ever engaged in. or, as stupid a war ever to take the time and talents of Americans. And a war that killed.

I knew nothing then of war. Oh, yes, wars were fought in places like Greece, where Stevie Crane and Dick Davis had gone. But the America I knew had been at peace for 30 years. War was old-fashioned.

I met many of the players in the game that led to the battleground. I don't mind admitting that at the time I didn't understand, or suspect their motivations, or drives. I didn't always understand my own. It took years before I understood the forces that pushed me. I'm not entirely certain now that I understand them completely. Maybe that's maturity. All I know is that the world seemed to be 1,000 yards ahead in that foot race.

I cannot honestly say that I realized that in one day. It took some time, but we had that in those days. Nothing but time.

Later that same afternoon, as I sat ignored by the irate Chapin, I noticed two other men at his desk. One was tall, with a Van-Dyke beard. He was dressed all in black, like a mortician. He was waving his arms, and I could hear his rambling oaths across the cityroom.

"That son of a bitch mayor is not going to tell me where my delivery wagons cannot go. I will not stand for it, you hear." Chapin and the other man tried to calm the tall man.

I heard Chapin say, "We'll take care of it, sir. Don't you worry about it. Don't you worry." The bearded fellow spun on his heel and waved one arm angrily. Then he started to topple. He had collided with a deep metal trash bin. For a second it was as if the bearded man would fall head first into it. The soft-spoken man caught him in time, however, and righted him. Then the tall man was led by the arm out a nearby door.

And so I got my first look at Joe Pulitzer.

CHAPTER TWO

Not Responsible

I don't want to give the impression that Joe Pulitzer called me to his office before he made a move. Far from it. Reporters conducted their business under the supervision of a set of martinets specifically hired for that purpose. Pulitzer was nearly blind, and the slightest noise agitated him. But he was a marvel when it came to arranging his newspaper so that all its parts competed. The parts, in the reporter's world, meant editors. The reporters were field hands, and usually paid as such.

I was truly ignorant, despite my seat on the curb. Many things I learned later, in conversations. other things I pieced together, and much I surmised. All told, I knew about as much about what was going on around me as anyone ever does, in that day, or this. I knew that Mr. Pulitzer disliked Mr. Hearst. Joe didn't care for competitors, and he would snub Mr. Hearst every chance he got. Later, from Hearst, and others, I learned about one of their early meetings from Hearst's mutterings. This is the way he told me about it later:

Hearst was uncomfortable. The stiff white collar cut into his neck. He disliked getting duded up for these affairs. The fat woman on his right babbled on, something about supporting the museum. She belongs in one, Hearst thought.

"What a bunch of farts," Hearst thought. "This was New York society! What fools. Pulitzer was the only reason that he came. The chance to be in the same room with the publisher was too much to resist," he admitted to himself.

Hearst arrived early, and endured the chatter of fools, for the chance to see and speak with his number-one competitor, and what happens?

Kicking himself mentally for not stationing himself closer to the door, Hearst found himself in the back of the crush that formed when word spread that New York's most illustrious and most powerful publisher had arrived.

The bearded man was surrounded by two of his English secretaries, young, tall men who protected their master. They seemed to guide Pulitzer by the arms.

So the little bastard is going blind, Hearst thought from his post by the potted palms in the hotel ballroom. Hearst had heard that Joe Pulitzer was virtually blind, but he had discounted such reports.

Hearst had waited until the pushers had their fling at the little man, then he moved in.

"Mr. Pulitzer, I'm Hearst," he had said simply, extending his hand.

He saw that the dark, shorter man smiled.

"Yes, yes, so nice to meet you," Pulitzer said, almost by rote, in a heavy German accent.

"I just want to tell you how much I enjoy your World," Hearst said in his high voice, louder than he usually spoke. "And to tell you that I intend to make The Journal the first newspaper in New York. I intend to compete, but I want you to know firsthand that there's nothing personal in my goals."

The older man seemed to shudder, twisting his head to the right, then the left, as if he could see Hearst better with side vision.

"Well," Pulitzer replied, "together we have, what, eight or nine daily competitors. I live for competition," Mr. Hearst," Pulitzer said. He pronounced the name "Hurtz."

Pulitzer shuddered again, and with effort, said, "Since I have come to this city I have every day been in fight with other publishers. We have beat them," he said loudly, causing some heads to turn toward the two publishers.

At the outburst, the two male secretaries took Pulitzer by the arm, and tried to lead him away. They looked at Hearst with an irritation reserved for a parvenu who had dared to bother their ailing charge. As the trio tottered away, Hearst felt there was room, room for all kinds of success in the booming city

William Randolph Hearst knew already that he was the stuff of which gossip was made. In San Francisco they couldn't leave alone his association with theatrical women. So what?

Thus distracted, Hearst allowed himself to be led to dinner in the big ballroom. He sat and stared at a ravishing woman opposite him. She wore a lavender gown.

He stopped his reverie. Yes, he knew what they thought of him, the bumptious Westerner. He knew he frightened them. They didn't know how far he would go. They all had something to lose. He looked across the table at Crosswaithe, the banker, talking to someone's wife. How would she react if she found out that he liked black prostitutes, fat black women. And, the hostess, up there with her blonde wig. Would she faint if she knew how many knew about her coachman, and his afternoon visits to her room?

They all had their squalid secrets, he decided. His secrets were out in the open. He didn't care. He didn't need them. He had the people. They were all he needed.

For a few pennies he would give them something to remember. Thrills and excitement, all legal. He would give them a show. And, these bloated fools would moan and deplore. These whited sepulchers, these obnoxious asses. He wished he could print a paper one morning which would lay before the world their flaws, their hidden lives. They would pee blood. He would show them before he was finished.

He left before the last course, and the speeches. Pulitzer was gone, a ghost, and he tried to recall what the man had looked like. It didn't matter, he would meet the ghost on the streets each day, in glorious battle.

CHAPTER THREE

I Get the Call

I was put on The World's staff about a month later. It happened the way Dick Davis said it would. My income from freelancing at The World, and The Herald, got to $40 one week. I thought I was rich. Chapin called me aside in the cityroom at The World one afternoon and offered me $24 a week. I asked what run he had in mind.

"Well now, we'll have to see about that. Something always comes up. You'll take assignments like everyone else." And that's how I spent six months in Brooklyn.

Brooklyn in 1896 was another city. I moved over the bridge, to another cheap boardinghouse. The bridge had opened the town, and there was much talk of joining Brooklyn to Manhattan under one government. I was assigned to Brooklyn police headquarters, and it was interesting work. Crime in Brooklyn was under the franchise of small groups of yeggs who practiced burglary on home-loving

Brooklynites. That generally was the yeggs' downfall, as the good burghers were not as likely as Manhattanites to go out evenings. Nothing spoils a good robbery like an irate burgher brandishing a loaded shotgun. A lot of burglars lost an arm or leg this way. I wrote what seemed like one thousand articles on the problem, and the dozen of other problems caused by the growth of what had been a community of small villages into part of a major city. Then I got the call.

On a cold November day I was called to the wall phone in Brooklyn police headquarters. It was Mr. Chapin. He told me to report to Park Row the next day. We "district men" seldom went to the main office. The occasion, usually was for some reprimand, seldom for praise. I wondered what I had done.

There is a telephone hanging on every wall today. In newspaper offices every desk has one. It wasn't so in'96. The World had three, one in the cityroom, in a large box. Most of the old time reporters and editors refused to learn how to use it. It took a very calm personality, that's for sure. You had to crank the machine a certain number of times to get the central operator, and if he was busy you had to wait. Once you had the operator you had to pray that he understood the number you gave him, otherwise you would be speaking to a butcher in Harlem when you wanted to talk to a lady in Madison Square. I understood how the old timers felt. I felt the same way about the typewriter. Never could get used to the machine. I know it writes faster and clearer than any hand, but I think there are many occasions when the brain should work as slowly as the hand.

The next morning I marched over the bridge, wondering what was in store.

Park Row looked the same: a few short, cobbled streets to Chatham Square. City Hall park to the west, and the drab and bulky newspaper delivery wagons in front of the doors to the basement press room, waiting for the next edition. A few printers wearing ink-stained aprons loitered in front of the loading sheds, discussing horses and women, their favorite topics, in that order.

I always got along well with these Knights of the Stone. Most reporters I knew never bothered to know printers. Printers in my day were educated men, if only that they were travelers. In'96 the journeyman printer was common on papers around this country. After many a form was locked up, and hauled to the stereotype room, printers and I shared a few cigars and spoke of Boston, San Francisco and the wild town that was Denver. They told me about the cities they had worked in, listing good with the bad. They had eyes as good as the best reporters. Printers have to make quick judgments. I knew a three-point rule from a linotype machine, and I knew how to edit on the stone. Some reporters and editors thought they were being kind not to inflict printers with intelligent conversation, but it was just snobbism. In many cases it was the printer who snubbed the bulk of the white-collar crowd.

What was it Mencken said later? "I always got along with the man in the work shirt. It was the fellow in the dirty white collar I could not stand."

Printers had their own saloons and restaurants, even their own boardinghouses. While publishers paid dearly in New York for good reporters and editors, especially, they didn't give much thought for the men whose fingers and minds put their papers together each day, often saving the publisher from embarrassment or worse.

Mr. Hearst was the only publisher I ever saw who could talk with printers. He never seemed to get over his awe of them. They generally responded with good natured ribaldry. Hearst laughed at their jokes in that high-pitched voice, and bought them sandwiches and beer after the presses started to roll.

But, I'm getting ahead of myself. That cold morning I walked over the slippery cobbles, I was not in any rush to get to The World. I stopped in the lobby barber shop for a shave. Spruced, I walked into Perry's Drug Store, and through it to the backroom bar where newspapermen grabbed quick drinks. Two copy editors and two reporters were ending a night's drinking.

"Looks like you're gonna be working days from now on," one of the reporters said. I asked how so?

"You're being shifted to the evening side. Chapin wants you with him on The Evening World." He shuddered. There are few secrets on a newspaper. It is an organism which has as its main purpose the pulling of secrets from every other levels of society, only a portion of which it can print.

Thus, in such an organism the only possible way for a secret to stay one is for the individual to keep his mouth shut. But this is an impossibility in an organization which is as fluid as an army in battle. Promotions, demotions, awards for valor and reprimands are always known first by the troops who hear first from their own commanders, the editors.

It was often said correctly that there were no secrets under Joe Pulitzer's gold-domed building on Park Row. That was true. The building literally buzzed day long. Now, I was armed with what was in store for me. It was not a pleasing prospect, however.

The Evening World was, to be frank, a step-child. Mr. Pulitzer and his top editors seldom read it. The star reporters did not come from the evening edition. They came from the morning edition which lived, or tried to live up to the owner's command of accuracy, terseness, accuracy.

High ideals. The morning rags had the jump on the news. You see, not much real news happens from 1 a.m., when the morning paper presses roll, and 7 a.m. when the evening paper staff begins its day. So, from 7 a.m. to 6 p.m. when the last evening edition rolls, the staff must scamper to freshen each edition. Time between evening editions is measured in an hour or two, so what counts is the ability to write fast, and to have speedy reporter's legs.

I had just begun to master the morning paper writing style, short, crisp sentences, and short, crisp stories. Now, I had to relearn the afternoon style, under a stern taskmaster, Mr. Chapin. In later years my colleagues called him "that bastard Chapin." On the evidence I would have to agree that they had a case. I have to add that over the years I never had a serious difficulty with the man. I thought he was a thorough martinet, a soulless, gray-faced, mean-spirited man wedded to his job, but he was never a fool. He knew the news business. He knew newsmen. He had a sixth sense about where news was about to strike. He read anything. Many afternoons I spied him reading society columns. He would glean some nugget which would cause him to send a reporter pounding over to the courthouse in search of a good divorce action. He was usually right, too. Chapin had no illusions about the business of the world. Or, of The World. What he lacked was an apparent feeling for those who worked for him. He took sadistic delight in pushing them beyond the limit. Occasionally he showed some compassion, in a backhand sort of way.

Whatever illusions I had about New York, The World, and its staff went west that year. It was an education more than I ever got in New Haven, I'll say.

In the cityroom that long ago morning, I had less than a spirited heart. Thus do we all greet change. Chapin called me to his desk, and for him, told me with cheery remarks what a fine time we would have together on The Evening World. I thought that he was trying to cheer himself, for the appointment didn't mean that he was on the ladder for promotion to the top places in the Pulitzer empire. But Chapin didn't mind that terribly. He was a newspaperman, and with a newspaper, any kind, he was happy.

Chapin told me to take the day to break in.

"Where?" I asked. He smiled again. "Police headquarters," he barked. And then he bent to copy on his desk.

I walked slowly down to Mulberry Street, where the city's newspapers leased an old tenement to house the regular reporters who covered headquarters. To work on Mulberry Street was an important assignment in Manhattan. The only other more important beat on a paper was city hall, and of course, to be a foreign correspondent. I laugh about it now, but Washington was then considered a backwater, a place where city editors put reporters whose table manners were correct, but whose legs minds and skills were not up to competing in Manhattan.

The reporters' tenement at 115 Mulberry was an old three-story structure of red brick and peeling paint. Its principal feature was that it was close to headquarters. There was no luxury within its walls. Each paper had a small office, and there was a common room on the first floor. The were be a dozen or so men and boys lounging in the building waiting for news.

I walked in the front door. A big, blond man sat in the front room.

"Hello, how are you?" he said in a German accent. He stood and introduced himself as Jake Riis. He was then the most famous police reporter in the country. Of medium height, straight blond hair, regular features, wire-rim glasses, Riis looked more like a clerk in a Broad Street bond house than the reporter who was successful telling the fortunate how the unfortunate lived.

"You must be Botwright," he said. "Yes, word travels fast. We're reporters, you I know." He smiled. At that very moment there was a crash, and the thump of a heavy object falling down stairs. We ran to the doorway. There was a body slumped on the stairway.

"Oh, it's just Cahill. He drinks too much and can't manage the stairs." Riis lifted the drunken man into a sitting position, checked his limbs for damage, and together we pulled the unconscious reporter into the big room where we deposited him on the floor.

"I hope you don't have a problem with drink," Riis said in a soft voice.

"No," I said.

"Well, this place could give anyone a problem. They only drink to relieve the pressure, you know. I don't know one of them that does it just for fun." Riis smiled.

I never saw Jake Riis take a drink. Whiskey, it seemed, was the all-purpose drink among newspapermen. They kept bottles of it by their desks. Some said they drank to relax. Some to spur the muse. After work most drank to forget. And, to postpone the inevitable departure for the bare room where they lived, or their daily reunion with their poor families. To be truthful, I have met only a bare handful of reporters whose families were cared for properly. The Riis family was one of those. Jake saw early what city life did to those unable to afford the luxuries. He moved his wife and children to Long Island, and he didn't mind traveling to work. His extra income from his books, and especially from his lectures, allowed him to provide comfort for his children.

Jake was a success story, all right. A poor, dumb immigrant in the'70s, Riis couldn't speak English properly, but he managed to get on The Sun, and stay there. Jake wasn't much of a writer, and he knew it. His style was borrowed, and stolen. I doubt if he could have remained on The

World's staff solely on his writing ability. He envied us, he repeatedly told me.

Riis may not have been a cunning writer, but he was one hell of a running reporter. Riis even ran rooftops to get to a crime scene before us. His contacts within the police department were formidable, cultivated for years, and now many of the former clerks he knew now commanded precincts, and they remembered the lanky, yellow-haired reporter who had bought them cigars in earlier years. It paid off in news stories. We didn't compete with Riis. We tried to keep up.

All this complicated my life, and I looked back on the quiet days in Brooklyn with fondness. I had to keep one eye on Riis, and also watch Mr. Chapin. It didn't matter to Chapin that I had managed to develop a few stories in a week that Riis didn't have. The one I missed was the reason for catching Holy Hell from Chapin. Whenever that happened, I would be called into the office, just as Chapin was ending his usual 12-hour day.

"Well, Botwright, you seem to have fallen down again. I'm sure that there is a plausible excuse this time," he purred in his sour voice. Chapin rarely raised his voice, but everyone in the cityroom knew that I was getting a cannonade.

"Botwright, I've already fired one man today. A fool from Princeton. Thought he was reporter. I disabused him of that foolishness. Now, just because you have a degree from New Haven, you mustn't think that you're a reporter, at least not today."

Chapin smiled without changing the flat Atlantic Ocean coldness in his eyes.

"Yes, sir," was all I said. My attitude then was that nothing I could say would save me the scorching. I had noticed early in my relationship with Chapin that if anyone argued with him, or gave lame excuses, it only added fuel for his bombast. I just soldiered it out. There was no need to reply. Just stand and take it. And, it worked. Without another player in the game, Chapin was a loss for more evidence.

He knew, better than anyone in the cityroom, that Riis was a tough competitor. He knew because he had tried repeatedly to hire Riis away from The Sun. Riis himself told me this, adding that his loyalty to The Sun was absolute. Only death would dislodge him. Chapin understood this, and I think, respected Riis for it.

I simply didn't have the connections which Riis had built over the years with detectives and precinct officers. They would call Riis before making their official report to headquarters. Riis then gained precious minutes, and minutes in our game meant the difference between a glowing story for the next edition, or a clean miss. Riis, the lone wolf, would help the tyro, if he was asked. But, God help those reporters who expected that Riis would share news with them. Riis shared his news with readers of the Evening Sun.

At this distance it seems humorous that I once placed such concern over who had the first story about two Chinamen hacking each other with hatchets in Pell Street. But, then it was important.

The city was growing explosively. Once respectable neighborhoods were turned into tenement warrens. Crime, too, became a major concern of the respectable. There were streets in Manhattan, actually whole areas, where it wasn't safe to walk day or night. The police did not really help matters. They were drawn from the same immigrant pool, paid cheaply, and asked to devote their lives to a system that was purely political. The system also rewarded many of them in the form of regular bribes and payoffs. Many of the brighter policemen saw how it was, and turned in their uniform for the outright political life. A few climbed through the thickets to the top.

At best the New York Police Department of 1896 was a uniformed patrol service run by politicians. Tammany used the department to control the underworld elements who ran the wide-open saloon and dance hall businesses. We reporters heard that promotions to the rank of captain in the department cost the candidate $10,000, if the post was one where the new captain would have a lunge at easy boodle.

We reporters knew this. We heard stories. We listened to our contacts within the department. We chatted with Tammany heelers. Readers didn't gain our insight. The way the system worked rarely made it into print in New York newspapers. Reformers would rant occasionally, but the system was arrayed against them. The reformers might even be right, as when they attacked Tammany for allowing wide-open saloons, dance halls, bordellos to operate with the connivance of the authorities.

The authorities always put on a hurt face, and asked for evidence. Temporary shutdowns, and a flurry of arrests would follow any serious attack from the reformers. But the system continued. It was entrenched. The poor benefited, running various deadfalls of vice, the officials benefited from the vice graft, and elements in the respectable world, banks and other institutions, benefited from the ownership of real estate that was used for illegal purposes. At one time, Riis told me, one of the worst slum blocks in the city was owned by one of the most respectable, and oldest churches in Manhattan.

By nearly running myself into the ground for a few-months I was able to stay abreast of Riis in news gathering. But not pass him. I often worked seven days a week, counting that Riis would spend Sundays with his family.

Every day that Riis had a story I didn't have I would reply with an article I had dug up on my own, often an update on an old crime, or a piece on the inner workings of the police department.

Riis was on good terms with the new police commissioner, that Dutchman Roosevelt. But I found ways to go around him. My secret was to go out to the precincts where headquarters reporters seldom, if ever, ventured. It paid off.

The Dutchman was changing the department every day. He was very active, but most of the changes were strictly on the surface. I'm sure that Roosevelt knew about the underlying corruption in the department, but he, like so many others, decided not to tangle with it. Roosevelt became a hero to newspaper readers when it was reported that he would stalk patrolmen at night, to see if they were marching their beats properly. He launched a major campaign to change the police uniform. Surface stuff, but effective with city desks. Roosevelt seemed to have an instinct about what would get him in the headlines.

Teddy Roosevelt had not yet instituted his regulation that precinct captains had to tell headquarters when a reporter nosed around, so none of the other reporters knew I was at the 30th Street precinct house the night they brought Annie Hampton in. TR put the rule in afterward, because of what happened.

CHAPTER FOUR

A Shooting—January 16, 1897

I had gone up to the precinct to do yet another feature story about the harbor police. It seemed then editors could not get enough articles about the harbor police.

I'm sure the situation is the same today—subjects that strike the interest of editors, and are done to death. Editors in '97 wallowed in stories about the fearless police department, especially those worthies who took to the boats to fight hoodlums on and under the docks. Mr Chapin insisted we reporters all had to be on the lookout for Saturday features. So, I decided that another article about the harbor police, this time a timely retrospective about the man who was first assigned to the squad, would keep Chapin from keel-hauling me. The night of January 16, 1897 I went to the 30th St. Precinct house.

I had arranged for an interview with Captain Michael Teague, but I found on my arrival that he was out to dinner. Teague, as a sergeant 15 years before, had formed the first regular river patrols.

Talking to this cop made better sense to me than going out on the frozen river in an open boat for hours, all in the interests of another Saturday story. It is terribly difficult to make legible notes in a swaying boat in the middle of the cold Hudson. I waited impatiently near the front desk for Captain Teague, while the desk sergeant fed the house cat. I was about to call off the interview, when the station house door opened and two uniformed cops entered, half-carrying a young woman into the light and warmth. She was sobbing.

"Sergeant. This lady has been involved in a shooting on West 28th Street. In a cab," he added. I edged closer to the desk.

"Patrolman Moriarity and I were patrolling over near Broadway. Some fellow ran up and said there was gunfire. I got to the cab, opened the door, and there was this man, and the lady inside the hack. The fellow was over on his side, on the street side. He had a bullet wound in his head, on the right side. We found this pistol on the floor. Only one chamber fired, it looks like. We took this lady from the cab. She says her name is Ann Hampton. And that the man was her fiance, William Fitzmaurice."

"Sit her down over there," the sergeant pointed to a chair. Something about the names made my ears tingle. The sergeant looked displeased. He beckoned the patrolmen closer. "Looks like you two have ruined my nice quiet evening. I had planned to look in at Muldoon's in a bit. Now Teague will have us tearing all around." He sighed. "Well, it can't be helped. Now, tell me, what did you brave fellows do with the body?"

The patrolmen smiled at each other. "We left it in the cab, sergeant. Didn't want to just dump it on the street, y'know. Well, that's careful of yez. Did you by chance go through the pockets to ascertain who this corpse is?"

"Yes, Sergeant. We told you. He's William Fitzmaurice."

The patrolman placed a wallet on the desk. The sergeant hefted it. I recognized the name. I recalled from reading the society notes in The World that there was a clubman around town named Fitzmaurice. His family owned one of the biggest coal and lumber yards in the city. The family was not in the Rockefeller class, but the Fitzmaurices were definitely wealthy. Fitzmaurice must have died instantly, the cop said.

He explained that he told the hackman to take his cab and the corpse to the hospital in 34th Street officers walked the woman to the station house. I looked at the woman again. There were only three weak gas lamps on the walls of the big room, but the shadows from these lamps were not cruel to the girl. She looked about 20 or 22, although I was no real judge, and she could have been older. Her hair, that part which peeked out from beneath a large cartwheel hat, was the palest blonde. The purple hat matched the light colored coat that tightly fitted her figure. She was a handsome specimen.

It was at that point that I knew I was on to something which would keep Chapin quiet for some time. The problem was keeping the story to myself. There was plenty of time for word to seep downtown, alerting all the morning newspaper fellows. They would swarm over the precinct house when they got the word. As an afternoon paper reporter, I would be in the position of picking up the crumbs later. No siree, I decided. "Okay Moriarity. Take her upstairs to the detectives' room. And don't leave. Stay with her. Teague will be back any moment now." I walked back toward the hallway in the rear of the station house. The only telephone in the building was on the wall. I picked up the receiver, as if I were making a call. Instead, I took out my pocket knife, and cut the two wires near the wall. I pushed the ends of the wires back under the wood frame. With any luck that phone would not work that evening. I did all this as if by instinct. I had never before damaged police property. I climbed the staircase to the second floor. The hallway was dark. There was a commotion downstairs and I could hear voices. Soon Captain Teague, one of his plainclothes bulls, and a natty young man climbed iron stairs and entered the detectives' room. I eased close to the open doorway, staying in the shadows. Something kept me from just entering the room. "What happened, Miss?" Teague asked quietly. She sat with her face in her hands. She appeared overcome. "Can you tell us what happened, Miss Hampton?" When Teague called her by name it jogged my memory. Annie Hampton was a musical, stage performer. I had read an article in The World about her just a few weeks before. She had been appearing at the Casino-in-the-Bowery. "He shot himself In the cab," she sobbed. The young fellow suddenly stepped forward and said, "Do you want a lawyer?" She nodded. "My name is Michael Lawlor, and I'm a trial lawyer," he said. She looked at him with tears streaming down her face, and nodded again. "Captain, I wonder if I could have a few moments alone with Miss Hampton. I believe you heard her say that she wanted me to represent her." Teague looked irritated. "Mike, you pick up business in the damndest places" Teague nodded to the two policeman. "C'mon. Let him have some time with her. We got a lot of report writin' to do, anyway." I stood quietly in the shadows. I was tempted to follow Teague downstairs, but something held me. Since that night I have often wondered if I did the right thing. Once I mentioned it to Dick Davis. He laughed, and thought a minute, and said, "Well, they could have shut the door. You didn't misrepresent yourself. You were just there."

Lawlor moved a straight back chair to where the girl sat.

"Tell me about it?" he said softly. She began to sob again, and nervously she began to wave her arms, as if warding off blows. Lawlor looked at her arms, and then gently took them in his hands. He pressed her hands to her lap. "Be calm. It's all over now."

Then he began to roll her light dove gray gloves down her arms. She didn't resist. He pulled them free of her hands. He stuffed the gloves in his coat pocket. I nearly stepped into the room at that point to ask why? I wished later I had.

Downstairs, I could hear, all hell was breaking loose because the desk sergeant had discovered that the telephone was out of order. Some of the older station houses had telegraph lines to downtown, but in this place I was in luck. When Teague returned I stepped out of the shadows. What's happened?"

"Who the devil are you?" the commander asked. "Botwright, The World," I replied. "Oh, I had forgotten all about you. Listen, we have a shooting case here tonight which will take all my time. We can't talk now, okay?"

Lawlor heard us in the hallway and stepped out. "We have a young lady who was found in a cab with a dead man," Teague told me,

"Can I talk to her?"

"Captain, I believe that my client is to distraught to answer questions from a reporter."

"Well, maybe you can tell me your name, then?"

"Lawlor. Michael Lawlor, counselor at law, Fourteenth Street."

Downstairs Teague stopped me, and asked if I was going downtown. "Yes," I told him. "Fine, maybe you could carry a report to headquarters for us. Telephone is out." After 20 minutes of slow penmanship, Teague gave me an envelope which he sealed with wax.

I carefully wrote down Lawlor's name, address and telephone number. I wished all a pleasant good night, and walked out of the station house at a measured pace.

It was all I could do to keep from running.

During the cab ride down Broadway, I decided that the only safe place to work was in the cityroom, but even there was danger there, because of the number of loafers always about. They could spot a payday at another paper if they got a scent of the story. I had to be careful. Luck was with me. Chapin was still there. I pulled the startled Chapin into a nearby office, and quickly told him the story. His eyes glittered like a snake's. "Are you sure of the identification?" he asked.

I nodded. "Are you sure that no one else will have this story?" I nodded. He paced the small office. "We must confirm that Fitzmaurice's body was taken to the hospital. You must go uptown and see if you can find the cabdriver."

Chapin suddenly relaxed, and smiled. "I'm going to my hotel, and have dinner with my wife. I will return by 10 p.m. We will work on this tonight. Don't tell anyone about this, hear."

At the hospital I found a nurse who confirmed that a dead man had been brought in by a hackman earlier that evening. She directed me to the basement mortuary. There I found a young intern, barely awake over some medical books. Feigning indifference, I struck up a conversation. I told him I'd been sent to check on the identity of a man shot to death in a saloon brawl on West Street. The intern checked the record, and showed me that the only. listing for that day was for Fitzmaurice. Killed by gunshot.

I rushed back downtown, and much of the remainder of that night is a blur to me. It was one of those rare times when being a reporter provided a pinnacle of excitement.

I spent six hours writing the story which began on the next day's page one, and spilled over two other pages inside the newspaper. The facts were clear. The girl and Fitzmaurice were in the cab. There was a shot. Fitzmaurice was dead of a head wound. The girl said he had killed himself. No reason was apparent. The girl was questioned by police. I was able to fill out the account with descriptions of Miss Hampton, her manner, and comments.

Mr. Chapin danced in glee as he read the copy. I gave it to him page by page. He bounded around the empty newspaper-clipping room he had commandeered for our headquarters for the night. I believe my story ran to 20 pages, handwritten. I included Miss Hampton's stage reviews, culled from the clip file.

Chapin found a copyboy in the cityroom, a hulking product of the Five Points section, the toughest part of the Bowery. Chapin suggested that the youth could make himself $10 if he were able to get Chapin whatever documents and letters that could be found in Fitzmaurice's office. The implicit order to commit burglary did not faze the youth. He returned hours later with letters he found in the dead man's rolltop desk. Some were explosive, and they caused further sensations later that week, when we published some. They were love letters to Annie Hampton.

CHAPTER FIVE

Bombshell

F itzmaurice left a wife and two children in his Gramercy Park brownstone. The 38-year businessman had been considered a pillar of the old New York society. He had been a member of the correct Presbyterian Church, and two of the most exclusive clubs in Manhattan. He was also dead.

One thing I have to say in Chapin's favor: he didn't ask me to interview the dead man's wife or family. I never met them. I'm glad I didn't, in light of what happened later.

"I've arranged for a later first edition press run today," Chapin told me at dawn. Theoretically he should have asked for an hour earlier, but the canny Chapin saw a chance to sow the most confusion among the competition. The paper sold itself that day. Chapin had put a thick eight-column headline on the main story:

SOCIETY NOB KILLED IN TRYST WITH SHOW GIRL. Underneath were line drawings of the girl, and of the slain businessman. I never saved a copy.

I was near collapse, drained. "Here, here, Botwright, I'm sending a copyboy out for a double order of Welch rarebit, and several of bottles of porter. You've earned it." I was famished, and the food revived me.

"I've done everything but carry the report over to headquarters," I told Chapin. He laughed.

"Here, give it to me. I'll send one of our slower dunderheads over there with specific instructions." That last twist gave us a couple of extra house before the report was found—later than morning by confused and angry top police brass.

Chapin put me in a cab, and I slept most the rest of the day. It was later on, from Dick Davis, and Jake Riis, that I learned about the commotion that I had caused. If I had set off a dynamite device in the middle of Broad Street, I could not have stirred up more activity in every cityroom on Park Row. I learned later that The Evening World's appearance that morning was greeted at first with amazement, then disbelief. There were assertions that it was all a hoax. But these same reporters and editors knew that professionals did not play hoaxes with real persons, or real homicides. It was too dangerous.

Then, came the frantic calls and messengers sent tumbling into the streets and to the police shack on Mulberry. Reporters there were as stunned as their editors. They ran to headquarters, to find that no one there knew anything about it. It was impossible to call the precinct; the phone lines were broken.

Some of the reporters, including Riis, jumped into cabs and bolted to 30th Street. Their pell mell arrival was greeted by amazement by the desk sergeant, and Captain Teague. The startled cops confirmed the major points. But, by the time the reporters were able to get it all down, and get back to their offices, they had missed many evening paper deadlines. Riis was able to get an abbreviated story in the last two editions of The Evening Sun, because he telephoned his office from a private home on 30th Street.

My joy from the enterprise was solely in besting Jake Riis. It was sheer luck, but I played the story the way he would have. I knew that he would hold no grudge against me for it.

"Young fellow, you really had us running the other day. That was a good job," Riis said, when I next saw him. He knew there was always another story down the street.

"Jim, I was having lunch at the Hoffman House and your story was topic number one everywhere in the building. It was a bombshell," Davis told me. Chapin called me aside the next day. "You're in line for a bonus. You did quick work in pulling the story together, but the bonus is for recognizing the elements of a first class news story. Respectable clubman, showgirl, shooting, mystery. It was all there." Storms broke in other cityrooms that day. Editors howled at other reporters. Angry police officials searched for Teague's report, and wondered why they had to read about a sensational murder in The Evening World.

And that wasn't the end of it. The story continued for four more days. We had the letters, of course. Chapin held them until the third day, when it seemed that the other papers would think the story had subsided. The letters were conventional love letters all dated about a year earlier. They were a potent circulation builder. I had to tone some of them down, as they were not fit for public print. I never learned how he had gotten them back. Fitzmaurice's death had caused a major stir in New York society. I learned later that strings were pulled, to try to get the story out of the paper. Society was not upset so much by what happened, but how it was reported. Society likes to appear in newspapers on its own terms, and dislikes to appear on page one under screaming banner headlines.

"Where is Ann Hampton?" Chapin yelled to me on the second day. I did not know. A week later she appeared at a coroner's hearing, where the crush of reporters and newspaper artists was overwhelming.

"He begged me to marry him," she sobbed. "I refused because of his family. Then," she said, "he pulled out the pistol and threatened to shoot himself."

"What did you do then?" she was asked.

"Nothing," she said in a low voice.

The day after the hearing I was ordered to appear in Police Commissioner Roosevelt's office. The Dutchman, we called him. I entered the large wood-paneled chamber quietly. Roosevelt stood by his desk. He began to read me the riot act about the loss of the official report from Teague. I resented being lectured by the big-toothed poseur. I supposed that other reporters and editors had complained en masse about the way they had missed the story.

"I'm surprised that a man like yourself, educated in New Haven, would be a party to this kind of deception," the Dutchman roared at me. I held my tongue. I wanted to shout back that any one of the other reporters or editors would have done the same. I had seen Teddy in operation before that day, and frankly, I was not too impressed. He had always struck me as an opportunist, using whatever post he held at the moment, for advancement to the next, regardless of who or what he had to step on to get to it. Not many of the reporters who worked at police headquarters liked the man. Oh, sure, after he became President, there were those who tried to make you believe that they had a close personal relationship, It become fashionable to appear that they were old pals. I was not among them.

Roosevelt was one of our first activist politicians, I decided later. He and Andy Jackson would have made a fine pair. They might have understood each other.

TR ranted for minutes that day. I kept quiet. I supposed that he was also feeling pressure from within the closed ranks of Society, of which he was a blessed member, about how the "mess" had become more than a short, sad obituary.

Chapin quickly put me on the chase, after Miss Hampton. I was not alone, as it seems that the entire Manhattan press corps had the same assignment. She had fallen off the earth for us, however. She was not to be found. My hero's laurel was wearing thin with Chapin. I knew I had to keep ahead. I trudged up to 14th Street, where I found Lawlor in a second floor office. His clipping file at The World said he was 32, and well connected with Tammany. He was one of those people, another reporter told me, you found elected officials deferring to at political dinners. He was, in a word, a "fixer." It was an important job in a day when many of the elected officials of the City of New York could barely read and write, let alone plan political deals. Lawlor worked in a paneled office. Instead of the usual rolltop desk, he had a flat, library-type table, which allowed him to spill legal papers over its acreage.

"I know what you want, but I don't think you're going to get it," he said by way of greeting. "My client wants privacy."

"She'll have to go before the grand jury."

"That's only because that assistant district attorney wants another batch of headlines. He won't listen to reason."

The day before the DA's office had announced that a grand jury would investigate the shooting. As I stood to leave, I wondered what I could say to this cold-eyed man to make him give up his client for an interview.

"I was impressed by you that night, Mr. Lawlor, the way

you kept Teague from asking her more questions. I saw it all, from the hallway"

Lawlor's head snapped up. "You were there then?"

"Yes, I was in the station house on another matter and I heard about all of it." I smiled.

To my surprise Lawlor jumped out of his chair, and began to pace the office. "You know, perhaps it might be wise for Miss Hampton to talk to a reporter, perhaps for your paper." I was surprised at the turnaround, and told him so. He shrugged.

"Look, I have her sequestered. For her own protection, you understand. If I took you to her, would you give me your word you wouldn't print her whereabouts?"

"Sure. It's not important where she is, but what she says. Besides, I'd like to keep the interview to myself.

Lawlor nodded. "Meet me here at noon tomorrow."

Chapin was glum when I returned that day to the city-room. "It must have been blackmail," he sneered. What was? The reason she shot him, he replied. Who? Annie Hampton, he yelled.

"I'll ask her. I'm going to interview her tomorrow."

"You get me an interview with that bit of fluff and I'll give you Saturday off, " he said. "Coming right up," I said. The next day Lawlor and I took a hack across the bridge, to Court Street, where Lawlor insisted we change cabs. He was afraid we were being followed. Lawlor told the cabby to take us to a hotel somewhere in Flushing. The ride cost $4.50 enormous sum, and we were deposited in front of an inn. Flushing was still a rural hamlet. I believe it had two inns. Annie was in the one on Main Street. When Lawlor knocked on her door, she opened it quickly. She was surprised to see me. She was wearing a white, floor-length wrapper, and her glorious hair was loose around her shoulders.

"Hello, Mike," she said, staring at me. I stared back. I

decided that her stare was an open and direct as a tigress's and it was no contest. I also noted that she had called Lawlor by his first name. Rather unusual, I thought. I was to learn that a lot of things were rather unusual.

She waved us into her rooms, which consisted of a parlor, and a bedroom. They were simply furnished. It was not the Astor House. Lawlor introduced us. Annie looked me over with that level gaze. I decided then that this woman was no sheltered innocent. At Lawlor's insistence, she agreed to answer my questions.

"Where do you come from?" She looked at Lawlor. He nodded.

"Buffalo."

Is Hampton your real name?"

"No. It's a stage name. My real name is Probst. Ann Probst."

"Where are your parents?"

"They live in Buffalo. They run a small store there." She looked down at her hands. " They don't want to see me since I went on the stage," she said in a softer voice.

"When did you leave Buffalo?"

"When I was 17. I joined a traveling troupe. That was seven years ago." So, she was at least 24, perhaps older.

Annie sat in a plush chair as we talked. Her wrapper fell open, revealing a white nightgown. And some ankle. But she made no move to close it. I thought it odd that it was nearly 3 p.m., and she was still wearing a nightgown. But, I didn't make a comment on it.

"How long did you know Mr. Fitzmaurice?"

"About two years. He saw me in one of my musicals, and sent flowers backstage. Then, he came backstage. That happens a lot," she said, with a sigh.

Before I could ask another question, she continued, "He was very nice at the beginning. I didn't know he was married. I didn't know anything about him. He told me later on. When he wanted to marry me."

"Had you ever seen him with a pistol before?"

"No.

"When did you see Fitzmaurice?" She looked startled at that question. She rearranged her wrapper.

"Ah, well, he would take me to supper, after my performances. Sometimes he would come around in the afternoon and we would go for carriage rides to Harlem."

"When did he tell you he was married?"

A silence. "I don't recall. Maybe a few months ago." She dropped her eyes, and it appeared that she would cry.

After a moment, she told me that Fitzmaurice had showered her with flowers and candy from the start. She said she tried to discourage him, believing that he was just another stage door Lothario. Then she found out he was married. Fitzmaurice persisted, and eventually she relented. She became his mistress, and he took her to suppers at Churchill's and Delmonico's. Davis told me later that he recalled seeing her at those restaurants, and noting that she didn't look like a woman who needed vigilant protection from a parental guardian. He said that she looked like a high-class whore.

"He begged me to go away with him, to Cleveland, to Chicago, on business trips. I went with him when I could."

"Did he say he was prepared to give up his wife and family to marry you?"

"Yes. He said it many times. But I would not agree. I didn't think it would last.

"That night I told Bill I would not marry him. At first he wouldn't believe me, and when I told him I was serious, he pulled out that pistol"

I believed her. She told a simple story simply, without theatrics, and it was impossible not to sympathize with her.

I looked around, and saw Lawlor sitting in a corner of

the room he looked bored by it all. I found it difficult to break away from the interview. Her magnetism held me. But a few minutes later Lawlor cleared his throat, and we made our departure.

The interview, naturally, wrote itself. Mr. Chapin chuckled over each page of it as it hit the city desk. "This is the real stuff, Botwright," he yelled.

The other reporters glared at me from under their derbies. They were envious that I was pleasing their tormentor. I would thus be exempt for a grace period from Chapin's scathing broadsides.

The interview ran on page one the next day, with a line drawing of Annie, as I described her to one of the World's artists, Frederick Remington. Fred was a nervous little fellow. He made a name for himself in the war, and because of his cowboy paintings. To us then he was just another staff artist. Every paper had them. They were almost as numerous as reporters. Pulitzer believed the public wanted pictures as well as words, if not more so. Pulitzer felt that he sold papers to immigrants who couldn't read well, but they could understand the pictures. I guess he was correct.

Of course, the interview was another sensation. It appeared on a day of February snow. I had a run of pleasant weeks afterward, basking in the warm glow of Mr. Chapin's good feelings. It was later that I imagined what she had done.

_____

CHAPTER SIX

Talk of Denver

I n March, Annie appeared before a grand jury. Two
weeks later, to everyone's surprise, she was indicted
for murder. I was stunned by the news. The courthouse accounts had it that the district attorney's
office had found the hackman, or rather, he had
come forward, and he told a story which indicated
that the couple had argued violently before the fatal
shot was fired. Most importantly, he said that Annie
had done most of the screaming. She would have
Lawlor as defense counsel.

One evening, after reinforcing my courage with
two drinks at Perry's in The World's lobby, I
approached Chapin at his desk, and asked if I could
cover the trial.

"We have reporters at the courthouse," he grumbled through cigar smoke.

"But, it's my story," I replied lamely. He looked at
me, shook his head, and said, "All right."

That was two days before I got the first phone call

from her. She left a message at The World, and it was sent down to police headquarters. I was surprised. The note said to call her at 5 p.m. that day. There was no mention of Lawlor. I was nervous when I called. She asked me to come to an apartment on Eighth Street. I arrived about 7;30 p.m., and found her dressed, but apparently upset.

"I'm out of work, because of this indictment." She paced the parlor room of her four-room apartment. It was elegantly furnished, I thought, for someone out of work. "I cannot get any bookings. The agents say they are afraid to hire me."

"What can I do?"

"You could do another article. I do need work." She pouted.

"I suppose." She smiled. Her golden hair, now piled high on her head, framed a fair, beaming face. "I would be so grateful. Now, that's settled. Have you had any dinner?" Within minutes we were on our way to the Hoffman House. We dined on crab and champagne. It cost me $8, but I was unaware of money. She was enchanting.

"You have no idea how hard life on the stage is. A woman alone has to put up with all sorts of things. Many think that going on the stage is the same as a life of sin. Imagine! Other women are the worst. It's hard even finding a place to live. Boardinghouses that will take in all kinds of drummers and scalawags turn me away."

I noted that the other women in the restaurant stared openly at her, as did their escorts. The women were judging competition. I don't think anyone noticed her because of the newspaper stories, but just because she was a beautiful woman. The newspaper drawings, in truth, did not do her justice. She was not exactly a Charles Dana Gibson beauty of the period. She was thinner, and not as full bosomed, but she could gather an audience.

It's hard at this distance now to recall which of her features were the most compelling. Her eyes were large, blue and somehow very chill.

They didn't laugh when her lips smiled. Her hands were small, and I recall that most often they were covered in public. She favored elbow length gloves of a pale gray.

"Why do you wear gloves all the time?"

"Tell me about your work?" She neatly changed the subject. I guess her compelling feature was her directness. She simply did not have female wiles. She didn't fall back on simpering or flattery, as many girls did and still do, I guess. She gave the impression of being as direct as a man. I guessed that was because of her work, singing and dancing and traveling the country.

Of course we went back to her apartment. It was natural. We sipped port on a small sofa. We spoke softly. She wanted to know about my work. I managed to work myself closer to her.

Within a few moments it all got serious. By then we were touching, then kissing. It was all very pleasant. I don't know what I was thinking, but it was all pleasant in memory. There was nothing hectic about it, just a slide into passionate embrace. She helped me unbutton the front of her dress. It had a dozen buttons, it seemed. I pushed the straps of her chemise down her shoulders, and revealed her breasts in the light of a single gas jet in the room.

I kissed each of her breasts slowly. She took both my hands and pulled me to my feet. She drew me into her bedroom, where I sat on the edge of her wide bed.

She quickly undressed, and helped me hang my clothing on a chair. It all seemed so natural.

Despite the chill of the room, we stood in embrace for some minutes, kissing each other on the lips, face, neck and arms. We could barely see the other in the darkness. She opened her legs to my growing manhood, and soon we were in bed, where I took her not once but twice.

I was not inexperienced. At New Haven I had gone with the other fellows to one or another of the houses. The discrete ones, which catered to the college. While a reporter in Pittsfield I had joined some of the older men from the office who occasionally went to a house. They usually went after a winning night at poker.

That night with Annie was a winning night for me. She was insatiable. Annie was a sensual woman, like some of the girls I had known in the houses. Annie was also beautiful and physically desirable. Our lovemaking was slow. The whores were always in a rush, to get to the next dollar, I guess. You may gather that until that night I had not been with a woman who was not a whore. You'd be correct, depending on how you define the word.

"Jim?"

"Yes."

"You'll help me, won't you?" Sure, I said, rolling toward her caress. I left about 3 a.m. It didn't occur to me to stay. I guess I could have. The truth was I was so involved with the woman that I could not stand talk of Denver or Chicago. We bedded regularly. My senses came alive. She was inventive. And passionate. I believe we spent more time in bed than in her parlor. I know we carried on more conversations after lovemaking then before.

One evening, after I had taken her to see the performance at the Casino, we rested after our exertions. Her head rested on my stomach.

"The trial is to start next week." I had forgotten it entirely.

"We shouldn't meet. The district attorney," she said softly, "might have a detective watching me."

"Did Lawlor tell you this?"

"Yes." That evening was the last time, I sensed. I ached with the loss.

"Then let's go away. Somewhere. Europe. California."

She raised her head to mine. "I can't. If I leave I'll convict myself. You wouldn't want that. We would have to run all the time." She was right, of course.

The next afternoon, in a fit of conscience, I approached Chapin and suggested he find someone else to cover her trial.

"What the hell is this? You made a gigantic issue of following through on this story. Now you come to me and say you want to pass it up? Get your goddam stupid ass over there, or you're through."

There was no way I could easily explain to Chapin that I didn't want to cover the murder trial of my lover. No way, then, or ever. I guess Chapin would have listened to my story, with his snake eyes impassive through the telling. At the end he would have laughed, I'm sure. "Why, you goddam fool. It's too bad we can't print that story. She's a whore and you're a fool." And, I'm sure he would have fired me on the spot, had he known even a part of the truth. His action would not have been based on any conventional morality, but because Mr. Chapin never allowed anything to get between him and a story. Chapin never socialized with his staff. Yet, others have told me that he would be seen occasionally at The Haymarket, and in other Tenderloin haunts, in the company of editors from other papers. The Haymarket was a notorious saloon on the Westside where the worst elements enjoyed riotously the life of drink, dance, and sex. The hall was a major display case for pimps' wares. Most nights the place boasted hundreds of young, and sometimes attractive prostitutes. The Haymarket survived for years because the owners paid the police handsomely. That was another argument I had with Roosevelt. He adamantly refused to look corruption in the face. New York was an open city, to a large extent, with the lower elements allowed to do what they wanted, provided they did not unnecessarily disturb the gentry.

And, Roosevelt was in place to insure that the gentry were not disturbed. Oh, yes, TR walked around Manhattan at night, trying to catch patrolmen asleep. But he never ventured into The Haymarket, where on any night you could have found a dozen policemen. The police controlled the underworld elements, and profited from them. Roosevelt, the reading public's pleasure, was more concerned with choosing new uniform styles for the force. He would not look life in the face. And that's not an unusual failing, or one that has diminished to this day.

The trial started on Tuesday, June 15, a hot day. Jury selection in the crowded courtroom was tedious, because Lawlor was careful to exclude all the late middle age and elderly men the bailiff drew from his list. When it was finally chosen, the jury was told to come back the next day for openings. The crowd was larger the second day. I've suspected that Lawlor played one or another of his political cards by arranging to have the Hon. Judge Michael Murrane sit as trial judge. Murrane was Tammany hack, and he gave Lawlor free rein in the courtroom.

"Your honor! Gentlemen of the jury. My client is innocent of this charge of murder. She is guilty only of being pursued by a wealthy, and single-minded family man who, when it dawned on him that he could not have his fancy, killed himself in her presence. What more punishment does the state wish to inflict on my client?"

Lawlor's opening made for a batch of headlines. That afternoon, the prosecutor, a short, red-haired lawyer named Travers Jerome, told the jury that Annie killed when her blackmail would not work.

"Why should Fitzmaurice kill himself? He had everything a man could want. He never owned the death weapon. He had no pistol. Before his death he did not act like a man about to take his own life." Jerome gave a straightforward, unemotional presentation. I was impressed. More grist for readers. I was kept busy, too busy to think. In my front row seat I wrote frantically all day long. I passed the scrawled sheets to a succession of copyboys who fled with them to make the next edition. After the trial ended, I was pressed into writing each day yet another story for The Morning World, an advance forecast of the next day's testimony.

Annie and I sat ten feet apart, but we didn't speak or as much as nod during the two-week trial. Lawlor had hired three beefy private detectives, as they kept the curious away from her, and shielded her from the other reporters.

Lawlor presented a few witnesses who testified that Fitzmaurice had pursued Annie in the typical stage door fashion.

The hackman, it turned out to be the prime witness, on whom the case could have turned. Jerome was smart enough to make the cabman his principal witness.

"Yeh. I heard them two in the cab. They hailed me at 23rd Street, and told me to take em uptown. She was a looker, all right," the cabman said, looking straight at Annie, and earning a gaveling from Judge Murrane.

"What did they argue about?" the prosecutor asked.

"Well, yr honor, that was hard to tell. It was just loud voices. Not at first, mind ya. I try not to listen to me passengers." He smiled all around the courtroom, begging the audience to believe him.

"Well, were you able to make out any of their conversation?"

"Well, you see, your honor, I did hear her yell the word marriage. Yes, I did." He nodded.

"Did you hear anything right before the gunshot?"

"I can't recall exactly. I was watching the traffic, you know how it is. It was busy on the street. You have to keep your wits about you, that's for sure. I did hear their voices, and I heard her yell. I heard, or thought I heard a few words."

Lawlor was on his feet in a second. "Objection, the witness said he thought he heard conversation. He either did, or he didn't." The judge thought that one over for a minute or so, and ruled that the jury had to disregard the previous testimony. The cabman looked puzzled.

Mr. Jerome started afresh. "Where did you pick up Fitzmaurice and the woman?"

"Downtown. By city hall. He was a smart looking fare. I thought" The hack driver stopped, and looked embarrassed.

"Thought what?" Jerome demanded.

The witness crimsoned. "Well when they got into the cab, well, I thought that I would get a good tip from this nob." Some of the jurors chuckled. The judge rapped for order.

"Well, as it turned out, I didn't get a cent, and it cost me money to carry his body to the hospital. But, I don't think he shot himself."

"Objection," shouted Lawlor. The judge looked puzzled. "The witness will answer the question about what he saw and heard, not what conclusions he drew."

Jerome tried another tack. "Was there something you observed that made you believe that Fitzmaurice did not shoot himself ?"

"Yes."

"Objection!"

Judge Murrane thought a bit, and said, "Well, the witness can answer if he saw something."

"What did you see?" Jerome asked.

"Well, when the fellow got into the cab I noticed that he was wearing a snug coat and trousers. No overcoat, even though it was cold and drizzling. I noticed that. I also noticed that he wasn't carrying no pistol."

"Objection!"

Judge Murrane asked the next question. "How would you be able to tell whether or not he was carrying a pistol?"

The coachman warmed to the inquiry. "Well, your honor, when you've driven a hack as long as I have, and been held up as many times, you learn to look quick as who gets in your cab. The gentleman had no place to carry a bulge like a pistol. But, the woman."

"Objection!"

We never learned how or where the woman could have carried a pistol aboard that cab. The judge ruled the jury had to disregard the last part of the hackman's answer. Afterward, Jerome called Mrs. Fitzmaurice to the witness stand. She was a gray little woman, neat and small-voiced. She was an unwilling witness, and I believe that Jerome damaged his case by calling her. Jerome may have felt compelled to, as there was no one else to speak for the dead man. Mrs. Fitzmaurice denied in a weak voice that her husband had strayed. Every man on the jury had the evidence before him in the form of the defendant that Fitzmaurice was attending to duties outside his home. Before his turn came there was major speculation that Lawlor would put Annie on the witness stand. Lawlor refused to tell us, and therefore the day he began the defense, scalpers were selling seats in the courtroom. Lawlor began that sunny morning with the assertion that Annie had no reason to kill Fitzmaurice.

He slammed one fist into the other. He said she was the one pursued. He yelled that she owned no pistol. Why, he shouted, would a woman shoot a man with a hackman nearby as a witness? It didn't make any sense. Lawlor made fine theatrics. The jury sat motionless through the harangue. Annie, dressed in a mauve, floor-length dress, sat composed at the defense table. She barely moved through the presentation. She looked at Lawlor with that level gaze. She did not cry out, sob, or faint.

Many of the other reporters seemed disappointed that she did not act the hysterical woman. They expected it. It added color to the already dramatic proceedings. The shocker came when Lawlor told the judge that his client would not testify in her own behalf. He said there was nothing she could add that hadn't been said. Somehow I wasn't surprised by this move.

The jury retired at 1 p.m. a day later, and by 5 p.m. Annie Hampton was a free woman, exonerated of all charges by the beaming jurymen. They appeared pleased by their civic action. Some said later that their deliberations took so long because they didn't want it to appear that they had reached a verdict even before entering the closed room.

The trial made me weary. I felt bone tired. I slept as if drugged., but it was not a refreshing sleep. On the following Monday I got a call to report to The World. A smiling Chapin met me and nervously told me that we would be seeing Mr. Pulitzer in a few minutes. I was in a daze. It was later I figured that she was making her plans with Lawlor.

CHAPTER SEVEN

Star Reporter

W orld reporters seldom saw Joe Pulitzer. His eyesight and nervous condition were so far gone by then that he rarely appeared in the offices. He remained most of the year in a soundproofed mansion uptown, or on his yacht, because he found the motion of the sea soothing. Folks sometimes ask me what he was like. The truth is that World reporters seldom thought about the man. Herald reporters, on the other hand, were always concerned that the wrath of James Gordon Bennett Jr. would come down on their heads, even from Paris, where Bennett lived most of the year. But Pulitzer, he was a ghost publisher. One worked for Joe, but only a few knew the man. I was not one of them.

But that day, Chapin escorted me to Pulitzer's plush office up under the gold dome, a richly paneled and carpeted lair. The tall thin bearded figure stood behind his flat, clean desk. Male secretaries stood at his side. They were English; he preferred the soft accent. They read Pulitzer every word published in his World every day.

In his soft, guttural accent, Pulitzer said, "Godammit, Botwright, you have done a fine job. The way you grabbed that story did The World a service. Anyone who does the World a service gets my respect." Chapin, usually the most outspoken person in the cityroom, stood uncharacteristically silent throughout the entire interview. Pulitzer said I had a fine future. And then he gave me the $100 cash bonus. In an envelope. Then he shook my hand.

"I hope you have something else up your sleeve, Botwright," Pulitzer said. "Something which we can hit the sonsabitches on the head." He meant the other papers, their editors, and reporters. I left Pulitzer smiling. Chapin and I backed out of the office, as if from royalty. We were especially careful not to make much noise.

I was supposed to go back to work. If I had everything might have been different. Instead, Chapin grabbed me by the elbow, once we got back to the cityroom. "Hey! Go take some time for yourself. I won't look for you till the end of the week. Take a slide." He walked away quickly, before I could reply. I could have protested, but with the $100 in my pocket, I decided to take the offer.

I knew what I wanted to do, but it was not possible. Annie had moved, I soon discovered from her landlady. She had moved during the trial, and had not returned. Lawlor, however, was still in his 14th Street office. He smiled, but did not rise when I entered his office.

"Well, how is the star reporter?"

"Where's Annie?"

He shrugged. "Maybe Chicago. Maybe San Francisco. Gone, perhaps for good."

"How can I find her?"

"Botwright, you don't want to find that woman. You

had your rendezvous with her. You came out undamaged. That should be enough. Consider yourself lucky. Luckier than Fitzmaurice.

"Are you saying that she killed Fitzmaurice?"

Lawlor shrugged, and reached for a cigar.

"Why did you take her case that night if you thought she killed him? I was surprised how quickly you became her lawyer."

"Botwright," he sighed. "A trial lawyer makes a career with successful cases. Acquittals bring business. I knew she could bring business."

"You didn't think she was innocent?"

"No. Of course not. She killed him, all right."

I was stunned by his blasé attitude. Then I recalled something. "Why did you take her gloves off the night you first met her, in the police station?"

Lawlor laughed. "I thought you knew. You were the smart reporter who saw it all. At least that's what I told Annie before she took up with you.

"I took the gloves off so the police would not see the powder burns on them. There were gun powder smears all over that lovely right hand glove." Lawlor laughed to himself. "She had planned it all carefully. Women are so vain.

"I really thought you knew all along," Lawlor said.

Later on I had difficulty recalling how I left Lawlor's office, or what, if anything, I said before I did. That is wiped clean in my memory. I don't recall where I started drinking that day, or how long I drank.

Dick Davis said later that I had been on my own for about three weeks, by his reckoning. It could have been that long. In this life, anything is possible. Even being a foolish accessory to a murderess.

CHAPTER EIGHT

Caskets on a Table

Now that many years have passed, I can look back without much pain. I still don't know if I went on that bender because Lawlor had confirmed what I already knew—that she had killed Fitzmaurice, or because she had left. Or, because I belatedly realized that I had been taken for a grand fool.

I wasn't missed in the cityroom. In those days reporters were expected regularly to go off on binges. That's why there was a floating crew of freelances around all the time. Most reporters drank quite heavily. It came with the job. Whiskey bottles sat openly in the newsroom. Most editorial workers said the alcohol relaxed them, and eased the tensions under which they slaved all day. It also helped to keep them sane. At least the ones it didn't drive insane. My colleagues drank heavily to blot out what they saw in the line of duty. And drink was cheap then.

You can only take so many corpses and deadlines. And meager pay.

Dick Davis told me years afterward that he came looking for me shortly after his return from London. He had covered Victoria's Jubilee for Hearst. Dick loved London. Most of his fans, even his enemies thought he liked nothing better than to suit up and run off to war. Wrong. Dick soldiered with the best of them, but he really preferred a suite in a London hotel, and plenty of fancy dinner invitations.

Hearst had paid Davis $3,000 for his London chore. Dick could afford to have his dinner clothing custom tailored in London. When he got back he came looking for me, he said, to recount his English adventures. He walked into the World's cityroom one morning and approached Chapin.

"Beats goddam hell out of me where Botwright is," Chapin said, noting Davis' discomfort with the strong language. Davis did not use oaths, or profanity, at least not in company.

"I gave him a couple of free days after that Hampton trial, and he hasn't returned. If he doesn't show soon, I'm gonna give his chair to a freelance. Can't hold it forever. This is a metropolitan newspaper, not a charity ward."

"Hold it until I get back to you." Davis said Chapin merely grunted. Davis returned to his apartment at 108 Waverly Place, where he had a telephone. Swiftly, Davis called around to the various reporters he knew, and asked that anyone who spotted me to call him. For a new nights Dick went out himself to search a variety of deadfalls. He knew them all, from places in Chinatown, to tough Bowery dram shops where you couldn't drink the liquor with safety. He patrolled the Tenderloin, checking a score of hooker halls on the Westside.

A plainclothesman spotted me eventually in one of these halls, and he called Riis. Riis called Dick. Soon Dick appeared at my dirty elbow. "Hello, Jim," he said. I must have looked a mess I tried to resist when Dick moved to take me from the place. Davis knocked me senseless. I was not match for his boxing ability. I woke at his apartment hours later. It was dark. I ached.

"Well, old man, how are you feeling? You look like the wrath of God. What's this all about? You were never much of a drinker." After I could stand, Davis hustled me to the door, and into a cab, and next to a Turkish bath on 14th Street.

I was surly, and tried to escape from the cab. My spirits were bleak. It was impossible, however, to elope from Dick's grasp. The man had a grip of iron.

We spent most of the night in the bath. The steam cooked the alcohol out of me, and I was left very weak. We were pounded by a masseur and shaved. I slept afterward, and in the morning Dick shook me and handed over some fresh clothing—his own. He had tossed my filthy trousers into a trash barrel.

I was weak, but sober, and I managed to walk down 14th Street to a restaurant.

We ordered breakfast. I drank about a gallon of coffee, before I found the strength to tell Dick the story. He listened without saying a word.

"And Lawlor seemed so damned unconcerned. He had gotten his acquittal, and was waiting for his new clients to come pounding through the door. She was gone, to God knows where, and I was a party to it all"

Davis sat quietly for a few moments, looking out the window at the crowds hurrying by on their way to the day's work.

"Well," he said, " I should think I would've tossed Mr. Lawlor out his office window, hunted down that woman, and then gone on a spree. You have come through a mighty big fire, old chap."

Davis smiled. He signaled the waiter for more coffee. "Today you go down to Park Row, and you apologize to Chapin. He has held your chair for you. I wouldn't speak to him of these events. There is no need now for others to know." I nodded agreement.

When Davis and I parted that morning, I felt I had a new parole on life, one presented to me by a man I hardly knew but felt I had known all my life. It was cool that June morning, so I walked downtown. By the time I reached The World I had begun to feel myself again. Even the musty air and stale cigar smoke smelled welcoming. I went to my chair, sat, and picked up a morning edition. The stories made little sense to me. I had returned to the world in the midst of controversies of which I knew nothing. It was as if I had been on the moon.

"Mr. Chapin wants t'see ya," one of the copyboys growled at me a half hour later. I went to Chapin's desk. He sat as usual, in coat and hat, reading copy, and scowling.

"Had to put Miller in headquarters. You'll work out of this office now. That's if you're still working. You have anything to tell me?"

"No, sir," I said. He grunted. I went back to my chair, while the other reporters and editors walked around me as if they didn't want to excite Mr. Chapin's displeasure by being too friendly. After a day or so, when they saw that I wasn't being punished, they approached. Chapin gave me small, time-consuming assignments. And, that helped, because they forced me to keep my mind on my job. I was busy. The Evening World had embarked on another of its crusades while I was away. The onset of summer had brought with it a diphtheria epidemic which was killing scores of children and adults in the city. The World felt, wrongly, it later turned out, that the widespread horse droppings from 25,000 horses in the city added to the disease's spread.

With all the medical advances today, it's hard to remember the fear and panic that widespread disease caused in the 1890s. Then it seemed like each year brought a new epidemic. And, through it all the constant problems, like consumption, struck men, women and children. Then the best medical specialists could only identify most diseases, not cure them. One lived with the constant fear and panic. I've often wondered how much that fact added to a form of fatalism about life.

Lately, there have been certain books, and films about the era, and a phrase has been coined, The Gay Nineties. It's a false phrase, I believe. There was little gay about the period, now that I look back on it. In the midst of that life we knew it was deadly serious. The major difference between that time and this is that now we have a feeling that we're more in control. It may be a false sense of security, but nonetheless it's there.

Then, we didn't know what caused diphtheria, but we saw that its ravages were quick and cruel, particularly in children.

One morning, I guess it was in mid-summer, I was sent to talk with parents who had lost children to the epidemic. I climbed to the second floor of an old tenement on Water Street. The apartment consisted of three large rooms, divided by old blankets tacked to the door frames.

Two white-painted, small caskets rested on a parlor table.

I had been wandering along the street, asking if anyone knew of recent deaths. One old woman pointed me to the tenement.

The boxes were about a yard long. Each was open and contained a shriveled little body, each dressed in a white smock. The children, a boy, six, and a girl, four, had died the day before. Their father, a burly man about 30 was named Michael Owens. He told me he worked for the Broadway Transit Co., as a hack driver. He answered my questions from a wood chair against a wall. He held a nearly full bottle of whiskey in one beefy hand. Three other men sat on chairs in the hot, gloomy room. A woman's wail punctuated our conversation.

"They came down sick last week. They've not been sick much. Just a sniffle here and there. In the winter, is all." Mr. Owens passed the bottle. The men took gulps from it. The day's heat was building up to stifle the tenement.

"I've been paying into a burial society, you know. Damn if I ever thought I would have to use it for them," he said in low anger. He turned toward the caskets, which looked like the only cool things in that room. His face crumpled then. He sagged, slid from the chair to the floor, and tears began to run down his cheeks and pelt the floor. I walked through to the next room.

Two women were attempting to pour whiskey down the throat of a disheveled woman whose face was bright red from grief and sobbing. She gasped, breathing through her mouth in big gulps, before muttering and screaming. She was near collapse. I beckoned to one of the women.

"What were their names?" She looked at the blanket-covered doorway.

"John and Alice," she said, "Why?"

I introduced myself. "My God," she said, "make them do something. The World can make them do something. We can't take more of this." She sounded close to collapse herself.

"Last week it was my nephew. Three, he was, Now this. Six babies on this street have died this month. When will it end?" she hissed.

I touched her shoulder, to comfort her. I had no words.

But I stammered, "We're trying to get better sanitary conditions," I said, lamely.

"She said them sanitary conditions was the problem," the woman said.

"Who said that?" I asked.

"That nurse, the one upstairs. She's the only one comes around here since this evil started. But she don't stop them from getting it. But at least she's here.

I climbed a set of rickety, smelly stairs to the roof. Tenants had made improvised shelters, and tied pieces of canvas to make sleeping tents there. They lived and slept on the roof, to escape the baking apartments day and night. The roof was small improvement. Children huddled under this makeshift shade; some were obviously ill. The tarry roof was soft underfoot. I looked around in the glare and saw a woman in a long, tan dress kneeling by a child's pallet, bathing a little girl with a large sponge from a basin of water.

"Where's the nurse?" I asked. The woman looked up at me from beneath a large straw hat. She had large brown eyes, a long straight nose, and a firm mouth. She continued to bathe the girl.

"I'm the nurse," she said. I quickly explained my mission. She stared at me. I asked for whom she worked.

"I'm from the Lutheran Settlement House on Grand Street." She sat back on her heels then, and used her left arm to wipe perspiration from her face. She was weary. She looked like she was on the losing side of a war. The girl on the pallet shuddered, and then seemed to fall into a feverish sleep.

"We must isolate them. Do you understand? So the contagion won't spread. But where can we put them? There is no room." She stood. She was a tall woman, about an inch taller than I was. She stooped, picked up her bag, and walked away. I followed. She stopped frequently to check on a child or an adult. She spoke her instructions in a strong voice, with hint of an accent.

"Will you tell me your name?"

She looked at me. "What for?"

"So I put in my account all the information about your work here." She turned away, moving toward the next tent. "My name is Hilda. Hilda Reiser."

I left her there on the roof, facing a score of sickly children and adults. I went to city hall, walking slowly in the steamy streets. A nervous under official, all the top officials being away at their places in Long Branch, told me that the city did not have extra money to clean the streets. This official, who sat in a darkened office with the drapes closed against the glare, said that city regulations forbade his department from accepting Pulitzer's $5,000 gift to clean the streets. Depressed by what I had seen, tired, and sweaty, I walked across City Hall Park to Park Row, and to The World. The third floor cityroom was virtually empty, even though it was 3 p.m. "What have you got?" Chapin barked from his desk. I told him about the dead children, their parents, the nurse and what the city official had said.

"Give me all of it," he said. "If this contagion goes on any longer we won't be able to print newspapers. I have six reporters out sick, or drunk, and the print shop tells me they have no idea how many men will show for work tomorrow morning." He sighed. "Give me all you've got."

I shed my coat, removed my collar, loosened my braces, and eased myself slowly into one of the warped and much used editorial chairs. It was a comfort to be seated, but it wasn't much cooler than on the street. We didn't have many electric fans in those days. We had palm fans you waved in front of your face.

"You might as well take your hat off," Chapin barked. I began the story slowly, describing the small caskets in the

70   YELLOW FEVER

front room. I wrote down what the father had said. The words were poignant. Three pages done, I got to the roof and its occupants. I described Miss Reiser in detail, calling her a tall strong angel of mercy, one of the few these unfortunates of that district would see before the real thing. I noticed that my scribbled notes did not contain any of her remarks. Yet, I was able to recall everything she had told me. My story went six pages. Chapin walked to my desk after he had read it. "Give me more," he said. I was able to write another two pages.

I left the deserted cityroom about 8 p.m. The sun was dropping in the Hudson, and it felt just as hot as night came on. I walked slowly toward the bridge. The others on the street moved as if drugged. Newsboys stayed in the shadows of buildings. Their normally raucous voices were stilled. I was approached by a woman as dusk settled. I curtly shook my head no, and she shrugged and walked on. I stopped in a saloon, and had three iced beers and a cold sandwich, before going to my apartment, and falling into my bed, weary but able to fall asleep for the first time in many nights.

CHAPTER NINE

New York—August 3, 1897

few days later I found a letter in my mail slot at the office. It was from William R. Hearst, publisher of The Journal. He asked me to call on him. I was surprised. That same afternoon I had a visitor, the Rev. Gunther Reiser, a Lutheran minister. I met him in the sales department on the first floor of The World. I shook hands with a tall, blond man with a smiling face.

"I just want to thank you for what you wrote about Hilda and her work. She has been too busy to come and thank you herself."

"She impressed me very much," I said.

"Well, there is so much to do, and not enough nurses and doctors who are willing to do it. We exist on church donations, you know."

"You have a wonderful daughter."

"Yes, I know. But I worry constantly that she will become ill from those she helps. Well, thank you again." He shook my hand, and strode from the building. I was too preoccupied with the letter from Hearst to have shown Rev. Reiser more courtesy. I was puzzled by the letter, and unsure what to do. There was one man in Manhattan who could help me. I called Dick Davis and told him I would like to see him. We made a dinner appointment. Later, a storm broke over the city. Afterward it was cooler.

We were quickly seated at our table in Jack's when the waiter recognized Davis. Dick was truly a man about-town. Over whiskey cocktails I told Dick about the note from Hearst.

"He's seen your work, and he wants your services, Jim. That's all there is to it."

"I don't know if I want to leave The World."

"Well, that's up to you. You can make more money with Hearst. What are you paid now? about $40 a week?"

"Yes, but it's not the money."

"Jim, don't ever forget the money. It's the only thing which will give you the freedom to do what you want to do. At least it's given me that freedom.

"Listen," Dick said, leaning over the table so as to keep the conversation between us, "Willie is in battle with Joe Pulitzer, and part of his strategy is hiring away World reporters. It's an opportunity. You may not like working for Hearst, but you'll be able to afford a better apartment, and pleasant dinners like this one we're going to have right now." Davis opened the big menu.

I changed the subject, and spoke of the contagion story, and meeting the nurse on the tenement roof. "Yes, I saw your story. It was well done.

"It's funny. I've seen death in a dozen places, and in war, but I don't think I could take seeing children die. Seems so senseless."

"It's happening every day, all over this city," I said. In the midst of such morbid talk we ordered bisque, broiled lobster, and a cold Chablis, and it was all excellent. Despite the talk of death, the mood of the restaurant led us to laughter. Davis spun anecdotes about himself, his family, and he spoke warmly of their home in Marion on Cape Cod.

"I'm going up there next week. You'll come along and we'll have a proper outing."

"If I go with Hearst I don't know where 1'11 be next week."

Dick laughed. "Let me give you a piece of advice. Before you see Willie, buy a new suit, and a pair of shoes-the best you can afford. It'll be a wise investment. You're looking a bit worn these days, old fellow. You have lost some weight, and your suit is just hanging on you. Willie wants the quality, and he's willing to pay for it. But you have to impress him with more than your writing. He'll ask you what you want to do. What'll you tell him?"

I chewed a mouthful of lobster. "I guess that I would want to work in the city, on some beat."

"Why not be a correspondent?"

"I don't think I would make a good correspondent." I took a sip of wine.

"You'll never know until you try it." Dick then launched another story, "Say, have I ever told you of the time I walked my pet snake down the street at Lehigh?" It was a funny story about Dick's introduction to college life. Even though Davis was then 33, his attitudes in great measure were those of a college freshman. He never lost his enthusiasm. His critics called him Richard-The-Lion - Hearted, but they were mistaken if they thought he didn't have his wits about him all the time.

After dessert, Dick suggested a drink at his club. As we were leaving the restaurant, I saw them.

She had red hair. Piled atop her head. She wore a white dress. He was leaning across the table, in earnest conversation with her. They were seated at a table against a far wall. I don't think they saw us when we arrived, although I couldn't tell who had arrived first. I stared at her in shock as Davis handled the bill. While Lawlor spoke to her, she looked up, in my direction. She stared for a moment, with no reaction, then she looked back to Lawlor. Dick and I left, went to his club, where I had two quick drinks. Davis watched me down the drinks. "Anything the matter?" he asked quietly. I told him that they had been in the restaurant.

"Well, I guess your tracks will cross in this town. I thought you had said she had gone west?" I nodded. "Does she still bother you that much?" Again, I nodded. I felt a combination of anger, disgust, and I must admit, a lust for her. Davis tried to bring me about.

"I think you should ask Willie for $100 a week, plus expenses." Dick sat in a comfortable chair, drink in hand. I smiled, and nodded, my mind elsewhere. My heated imagination saw them in bed, doing what we had done. No wonder Lawlor had been so ardent a defense counsel. He had been, no doubt, an ardent lover before he ever got to the courtroom. She may have been the ideal defendant on all counts, I thought. The more I mulled over these possibilities, the angrier I became. Davis and I parted an hour later, he to play billiards in a room upstairs. I spent two hours plodding down the quiet streets to calm myself so I could sleep.

The next day I called on Mr. Hearst. His office in The World's tall building was two floors down from The World's. The newspaper world was small, and its inhabitants, reporters and publishers, lived on a small piece of turf. It was not unusual for reporters of one paper to go into the cityroom of another. It was common, if only because reporters were looking for available drinking companions. The Journal's cityroom was on the second floor, a large, dusty, and badly lighted room which looked in most particulars like The World's. I found Hearst sitting at the city-desk, reading copies of other evening newspapers.

Hearst by now has become something like a force of nature. His name scares up a tornado of wrath and scorn. But few Americans then or now knew what he was really like, or even what he looked like. I bet that Hearst could walk down the Main Street of any city in America unrecognized, despite the cartoons which have depicted him all his professional life. As I saw him that afternoon he was a tall, man in his 30s. His sandy brown hair was parted neatly in the middle, and he was in his shirtsleeves, though he wore a collar. A clean one.

Hearst was pleasant-looking. He could have passed for a small-town banker. He never took on the sharp, angular looks of New York moguls. He did not seem to look down his long nose at his fellow man. He spoke with reporters, printers and copyboys in the same tone. When he was angry, or upset, he never raised his voice. He once complained that, for a man who did not drink, he had suffered greatly from alcohol. But he did not begrudge his editorial staff its drink. His pleasures were women and song, and collecting.

A copyboy interrupted his reading, and introduced me. Hearst looked up, and I stared into an unusually long face, and two closely-set light-blue eyes which were his most youthful attribute.

I nearly lost my life in Hearst's service, but even years later it's impossible to dislike the man.

"Yes, yes, Mr. Botwright," he said, standing and extending his hand. For so large a man, Hearst had a very high tenor voice which he used softly. I never heard him shout. Taller by three inches, Hearst took me by the arm and walked me to an office in the rear of the cityroom. He closed the door and sat down. He opened a desk drawer

76

and pulled out a bottle, and two glasses. We drank.

It was applejack, about the strongest drink Hearst allowed himself.

"You have been doing some very nice work for The World. I would like to have you do the same for The Journal. Your story about the Fitzmaurice shooting was talked about town for weeks. Very nice. I want that kind of reporting in my paper. I'm prepared to pay for it. How much do you make?"

I noticed that Hearst was looking at my suit, which, though pressed, had seen much wear that year.

"Mr. Hearst, it would take $100 a week for me to work for The Journal."

"Fine. Now that we have that solved, what would you like to do?"

"Well, I usually leave that up to the city desk." Hearst smiled. "Yes, but I think that if I'm to pay you $100 a week you should be doing something more enterprising than covering police headquarters.

"Would you like to be a foreign correspondent? The Journal, you know, has the best correspondents I can find."

"I've never done that kind of work. I had a bit of French in college, but not enough to operate where it's spoken."

Hearst laughed. "Where did you go to college? New Haven, wasn't it? I went to Harvard, at least until they threw me out. Had a damn good time there. Now I don't think they'd even let me attend the football games.

"But, let's be serious for a moment. My aim in this town is to put out a newspaper that will sell a million copies. There are too many newspapers in New York now. Not all of them can succeed. I intend to succeed. Pulitzer wants the same thing, but I don't think he'll fight as hard for it. Time will tell." He poured us another drink.

"Well, there's time enough to decide what you're going to do for us. Glad to have you with us. Davis has told me about you. Anyone Dick Davis recommends is enough for me. All I ask is loyalty—to me and to The Journal. Unlike Mr. Pulitzer, my staff sees a great deal of me. I'll be around the cityroom. I like to keep my hand in. We'll see that you get to do something grand. Something you'll enjoy.

"You see, Jim, this old century has had it. There're new times coming. And this country is going to have a big part in them. I want to be part of them, with this newspaper, and maybe." Hearst let his thought end there, but I had the impression he was talking about public office. He had dreams and ambitions, but he was never able to realize them. Not with all his money. Not with all his power. Willie was always reaching, but he never got to the top in his own mind. He was considered an ogre, a monster who preyed on the people's fears. Maybe so. That day we agreed that I'd start in mid-September which would give me two weeks to settle up with The World. Chapin was at his desk when I returned. He started at me as I walked the length of the long room.

"Has Hearst bought you too?"

I smiled. There were few secrets on Park Row. "That's what I want to speak with you about."

"Nothing to talk about." Chapin grabbed a handful of unedited copy. "You're fired. Get out." I stood there, stunned, and unable to speak. At length, I mumbled, "I wanted to give two weeks notice."

"Not necessary," Chapin growled. "Get out." He turned and roared for a copyboy.

With the stares of the silent copy editors on my back, I walked to my desk, and took the few personal things I kept there. It's truly impermanent working for a newspaper, like life itself. Papers have their star reporters, but when one leaves, the loss, if there actually is one, is filled as quickly as a swell in the ocean.

On my way out I stopped at Perry's in the lobby. Two

World reporters hailed me, and asked me to join them.

"Now that you've joined Mr. Hearst's army, you can buy a round," one said.

"How did Chapin react?" the second asked. I shrugged.

"He growled at the last fellow who went to Hearst. Said he could never return to The World. If the fellow gave a thought to coming back. A couple of years with Hearst and you can retire to Saratoga and sail your yacht."

"Only Hearst and Pulitzer and Bennett have yachts," the second fellow said. Their cynical mood matched my own. I changed the subject, to news of their beats. Al Coyne, the courthouse reporter, told me that Lawlor was the most sought-after defense lawyer in the building after his acquittal for Annie. "They say he's asking one thousand to handle a case now he'll have his yacht soon enough.

"The only good to come of all this, besides your good fortune, Jim, is that Chapin will be forced now to hire Jameson. He needs the work."

"Do you know Jameson?" Coyne asked. I shook my head no.

"Chapin fired Jameson last year. He had stayed home a few days to care for his sick wife. She died last December of the consumption. Chapin would have none of Jameson's excuse for staying out. Poor bastard went on a terrific bender after Chapin fired him. He had been close to his wife, and it really set him off when she died. And, then there were the children. He spoke of getting a gun and shooting Chapin. Well, as much as we all liked the idea of seeing Chapin with a few new holes in his head, we talked Jameson out of it. We pointed out the fact that he had to care now for his sons. He put him with relatives upstate, and Jameson has cleaned himself up. He's been working for the Commercial-Advertiser as a freelance. And any other pickup work he can find."

"What makes you think Chapin will relent and hire him?"

Coyne smiled. "The bastard delights in punishing his victims over and over. He knows that Jameson has been on the wagon for months. It will tickle the bastard's iron mean streak to torment Jameson until he slips off again. And, then he can fire him all over again. It's a rotten game we're in, boys," Coyne said, lifting his glass.

"Chapin will take his fall someday," Coyne's pal said. "And I want to be around to see it, too."

We all laughed.

CHAPTER TEN

The Haymarket

The next day I reported at The Journal, and was greeted by courtly Arthur Brisbane, Mr. Hearst's managing editor. Brisbane, as urbane as the chief, told me to call Hearst "the chief."

"The chief is in San Francisco, visiting his mother. However, he left instructions to assign you to a couple of projects." Chatting smoothly, Brisbane quickly elicited my family background, and schooling with a few discrete questions. Then he told me that Hearst wanted me to interview a small group of Cuban insurrectionists then visiting New York.

I told Brisbane that I didn't speak Spanish, and that I knew nothing about Cuba. He laughed. "We can buy translators by the barrel, Botwright. He had one other order.

"Oh, one other thing. Mr. Hearst asks that today you go to Brooks, his tailor, and get fitted for five suits. Pick any material. They will also fit you for shoes. Don't worry about the cost. Brooks knows to bill Mr. Hearst's account.

"Mr. Hearst cares how his reporters dress."

And that's how I came to have those three fine suits in my closet for years afterward. I was fitted for five, but one got lost in my baggage between Washington and Florida, and the other was ripped during a bar melee over some insurgents. I never had it repaired.

Before I left him that day, Brisbane told me that I would report directly to him or Mr. Hearst, and not the city desk. I would not have the usual cityside run. I was on special assignment. Surprised as I was at this news, I had the clearness of mind to remain silent, and await developments. I remained silent too long, and developments overrode me, I decided later. I decided that after the events. In the midst of all of it, it was too difficult to figure out what was happening, and where it would lead. My life for the next year was a perfect example of that. I was carried along, willingly, I must add, like a leaf in a stream. On some reflective thought I would have carefully skirted many of the events.

"All right, Botwright. At noon today you have an appointment with Senor Manuel Sanchez. He's a major figure in the Cuba Libre movement. He's at the Astor House."

At the announced time I knocked on Sanchez' door. it opened a few inches, and a dark man peered out. I introduced myself. He asked for a card in an accented voice.

Reporters, I told him, did not use them. I said that Mr. Brisbane had arranged the meeting. The name caused him to open the door wider. With some reluctance, Sanchez allowed me to enter the room. I learned later that he had been receiving death threats, which he believed came from Spanish government agents.

Sanchez had a pungent smell about him, which I later

learned was garlic. I came to like the herb myself, but only in small doses. I looked beyond him in the room's gloom, and saw a woman.

"May I present Senorita Evangelina Cisneros. Her father is a leader in our movement. The senorita performs valuable services for us."

The girl was short, no more than five-foot tall, slender, but with a good figure. Her thick black hair was tied tightly in a bun. She had clear, white skin, and bright black eyes. She looked like a revolutionary. But I must admit that I was then no judge. I had never met one before.

I sat at Sanchez' motion. "Mr. Brisbane told me that you would explain what has been happening in Cuba. I must admit," I said, looking from one to the other, "that I'm not familiar with your country. I do not know much about it. And, I do not speak Spanish." They looked at each other, and Sanchez smiled.

"Well, we will begin now."

They began my education that afternoon. I learned about more than 200 years of heavy-handed Spanish rule, of deprivation, of theft, and confiscatory taxation, slavery and the refusal of the Spanish royalty to allow local rule. I learned about the movement of 1873, and how the United States almost went to war a few years before over filibustering expeditions of American forces from Florida, and their capture by the Spanish.

I left the hotel that evening with my head buzzing with strange names, pronounced in that lisping Spanish fashion. I hadn't known that many Americans wanted to free Cuba. Or that they had mounted armed expeditions for that purpose. The forays were called filibusters. Many ended tragically because the filibusters had not taken into account the strength of the ruling government, the apathy of the largely uneducated, ill-fed populace. The average Cuban obeyed his district Don, the landlord who owned his farm and the rural pastor who preached in the village church.

I was surprised to learn that the revolutionary movement was kept alive from 1870 to 1897. In large measure it was the students who fueled the rebel populace. The Cuban government aided in its own downfall. For every dozen illiterate farm hands who took up arms against the Spanish flag, the Spaniards added to the insurrectos by letting hundreds of young people go abroad to university. The Spaniards exported the raw material for revolution, and then imported the explosive mixture which eventually ignited the island. I must admit that I wasn't really caught up emotionally in all this history. I hadn't been there, and I had no idea what life was like on the island. Sanchez' enthusiasm held my attention, and, of course, I was attracted to Miss Cisneros.

That evening I found Crane sitting morosely in The Journal office. He had returned the week before from Europe. He wanted to have a few drinks. I had no objection. We started at Perry's, and moved from there to Churchill's where' I thought we would have dinner. We didn't. We had more drinks. Crane was in a quick-silver mood. He kept showing me a roll of greenbacks which he said was royalty from his book." This will get me back to Cora," he kept saying. I told him of my Cuban assignment, and he laughed.

"Those people will get you killed," Crane said pleasantly, before downing another cocktail. Suddenly he asked if I had ever been to the Haymarket. When I said no, all thoughts of food vanished, and we rolled off to look for a cab, to take us to the number-one Westside tenderloin spa.

The Haymarket was located in a shabby Sixth Avenue building, a hall actually, with two long bars running its length.

There were upstairs rooms, and balconies, and even

downstairs rooms in the basement. We arrived about 10:30 that night and the rowdy customers, and underworld ruffians were already in full cry. There were two entertainments at The Haymarket—the bottle, and the women. The men enjoyed both to the fullest. Girls danced the can-can, usually with nothing on underneath their skirts, the way the dance originated in Paris. Crane and I were both overflowing with spirits by then, though we had enough wit about us to ignore the bunco steerers and pimps who tried to tout us their grift when we pushed through the doors. We stood at the bar, and Crane was recognized by more than a few of the burly men there. They all looked alike, battered, and no doubt many were thugs. The bar was the longest I had ever seen. Crane said it was 200-foot long. I believed it. It, it was nearly covered by a pushing, laughing group of women and men. They drank huge schooners of beer, and shot glasses of whiskey. Bartenders stood every five feet, handling the crowd. They tried feverishly to stay ahead of the mass thirst.

"Many of these women are prostitutes," Crane said softly. "But some are just pickpockets.

"Whatever you see in here, don't go for it. Not a straight play. No matter how pretty she is, she'll have a Murphy man upstairs to rob you fast, after they shoot you the drops."

"What do you mean?"

Crane translated by saying that the hookers worked with men who would strip a victim after the hooker got him to a room, and after the victim had imbibed a drink with knockout drops in it. Just then a band struck up a fanfare, the curtains up on the stage at the end of the hall parted to reveal a chorus line of ten young women. Most were attractive. They began to dance a can-can, and I must say later that I can still recall my shock at what those women revealed when they tossed their skirts, legs and bottoms in the air. Crane just smiled.

Behind us, two women jumped up on a table and began competing with the program. They had obviously been drinking quite heavily. I was distracted from the stage performance when one, a quite voluptuous blonde decided that her corset-like bodice was too constricting. She undid it. She revealed big, white breasts. She held them up for view. A big, burly fellow in a striped suit, wearing a hat, reached up and pulled this woman down on his lap. She did not put up much of a struggle. But the removal of her dancing partner angered the second woman. She reached down and grabbed a beer stein. She swung it at the lecher's head. It, connected, and I suspected the thud was heard in Hoboken. The man slumped to the floor. The blonde toppled with him, but she quickly regained her feet. The attack inflamed the blonde. She climbed on the table, and began pushing the other woman, who quickly toppled off to the floor.

Crane just smiled at all this. Each of the hundreds at The Haymarket seemed to be putting on his or her own performance. I looked up at the balcony, and saw that many of the small rooms there were being used by couples, some of whom did not bother to close the drapes. One couple appeared to be dancing slowly, until I looked closer and saw that neither was dressed below the waist. The heat, smoke, music and throbbing sensuality of The Haymarket smote the senses. The bartenders never let an empty glass stand before a customer. Without asking, they refilled each, until the customer fell, or otherwise turned off the flow. The laughter, shouting and noise struck the ears like the constant crashing of an ocean surf. I must admit that I enjoyed the place. I was in mid cups. Roving hookers sought us out. Some recognized Crane. He was most pleasant to them all, refusing their services. He sometimes would neatly slip a coin in the bodices of those who spoke kindly to him. The women were mostly young. The kind of girl you would find in shops around the city. Crane told me that most of them had been driven to The Haymarket from exactly that kind of shop.

"Economics, it's all a question of economics," he said. A few of the men in the place were better dressed, and they were skirted by the bearded thug-types. Crane said the better dressed ones were most likely policemen.

CHAPTER ELEVEN

Close Range

aughing as only drunks can, and nearly falling over each other, we eloped in a milk wagon we found at the curb, its patient old mare waiting for the deliveryman. God knows where he was.

We made it to 14th Street before we were hailed to the curb by two mounted policemen alerted to the prank by our shouts and erratic course.

It took much quick talking, and hasty phone calls downtown to police headquarters before we were sent on our way—on foot. The police confiscated the wagon. It was hilarious to us then, but sobering later to realize through a most massive hangover that we could have been arrested and charged with larceny. The story somehow spread from police headquarters, and within a day virtually every reporter on Park Row knew what we had done. Carrying my hangover, I spent the next day trying to make sense of Sanchez who droned on about Cuba.

At 4 p.m., somewhat refreshed by ten cups of

coffee and a light lunch, I returned to The Journal.

After slowly easing myself into a chair, I picked up a late edition of the paper, and nearly fell off the chair upon reading the main page-one headline: Lawyer Slain in Office. While Crane and I had been plunging into the underworld the night before, someone had shot Lawlor to death in his office. The murderer had left the weapon behind. A pistol had been found on the carpet in front of Lawlor's desk. The story said that Lawlor had been shot at close range. Leaving the weapon behind may have been a ruse to indicate suicide, but it didn't work because the pistol was too far from the body.

Lawlor's legal associates and Democratic party officials were quoted as saying they were at a loss to explain the shocking crime. Lawlor, they said, had no enemies. Police, the account stated, suspect that Lawlor was meeting late at night with an irate client who shot him to death.

Despite the lingering headache from the hangover, I felt a cold chill. I knew who the killer was. I didn't sleep much that night, wondering what I could do. To go to the police with my suspicions would not help. I had no evidence to back up my feeling. All I had was a theory, and a story that would not hold up in court. I felt sure that Annie went in and out of Lawlor's office without being seen. I also developed a chilling realization that I might be next. And there was no way I could appeal that sort of execution.

The next afternoon, dazed with my realization, I was called to Hearst's office. He was there with Brisbane and a young, bushy-haired young fellow. Hearst beckoned me to a chair.

"Oh, gents, let me introduce Jim Botwright. You know Mr. Brisbane, Jim. And this is Morrill Goddard. He runs the Sunday Journal. You may have met when you both worked at The World." I shook hands with Goddard, the reputed boy wonder of Sunday newspapers in New York.

I had not met him before. But I knew who he was. He was the wizard who redesigned The Sunday World, making it a paper with huge, nearly full-page illustrations to go with stories. Word followed art in Goddard's editions. And the Sunday papers flew from the newsstands. Hearst had hired Goddard months before. Pulitzer reportedly went berserk with anger and he rehired Goddard. Hearst upped the ante, and Goddard returned to The Journal for a salary reported to be $500 a week.

Goddard was not the average newspaperman of the period. He had little interest in reporting or writing. His sole concern was with how the paper looked. Goddard devoted his days to designing new sensations for Sunday. A fairly routine murder story in Goddard's hands became an illustrated text, with line drawings from photos that were almost life size. The pictures jumped off the page at the reader. If anyone was really to blame for "Yellow Kid" journalism, it was Goddard. In fact, he was the editor who promoted the Yellow Kid comic full page in The Sunday World. It was about the first of the color comic pages, and it was a sensation.

The mechanics of printing had changed. Newspapers for generations were black with page after page of tiny words. Fifty years before newspapers were so small you could fold them up and put them in your pocket. Then the machines changed. First it was the linotype machine, which enabled a fellow to set a column of type faster than any two of the fastest printers. Then came improved presses that enabled colored ink to be spread on newsprint. Graphics, cartoons, drawings replaced old-fashioned line cuts. You could sell newspapers with pictures to immigrants who could not read a complete sentence. They could understand the cartoons. They enjoyed them. It was entertainment. Hearst, however, had bigger plans than cartoons. He wanted to make The Sunday Journal an organ of United States policy, nothing less. It didn't occur to me once in all our subsequent conferences to question whether it was right or proper for the paper, or Hearst to do this. In the midst of it all we assumed that we had a natural right to do as we wished. My education came slowly, and painfully.

"Jim, we're called you in to see if you could do a Sunday piece this week about the Cuban situation. I understand that you've interviewed Sanchez and Miss Cisneros."

Goddard added, "We need something which tells the reader about the Spanish atrocities, towns burned and all that sort of stuff. Can you deliver?"

"Well, I guess I have enough background to get up a story," I said. Brisbane beamed. I knew then that it was easier to write a news story when you don't understand it all, or have all the facts. The more knowledge you have, the more difficult it is to write smoothly.

"What does Miss Cisneros look like?" Goddard asked. He smiled widely when I told him. "Fine, we'll use her in the paper. I have a young fellow in my office today who could go along with you and sketch in the outline. Do you intend to see Sanchez today?"

I nodded yes. Hearst pushed himself back from his desk, and put both heels on it. In all the time I worked for the chief, I never actually saw him at work at his desk. He was either reading newspapers spread on the floor, talking about an edition, or his beloved antiques. The chief was, however, always pleasant, a natural gentleman whose language and conduct were always proper. He was not the ogre of his later reputation. He had a wide sense of humor, and did not excuse himself from its sting.

Later Goddard introduced me to a young, dark-haired youth who kept nervously adjusting his collar.

"Jim, this is Jack Barrymore. Jack wants to be a Journal

artist, so we'll give him a chance on your assignment. Jack is a pretty good penman." Goddard told the youth he wanted profiles, and a full page of outrages, pillage, beatings, prisoners. The youth nodded nervously.

On our way across City Hall Park to the Astor House, I asked Barrymore if he was related to the then popular ingenue, Ethel Barrymore. "She's my sister," he said softly.

At the Sanchez apartment Barrymore sat quietly and quickly sketched the man and woman for my article. Barrymore had a flair with a pencil, and within a half hour he had roughed in portraits of both insurrectos. The girl complimented Barrymore on his skill. He smiled modestly. Jack Barrymore, of course, has gone on to worldwide fame as a stage actor, and in film, but that day he wanted to be a newspaper artist. The family trade exerted the stronger pull. We worked together for a few days, and during that time Barrymore never relaxed. At lunch one day I noticed that the boy gulped two cocktails before our plates arrived. He had about him the hot-eyed look one sees in heavy drinkers. But he was always polite. But Jack Barrymore did not stay long with Hearst. I was busy launching Mr. Hearst's war, so I didn't notice Barrymore deserting the pencil for the stage. The Sunday article about Sanchez and Miss Cisneros appeared the following weekend, and it was a sensation. The article and artwork were unsigned, the style in those days, but most everyone on Park Row knew who had done the work. Hearst called for another article the next week. Goddard suggested that I collect information enough to do a piece a week until further notice. Hearst also suggested that I go to Washington to talk with diplomats and U.S. officials about the Cuba problem.

"My man Bierce is down there. He'll show you around. Ambrose knows where all the bodies are buried." Hearst chuckled. Bierce was a columnist for the chief's San

Francisco Examiner, a cynical crusader who had been waging a long battle with the western railroads.

Early the next morning, after a fitful night's tossing which couldn't be called sleep, I slouched into The Journal office early. I felt like I had a massive hangover, and it would continue for a week. The ache was not brought on by the earlier carousing, but the murder headline.

The morning was sunny, and through the big windows the rays shone, catching all the dust motes in the disorderly room. I went through the edition, and was tossing it aside when my eye caught Dick Davis in the doorway. He motioned to me, and I followed him, down the stairways to the ground floor, outside to Park Row, and across the street to a shop "You know about Lawlor?" he asked. " What do you think happened?" he asked.

"She killed him. I guess, I suppose, Oh, I don't know, Dick," I said.

"I went to see Lawlor last week," Davis said calmly. I nearly jumped up from the wooden bench.

"Yes. I wanted to beard him with the story. See what he would do," Davis said.

"What he would do?" I nearly shouted. Fortunately the room was crowded with boisterous printers.

"What the hell did you tell him?" I asked.

"Relax. I told him I knew all about it, and before long everyone else in Manhattan would, too, and how long would it take Tammany to unload on a lawyer who bedded, and defended a murderess. That got to him."

"He told me what he knew about her. I guess he knew that I was whistling in the dark. I couldn't just write a story about her and accuse her of the murder she had been acquitted of. And, could she be tried again for the same murder? No. So it was a gamble,"

Davis stirred his tea. "She killed Fitzmaurice, all right, and Lawlor thought he wasn't the first one, either. In fact, he gave off the sweat of fear, the kind of fear men get when they know they're targets.

"He knew he was going to be killed?" I sputtered.

"Yes. He had done some checking into her background, what there is of it. She was born in raised in the coal fields near Scranton, spent time in a parlor house in Philadelphia, and then found a place in a theatrical company in the sticks. Lawlor says he was lucky to run across a booking agent in Pastor's Theater one night when he was down next door at Tammany Hall, who knew her. Said she was not company. Meant that she wasn't one of the show folks. Cold, distant, they thought, and accidents had a way of happening to those around her. She was a jinx, he said."

"But why," I asked, "didn't Lawlor go to the police?" Davis smiled, and jutted his chin at the same time. His collar was too tight.

"And who was he going to tell all this to? Teddy Roosevelt? Or what other policeman? None of it would stay put. The woman had her day in court. It was all hearsay anyway."

I stirred my lukewarm coffee with a bent spoon. "Well, what the hell are we going to do now?" I asked. I was torn from the pain of knowing what she had done, and my part in the whole matter. I also longed for her.

"I'm telling you this, scout, for your own good. Honestly, I thought there might be a story for me, something I could wrap up in fiction and sell to the magazines." Davis waved his hand at me. "I know it was your story, but it was too good to let go. And, I don't think you're about to write it.

"The problem is a second murder has been committed. We can go to the police. They might even get excited about it, but we have no evidence, no witnesses. It would be a waste."

"Yes, but she wouldn't have Lawlor to defend her this

time," I said. Davis gave me a wintery smile.

"No. What we have is a situation where you are a prime target, you know that, don't you?" I nodded.

"It's really too bad that Roosevelt has gone to Washington. I can't see him running the Navy, when a good murder like this would get him all the headlines he'd ever want right here in Manhattan," Davis said.

"I wouldn't tell the Dutchman anything," I said.

"He'd be the only one who'd see this thing through," Davis mused. "And now it's too late for his help." He slammed the table. "Well, if you've had any thoughts about becoming a roving correspondent, now might be the time to act on them. We ought to put a rail line between you and that pistol."

I walked back to the paper, numb, and wondering if I would escape.

I called on Sanchez and Miss Cisneros that afternoon, and told them of my assignment. Sanchez didn't seem disappointed.

"Senor, I cannot speak with you today. I have to meet with others in our group." He quickly left the room. I looked at the girl.

"Would you like to take a cab ride?" She looked at me, and shrugged. At that point I was not entirely sure of her relationship with Sanchez. He sometimes acted like her chaperon, and occasionally she flared at his protective attitude. But at other times he left her alone.

"Are you married?" she asked, after we had settled ourselves in a cab headed up Fifth Avenue.

"No," I said. She smiled. Her eyes were lively and inviting. By the end of the ride we were holding hands. I escorted her back to the hotel room, and she did not resist when I entered it with her. She did not resist when I took her by the shoulders, and kissed her beautiful mouth. We kissed for some minutes, and I gently moved her toward the bed. After seating her, I began to undo her shirtwaist. That's when she responded, but not the way I had hoped. She slapped my face, hard, and stood quickly and shouted at me in Spanish.

I smiled and told her that I did not understand. She switched to English.

"What do you think I am? Whore?" she screamed, and I was sure that she was heard on every floor of the hotel. I tried to placate the spitfire. It was no use, and I left her room quickly, with my composure in disarray. I decided later that Miss Cisneros actually spared me. She possessed two pistols, and was a trained shot. I suppose I was lucky to get away.

She never mentioned the incident thereafter. I don't know if she told Sanchez of it. But he didn't change his aloofness toward me. I was happy the following week to pack for Washington. Before I left Goddard introduced me to Frederic Remington, who had replaced Barrymore as the artist on my assignment. The wiry, neat little artist was as outspoken as Barrymore was quiet. Remington had worked for Pulitzer, too. He went to Cuba later to draw on-the-spot illustrations for Hearst. Remington was cocksure that he could survive in an unfriendly nation where the government did not worry much about jailing troublemakers, particularly Americans bent on stirring up trouble. I asked Remington how he would mask his mission.

"Ah, I just tell them I'm a traveling artist. Do a few portrait sketches here and there. Give them away free. Makes a big hit. Everyone likes a drawing."

"They might consider you a spy."

"What the hell are you talking about. I'm an American," Remington said irately.

I laughed. "No. I meant that if the Spaniards decided that journalists wandering in Cuba were more than troublemakers, they could decide to line them against a wall, and shoot them."

"Well, Hell's bells, they'd better not try that with me. Mr. Hearst would be powerful upset about that, I'm sure."

I nodded. Remington was a typical American of the period. He could not believe or understand that any foreign government could take any action against an American citizen, or would want to. Americans were close to Godliness, in his book. It was un-Godly to take offense at anything an American would do. Even in a foreign country. I did not envy Remington his assignment. I had no suspicion then that I would soon join him on the island. Yet the aggressive artist beamed when Hearst gave him his instructions. "You say when, chief, and we'll be on our way," Remington said.

For his part, Hearst enjoyed all the dare-deviltry. He told Remington he would send him to Cuba on his yacht. The boat would carry the artist and Dick Davis back to New York. Davis had been roaming the island in the guise of foreign correspondent, but he was not writing any reports for print about the guerilla war.

Davis was really Hearst's private spy. He was roaming around, as seeing conditions as they were in Cuba.

"My country is a military camp," Sanchez told me over one of his long dark cigars. "The Spanish don't know what to do with us. In Spain there are warhawks and what they call appeasers. The warhawks want more regiments to crush us. The appeasers would give us limited self-government, limited to what Madrid wants.

"This General Weyler," he said, "is a major warhawk. He started the camps. They keep all our people in fear of them. To go to one is death."

Davis told me later that he got close to one of the camps and confirmed their dreadfulness. Dick said, "I spoke to a few Spanish officers at one camp outside Havana. They bragged about the unsanitary conditions, and their cruelty to the prisoners."

Sanchez explained, "The death toll is high, but for the Spanish authorities it was a cheap price to pay to cut down the number of rebels."

Davis wrote all the details in letters to Hearst. I did not see the letters, and the chief did not publish them. He wanted pure information on which to base his crusade. No correspondent was better than Davis to provide the information. Afterward, Hearst was accused far and wide for sensationalism, but in my experience he always based his "sensational" news on fact.

"No one who has been in Cuba can say our cause is unjust," Sanchez said repeatedly. The Spanish were treating the Cubans badly, and there was no getting around that. Cuba may not be better off today under its own flag than it was in 1897, but there was a fever current then running through the American people. It was as if the nation had gone too long without a war. The truth was, of course, that the U.S. was not in any position to carry on a war with any nation. That fact we learned the hard way later, after the casualties were added up. For Hearst, however, the issue was never war. It was Pulitzer and newspaper sales. For a six-month period, the pair engaged in an orgy of sensation, reporting alleged insults to the American flag. It was a most interesting time, and I was right in the middle of it. Frankly, at the start I thought it was all grand, a great opportunity to be in the thick of things, taking orders from the chief, and Goddard. They stage-managed the whole affair. It was a big adventure, for me, for all of us, and for the country. We didn't at any point stop to ask the cost. We had warnings, many from responsible persons in office, but we refused to listen. Hearst would not tolerate criticism or any questions of his desire to beat

Joe Pulitzer on the streets of New York. If it took a war, well, that was all right, too.

And that's what happened. My education came slowly. Goddard told me one day to chase Sanchez and Miss Cisneros to Washington, where they had gone to raise money for their cause. It was one of the ironies of the period that as 1897 waned the war was launched in the Sunday newspaper columns. But the public seemed tight-fisted when it came to kicking in toward the rebels' effort. The daily newspapers, ironically, continued to reflect the more mundane concerns of tax bills in Albany, murder in Brooklyn, and the usual finagling among Broad Street traders. It was the difference between the routine, and a new expansive feeling on weekends. The latter was enterprise material developed by publishers at great cost, all for reader interest, and it was copied from coast to coast. The American newspaper was changing before our eyes, becoming more concerned by the world at large. And, as circulation-getter, it worked.

The American public was ready for the warhawks. The Jingoists, we called them. The nation had 30 years of peace, and reading about other peoples' wars. It was time for one of our own. I didn't want to be cynical about it, but that's the way it was.

When I got off the train in Washington, a beefy, middle-aged fellow who said he was Ambrose Bierce met me one bright December morning. He had a carriage. At dinner Bierce was caustic about our work, Washington, the government and New York. "Well, what do you think?"

"It seems a very small town with very wide streets," I said.

Bierce laughed. "They built them that way so the politicians could make a clean getaway before the posse. You're right. This is the country's biggest small town. For any intelligent conversation you have to go all the way to Baltimore." Bierce dug into his steak.

"This new crusade of yours has removed some of the pressure on me. I'll help you as much as I can. But the one problem we have is that I'm not too tall in diplomatic circles. Never paid much attention to those dudes. But what are your orders? Has Willie asked you to start war before Christmas?" Bierce laughed.

I told him that I was to scout around, and get the feelings of the McKinley Administration toward American intervention in Cuba.

"There are some on the Hill who itch for a war," Bierce said. He shook his head.

"Son, I was in the last war, and I don't want another. The only ones who profit from war are shoemakers and those who sit home by a warm fire, and write about it. War is dirty. If one comes, I'm going to scoot to San Francisco, and do my fighting with editors." Bierce was serious. Every uniform we passed in Washington drew a scornful glance and remark from the Civil War veteran. From the way he spoke I thought he had been a Confederate. He had fought on the Union side, among Ohio volunteers, he told me one night.

The city looked half-finished to me. The buildings were ancient. Many were tumble-down. Three times a day the streets were crowded with clerks going to, or leaving their offices in the massive stone buildings. The streets were badly paved, and when it rained they were worse than anything in Manhattan.

I asked Bierce how he withstood the boredom of the place, and why he didn't move up to Manhattan.

"Son, don't let the lack of rheostats fool you. This is a city of simple pleasures. There are some of the country's nicest parlor houses within a few blocks, and Congress likes the comfort and quiet. Drink is readily available, and cheap. There are plenty of young women around, and alliances are easy to arrange if your income allows that sort of thing. Don't be fooled. The men who run this town have learned from experience that it doesn't pay to be too loud in one's pleasures." He winked.

That evening Bierce and I ventured into the cold, rainy streets, to sample the dens. We stopped at two quiet drinking clubs, where we played a few games of billiards with men whose Southern accents were strange to my ears.

It was about the same time, Dick Davis told me much later, that he was in London, making his arrangements to get to Havana. Dick felt it would be better to arrive in Cuba from England, rather than the United States. I didn't see any difference, as everyone knew who Richard Harding Davis was. At least everyone should have known.

"I met Steve in London. He was with that peroxide blonde of his. I don't care for her, Jim, and I don't mind saying so. She's latched onto Crane for a meal ticket and I don't think that's right. I don't think she's right, either, not a woman with her background." Davis seemed embarrassed. He rarely spoke ill of any woman, but he didn't have a good word for Cora, and I believe that she knew it. I believe that Steve knew it, too, though he was too much of a gentleman to ever bring the subject up.

"There was a round of parties. London is such a swell town, and I was invited so many places. I questioned everyone I met in the diplomatic service about Spain, and Cuba. The British saw the whole thing as an embarrassment, something that gives empires a bad name, y'know.

"Anyway, the steamer trip to Havana was uneventful. I got to write two more stories, and mailed them to the magazines after I arrived. After the cold of London, the heat in Havana was nearly overpowering. I don't care for the tropics. It's the difference between the Anglo-Saxons and the Mediterranean races. We function better in cold climates.

"I had a letter of introduction to the British ambassador. I used it, too, and it paid off handsomely. I was welcomed as if a long-lost son. They put on a dinner for me, one of those outdoor things. I've never fancied eating outside. But it was pleasant, I must say, colorful, with the flowers, and all the women dressed in summery dresses. They all wanted to know why I was in Cuba. I told them the truth. That I was spying for Mr. Hearst. They all laughed. That's the way it is with the truth sometimes. It makes people laugh.

"I had a carriage at my convenience, and I saw much of the town. Shabby kind of place, even the homes of the nicer elements. It looks like they're too lazy to collect the trash. The British and the French maintain large embassies in Havana, mostly because they do much trading with Cuban firms, sugar, rum, that sort of thing. I met dozens of Cubans, the business types, usually. To a man they refused to talk of the independence movement. Not surprising. It affected their business.

"One night a young British diplomat, I believe he was a military attaché, though he said he also wrote for the London papers, introduced me to a Havana newspaper editor."

"What was this English fellow's name?" I asked Davis.

"I don't know. I can't recall it exactly. Something like Churchman, I think.

"Maybe Churchill," Davis said. "Well, we met in a cantina, and this Cuban told me about the independence movement, and he urged that I go into the countryside. The Englishman endorsed this suggestion. We met the next day, and hired horses for the trip.

"It was an experience, I'll tell you. Churchill, or whatever his name is, knew where to take us, and the Cuban explained what we saw. It was not pretty. Small villages, mostly hovels, and large plantations, where men, women, and the smallest children worked all day in the sun, cutting cane. There seemed nothing to make life interesting. Just never ending work, and disease. The people looked starved, especially the children. After three days we had seen all there was to see."

"And these people were all insurrectos?" I asked.

Davis scowled. "No. Few were. They were more like victims. They had little hope. And everywhere we went there were soldiers. Spanish soldiers, and Cuban soldiers. And they acted as if there was nothing they couldn't do to those people. It was depressing, Jim."

I believed Dick implicitly. And, when I saw Cuba myself it looked exactly the way Dick described it.

That day, however, when Dick was perspiring in the tropics, Bierce and I were making our way across the frozen slush of Washington streets. I was getting to know the nation's capital, a place that was more symbol than city.

We completed our tour at a parlor house, which from the outside looked like one of those fashionable brownstones in Gramercy Park. Bierce was on intimate terms with the large, brown-haired woman who ran the establishment. Even though it was a cold, damp mid-week night there were four or five men in the main parlor, some sipping champagne, and chatting with a half-dozen young women. The liquor was served by black women. I was not used to seeing so many Negroes in one place, on the streets, in the stores, and restaurants. They were everywhere. This was before the Jim Crow laws, of course, and I must say that the Negroes were well-behaved. In Manhattan a hackman would be Irish, but in Washington he would be a black man.

We sat sipping wine on a high sofa. Bierce joked with the madam about her trade.

"I'll bet these Ohio Republicans are tight with a dollar.

Know them well, used to be one myself. Bet they stay home with their wives," Bierce said.

The woman, Mrs. Sampson, laughed. "Now, Mr. Bierce, every change of administration is slow to find the most entertaining parts of this old city," she said in a soft voice. She rearranged her gown.

"Well, Mrs. Sampson, I thought you might like to know Mr. Botwright, here. He's one of the star reporters from New York. Can't go anywhere in the city, but all know and respect him. A real man of affairs."

She looked at me with a small smile.

"What brings him down here?" she asked.

"Well, hell, Mr. Botwright is on special assignment from Mr. Hearst. We can't speak about it, but you can know that it's mighty important to our country."

She rose. "Well, that's fine, but I don't believe that Mr. Botwright came here to talk over affairs of state. I would like to introduce him to a young lady who has had her eye on him since he arrived." She motioned to a tall, dark-haired young woman across the room, who rose and joined us. She wore a short, plain nightgown and not much else.

"This is Jeannie," Mrs. Sampson said. I nodded.

"Aren't you chill in that nightgown?" I asked. She laughed. Mrs. Sampson wandered away. Soon Bierce had his arm around a short, heavyset blonde. I spent the rest of the night in a comfortable, big, soft bed, with a big, soft woman. Looking back it is apparent that I never gave a second thought in those days to patronizing parlor houses. I don't mean to imply that I made a practice of it, but it didn't bother me to be in one. In fact, those I did patronize were run more genteelly than most saloons. They served a purpose. The girl I stayed with that night told me that she had come to Washington from West Virginia to work for the government. She soon found that she could make more money in a parlor house. It was strictly economics. The myth in those days, at least the public myth printed in newspapers and magazines was that women were lured unknowingly into the life. I don't think that was true at all. It was a matter of economics.

A single woman in the 1890s on her own could make a living in only a few socially acceptable ways, mostly low paying positions. There just weren't that many jobs which paid a woman a decent income. Of course, many prostitutes had other problems besides economics, such as alcohol and drugs, but hell, I saw ministers who had those problems, too.

After a big breakfast provided by Mrs. Sampson, Bierce and I went on our morning rounds. It was another clear, cold December day. After the dark of the house and its rooms, the sunlight made us grimace.

"Well, Botwright," Bierce said, after we had settled ourselves in a hack, "Willie said not to spare the expenses in setting you up here, and we haven't. After what last evening is going to cost Willie, it's too bad he couldn't have at least had a tiny bit of the pleasure."

Bierce blew his nose. "That's one thing about Willie, though. For as long as I've known him, he has never refused himself the fleshly pleasures. He enjoys them to the fullest. And, he's never been a hypocrite about others having their enjoyment, too. And, that's something rare, Botwright."

I agreed, and only half listened thereafter as Bierce explained the buildings we were passing. Bierce had arranged an appointment for us with Theodore Roosevelt, at his office in the War Department. The Dutchman had been assistant secretary of the Navy, a post he sought after working for McKinley. He was as qualified for it as I was. As we got out of the hack, I looked up at the gray granite mass of the War building, with its scores of tiny windows. The building looked like it could withstand a siege. Bierce said that all the buildings in Washington looked strange because they were designed by an architect, and at least three congressional committees. The halls smelled of heavy wax. The place was dark, and occasional gas lamps relieved the gloom. We found the Dutchman's office on the third floor. Roosevelt wore a crisp tweed suit, buttoned all the way up, of course, and a happy expression. He looked as if he was about to bound across the room and wrestle us to the floor.

He launched his tirade after hellos. He asked how things were in Manhattan, and said he was pleased to see us. TR then spoke as if we weren't in the room. I had noticed this trait before, but it had seemed as if Roosevelt was so tightly wound that when his main spring let loose, it did so regardless of the attention or inattention of the audience. That morning, neither Bierce nor I were brightly alert after our exertions of the past night. TR did not notice, and he roared on about preparedness. And how the great powers would surpass America in controlling the sea lanes, and world's minerals. And didn't we agree with Mahan that it was the duty of the United States to take its rightful place among the imperial powers? We nodded, and took few notes. Bierce seemed to be sleeping with his eyes open. It was impossible to be passively rude to TR. He just didn't notice.

"Gentlemen," Roosevelt roared, slapping one fist into his other palm, "This nation must control its own sea lanes. We must have an end to old world powers controlling colonies in our backyard. Our sphere of influence must extend to the South American continent. Otherwise the British, Spanish and Prussians will move right in, and then where'll we be?" Truly a pure rhetorical outburst, requiring nothing but implicit assent. I didn't know much about international affairs, but I suspected then that TR had a grasp of them about the same depth he had in New York police matters. He seemed to be working with the same bluster.

When Roosevelt took a breath, I slipped in a question about Cuba.

"Terrible situation," Roosevelt fumed. "Weyler rounds up the natives and puts them in camps, his troops shoot and pillage, and Spain refuses all pleas for justice. Gentlemen," Roosevelt said in a lowered voice, "the main problem is right here in Washington, too." TR explained that there were too many in the White House who believed the U.S. should solve any problems with Spain amicably. When TR discussed Cuba at length it dawned on me that I had heard the stuff before. I had, it was all material from my Sunday Journal special article. Could it be, I asked myself, that officials like TR get their information from the Sunday papers?

CHAPTER TWELVE

Winston Churchill

oosevelt ranted for another hour, shoving papers around his rolltop desk. Bierce awoke from his torpor, and loudly announced that we had to go to a luncheon appointment. I nodded, and we flew out of his office. "That son of a bitch would talk you deaf, dumb and blind, and then he wouldn't put a penny in your cup," I said.

Bierce and I parted after we left the War building.

The days afterward passed swiftly. I met with Sanchez. Miss Cisneros, he said, had returned to Cuba, to visit her father. It was a trip which was to make her internationally famous, but at the time I was relieved that I didn't have to face the girl again.

We saw Roosevelt regularly, as Hearst wanted the New Yorker featured in my reports. Bierce went back to his anti-railroad crusade, and we met occasionally for lunch. Ambrose had little interest in the Cuba situation. One afternoon I met Sanchez at his hotel. He told me how the Spanish envoys under Ambassador de Lome were lobbying at the White House against the rebels. Sanchez said the Spaniards were discounting all reports of terror on the island.

"He wants to believe them," he said morosely.

"Where are you getting your money from?" I asked gracelessly that day. Sanchez looked at me darkly.

"That is one of our big problems," he said.

"This is not for your paper. Mr. Hearst has been most generous, but the others..." What others? I asked.

"The sugar companies. They had been giving us money to buy rifles in New Orleans, but no more." He explained that the rifles cost $50 each, and that was not for the best European Mauser. He said the insurrectos were trying to buy old rifles in Texas, but the operation cost a lot of money, for shipment, for bribes, and his organization did not have it.

We were interrupted by a knock at the door. Sanchez gave me a puzzled look. He admitted a young man dressed in a neat dark topcoat, gloves and bowler, which he carefully removed, and tossed on a chair.

"Allow me to introduce myself, gentlemen. My name is Henry Lee, captain of Her Majesty's Guards." We looked at him in silent surprise.

"I'm military attaché to Her Majesty's embassy here. I think we should sit and talk about the Cuba situation. Mr. Botwright, I know you have been writing about it for Mr. Hearst's Journal."

It would be understatement to say that Lee's appearance took me by surprise. Lee sat down and filled a long, curving pipe. We stared at him.

"Mr. Sanchez, I realize my coming here like this takes

you back a bit. Perhaps I can ease the situation by showing you a letter from Senor deLome to his home office." He reached inside his suit jacket. "Don't ask me how I got this letter, but you are welcome to use it as you wish, provided of course that you do not reveal its origin. Agreed?"

Sanchez nodded dumbly. I read over his shoulder, but the letter was in Spanish handwriting. Sanchez caught his breath at various parts. Finished, he folded it up and put it in his pocket.

"You do us a favor, Senor. Why?"

Lee smiled, and puffed on his pipe. "Let's say that her Majesty's government sees no point in allowing Spain to give imperialism a bad name by her mismanagement of her colonies, particularly Cuba.

"Why, just a month ago, I was in Cuba. The conditions are just as you have been reporting them," he said, turning to me.

"Mr. Botwright, perhaps we could meet for dinner tomorrow." I nodded. Then he surprised me by asking if I knew Dick Davis, whom he knew from London and Havana. He beamed when I said we were old friends. "Fine, by the way, this letter is bona fide. It is not counterfeit. Use it. Publish it, it will cause a big uproar. But you can be assured that it will not blow up in your face.

"Again, all we ask is that you do not divulge the source." And, with that, Lee left. Sanchez and I stared wordlessly at each other for minutes.

At dinner the next day Lee had a English translation of the letter. It recounted deLome's feeling that McKinley was not strong enough to withstand the Jingoists in Washington, and that the President was a weak politician who would go with the crowd.

I looked up from the letter to see Lee waving at a round-faced young man who was striding across the hotel dining room to our table.

"Ha. Here's Winston," Lee said. "He's a reporter, too, you know." I didn't know. I stood and Lee introduced me to Winston Churchill, correspondent for The Times of London. Churchill grinned at my name. "Yes, of course, you're Dick Davis' friend." I nodded, wondering how many persons all over the world Richard Harding Davis had told about our association. And, why? Churchill sat, and ordered a large rare steak. "Rare, it must be, and with a bottle of good burgundy." Churchill spoke about Washington, Americans and the Cuba situation in a rushed way. He said it all seemed headed toward crisis. Later it struck me that my end of the conversation was an occasional yes or no. "We've just come back from down there, you know. I toured the island, seeing conditions. Not good, not good at all. Well, Botwright, what do you think of the situation?"

I was startled by the question. I mumbled something about how McKinley seemed to be trying to keep the country out of a conflict with Spain.

"Maybe so," Churchill said, "but your Mr. Roosevelt and the others will see to it." Lee laughed. "Undoubtedly," he added. After another full glass of wine, Lee asked Churchill, "Well, where are you off to now, Winston?"

For the first time since he sat down with us, Churchill's face clouded. He looked at me, and said, "You know, I've always wanted to work as a journalist in New York. Do you think I could get a post on one of the papers?"

I smiled. I knew the question was a sly move to change the subject. I told Churchill that anyone like himself who arrived in Manhattan with clippings from The Times of London would have no trouble at all finding work.

"You must be careful, however, it's a very dangerous town."

Churchill's face got grim. "I'm used to dangerous work." He then excused himself and left as quickly as he had arrived. Afterward Lee said that Churchill was an awfully good fellow for his line of work. I was left with the strange impression that Churchill's work included reporting for other than the Times of London. I had the strong impression that Winston S. Churchill, pal of Dick Davis was some kind of spy.

CHAPTER THIRTEEN

The Real Stuff

I returned to Manhattan that week. On Sunday The Journal printed my piece about Captain-General Valeriano Weyler, the Spanish-born Prussian who ruled Cuba with iron discipline. It was, to be modest, another sensation. The insurrectos called Weyler the Butcher. He built concentration camps for Cubans. He issued decrees, which if broken could result in death. The roads of some provinces were littered with corpses of insurrectos, and just plain citizens who ran afoul of the Spanish regiments. Sanchez had told me that the rebels were hampered by a frightened, ignorant populace terrorized by the great number of Spanish troops. The hard-pressed rebels succeeded only in making dead heroes. Antonio Maceo, the one man who could have united the rebels into an effectve fighting force had been killed by the Spanish in a small town skirmish in 1895. Weyler's firing squads were effective in keeping many a replacement from stepping into Maceo's shoes.

The day I got off the train in Manhattan it was wet and cold, but Hearst threw a smile at me that glowed like two suns. He was happy with my work. Frankly, I was not. It was all too secondhand. I told Hearst as much that day in his office.

Hearst was slumped in his chair in the gloom of his unlighted sanctum. "Sure. I understand that. You want to see what you're writing about," Hearst said pleasantly. He took a penknife from his vest pocket, and began to pare his fingernails.

"Jim, I have Dick Davis down there now. He'll supply us with firsthand stuff. The problem is he can only see so much, and it's been a major problem getting written copy to cablehead outside the island. It has to be taken by boat to Key West, or Tampa. It's not easy. But, perhaps when Davis returns you can replace him. How'd that be?" I said that would be fine.

After I left Hearst chatting with Goddard, I found a note in my mail box from a Detective Rooney, who asked that I call him. I found Rooney at the East 14th Street Precinct. He was a short Irishman with a soft voice, and elaborate manners. You would not take him for a policeman, which obviously helped him in his work.

"We're still investigating the killing of Mr. Lawlor. Tammany don't like it that one of their best brains got killed like that, Mr. Botwright. We understand that you had worked with the deceased on the Fitzmaurice case. I wonder if you could tell us about that." I asked if I could sit down.

Pencil and paper before him, Rooney took notes as I told him an edited version of the murder, and subsequent events.

"Do you have any idea who killed him?" Rooney asked.

I said I had a suspicion who did it. Rooney said, "The district attorney who prosecuted Miss Hampton still insists that she killed that man. Do you know how she got along with Lawlor?" Rooney asked.

"They got along-very well. He defended her. I saw them together in a restaurant after the verdict. Others no doubt have seen them together." He scribbled, asking what restaurants I told him.

"Do you have any theories about what happened?"

"Well, he did have a few political enemies, but they don't kill each other in Tammany," Rooney laughed.

"He was just a good defense lawyer, and he had a roster of some of the biggest criminals in this town. But they don't kill their lawyers. He was married, and a father, but he liked the skirts, we know, and we know he liked Miss Hampton, and we know that the last man she was involved with got made dead, too. But Lawlor was not about to toss over an early judgeship from Tammany for another skirt.

"The trouble is we have nothing to pin on her. No witnesses. I could arrest her, but there's not enough to convict."

"And she'll never confess, either," I mumbled. "Where is she now?"

"We heard through theatrical booking agents that she had gone out west—Chicago, I believe." He smiled a lop-sided grin.

"Well, what are you going to do?" I asked.

Rooney shrugged. "Just hope to hell the next one she kills is out of town." He laughed, and shook his head. "There are a lot of em like her," he said before I left the police station. I walked slowly back to The Journal.

I met Hearst and Goddard on their way out to dinner. They invited me to join them. "They have a good cinemapantograph this week at Koster and Bials. It shows a steam locomotive coming straight at the audience. It's the real stuff," Hearst enthused. We adjourned to the Astor House for a five-course meal, during which Goddard worried aloud about what to display in next Sunday's edition. I ate happily, listening to the chief tell stories about San Francisco days. Willie spent many years in New York, but he was not thought of as a New Yorker. The chief seemed to be "visiting." He mentioned Bierce.

"They call him Bitter Bierce out there. He has written stuff so incendiary that a couple of times I thought the victims would burn the paper down. We had fun, though. Ambrose is good company. I'm sorry he won't come to New York. He's afraid of this town. Though, God knows, it would soon be afraid of him." Hearst laughed loudly.

The cinema show was as thrilling as promised. It was the first I had ever seen. The audience gasped when it thought the locomotive was going to rush right over them. I could not figure out how it was done. Later, during the war, I met a cinemaphotographer in Tampa, and he showed me his camera. It was a mystery to me for years how they worked. Hollywood cured that much later.

Film in the 1890s was sheer novelty. It was shown in musical halls between acts. The audience did not come to the hall solely to see the film. They came to see the performers. At about the same time the cities of America began to have nickel shops, usually in the slum sections, where film was shown to gaping audiences for that sum. They were very popular because the audience didn't need to be literate to understand the program. The silent film was a universal language.

Despite the fact that I was hobnobbing with the chief and his first assistants, I can't say that I was happy during the period. I suffered from waves of guilt about my part in the Fitzmaurice case, and my longing for a woman I knew had killed twice. I wondered how many other victims there were that I didn't know about.

I came to the office late the next morning. "We have a dispatch from Davis," Hearst yelled to me. We looked over the long cable from Key West. Davis said that worried Spanish officials were clamping down on arrivals and departures from the island. In one case, he said, the authorities had stopped a U.S. flag steamer in Havana harbor and searched it for contraband, including some of the passengers. One, Miss Evangelina Cisneros, was personally searched, Davis wrote.

"This is it," Hearst yelped as he read on. "This is our Sunday article. Get Goddard.

"I want a full page sketch of the Spaniards searching the girl. Take her clothing down. I want her naked."

Goddard arrived at a trot, listened, and then suggested that perhaps Davis ought to be queried how the search was accomplished. Hearst waved his hand no. "It's all here. In the long run it would have been better for Willie if he had listened to Goddard. But in the longest run it didn't matter at all.

Hearst gave me the Davis dispatch, and orders to turn it into a sizzling Sunday article, to go with a drawing of a girl stripped and being searched by the Spanish. Remington had just returned from Cuba, so he drew the assignment.

A few days later we all met in Hearst's office. Remington arrived with a large sketch. It showed a group of leering, bearded Spanish officials staring at a demure young girl who stood naked before them. The girl's back was to the reader. It was a shocking illustration for a newspaper of that day, or even today.

"That's the stuff, Remington," Hearst said. Goddard looked less pleased by the prospect of putting a naked girl in his Sunday newspaper. But the point of it all was that it wasn't his Sunday paper. It was Willie's.

Hearst looked over my article. "Good, good." The piece that was printed was heavily edited. Fortunately, it didn't have my name on it, considering the blaze it caused. You must understand that in those days the byline hadn't been invented, not in the form used now. Now, even the women who write up the recipes get their name in the paper. Most if not all news accounts then were printed without a notice for the author. Rarely, when a publisher or editor had to pay dearly for some piece of reportage, a headline would inform readers that the dispatch they were about to read had been prepared by Dick Davis.

I looked for Dick the next day, but he wasn't home. He was somewhere between Havana and Key West. Anyone who has doubts that Davis was a brave fellow only has to consider that it was very dangerous to wander in Cuba in those days. Anything at all could happen to a lone American, especially one that the authorities suspected of being a spy, or worse, a troublemaker. Any kind of accident could have been arranged. Davis told me later that he slept regularly with a.45 caliber pistol in his bedroll.

Goddard and I ran across Steve Crane one evening in The Lantern Club. He looked well, and told us he had just returned from London, to see his publisher, and to ask if the firm was interested in a book about his recent experiences as a war correspondent in Greece.

"I didn't know you've been covering a war," I blurted.

Crane laughed, not at all offended. Yes, he said, Davis had introduced him to the game. "He claims we can make a pile of money just on war, just writing about it. But I have yet to see any of the money." Despite his good spirits, Crane looked older than he had just a few months before. He had aged. Over drinks Crane told us that he was happy living in England.

"When are you going to come back?" I asked.

Steve looked moodily into his glass. "I don't think I'll ever live here full time again. It's too difficult for me." He added that it depressed him to make a half-hearted living from pick-up freelance newspaper work.

"What are you doing now, Jim?" Crane asked.

"I'm with Hearst. He's got me dealing with Cubans. And I've been in Washington," I told him succinctly.

He sat quietly for some minutes while Goddard and I dug into our meal.

"Don't get too involved in it. If it blows up in Willie's face, he'll blame you for it. He's like a big child." Goddard laughed. We drank the night away, and before we parted Goddard suggested to Crane that he accompany me to Washington and do some pieces for the Sunday Journal.

"There's a war coming. This country wants blood. We will pick the place, and do the thrashing. It's funny, but I don't think people even care who the enemy will be. It's our job to pick the enemies." Goddard was drunk, but I listened respectfully. He was right, of course.

After Goddard left in a cab, Crane, standing with me at the curb, said he had seen it already in Europe.

"The small nations want freedom. The large nations want to control them because control means empire. I think the big nations declare war just to have an excuse to use their battleships and troops."

Crane spat in the street. "Do you know that there are factories in England and France which make war goods that they sell to all nations. These factory owners cannot lose. Whichever side wins, they win." Prompted by his mention of England, I asked if Steve had ever run across Captain Lee and the mysterious Churchill.

"Don't know either of them. But it wouldn't surprise me

if you're right. They have given you information which is incendiary. You must be careful about how you use it."

We slept off the alcohol the next day on the train to Washington. It was snowing when we arrived, a bleak white day which did nothing to enhance the drabness of the city. We took a hack to the hotel. Sleepy as I was, I noticed a theatrical poster in the hotel lobby which advertised a company currently in the city. Her name was prominent on the poster. I stopped dead in front of it, and Crane noticed my reaction.

"What's the matter?"

Nothing, I told him.

The next morning Crane suggested that we ask deLome for an interview. "You can show him the letter. We can tell from his reaction if it's bona fide. I suspect it is."

CHAPTER FOURTEEN

Not a Star Act

L ater that morning we were ushered into Ambassador deLome's office, where we shook hands with a short, balding man with a long nose, and a foppish manner. Yet, he had a forcefulness about him. He bowed. "Ah, yes, the young author of The Red Badge of Courage, and Mr. Botwright of Mr. Hearst's Journal. How may I be of service to you?"

We told him our mission. Crane, with his boyish politeness, said we owed the Spanish government the courtesy of hearing its explanation of the Cuban situation. deLome sat back, and puffed on a long cigar. "That would be novel." deLome said he could not understand why Mr. Hearst wanted to make war between the two nations. He said the Spanish government was doing its best to make peace with the Cuban rebels.

"I have found Mr. McKinley to be sympathetic. Unless I'm mistaken, he doesn't want war. However, he has advisors who feel otherwise. It would make no sense for the United States to go to war with Spain. For what? You do not want Cuba. Do you honestly think the insurrectos are capable of governing the island?"

Without waiting for an answer, deLome swung out of his chair and opened the curtains behind his desk. Bright sunlight, heightened by the recent snowfall, filled the room.

"Gentlemen, Spain has no wish with anyone to make war, especially the United States. We have been looking for an honorable solution to the Cuba problem for years. Your suggestions are welcome."

At this point, Crane unfolded the copy of the letter Lee had given me, and placed it before deLome. He took it and read it swiftly. "Where did you get this?" His hand shook. "This is private correspondence, not an official document."

"You do not speak too highly of President McKinley," Crane said mildly. deLome reddened. "Every diplomat here has his own opinions of McKinley. That is part of our job, to study government leaders. You would do the same thing in my country," deLome said.

deLome demanded return of the original of the letter. We told him no. He got angry, and spat Spanish oaths at us. Later, on the street, Crane turned up his coat collar against the cold, and looked up at the solid brick embassy. "Well, he told us that it was his. You have to hand it to the British."

That afternoon I wrote a lengthy Sunday article based on the letter, and mailed it off to New York. Then I made reservations at the theater for that evening. I did it hurriedly. I didn't want to think about it, and perhaps decide to see her again was dangerous folly. Crane decided that he wanted to attend the program, too.

The theater was a shabby imitation of the music halls on the Bowery. There was a full bill of performers. She appeared half-way down the bill. Not a star act, but very effective despite that. She did a turn in a set of tights suitable for riding the bicycle she had wheeled on stage. Her voice was clear and firm. When she loosened her hair and rode the bike around the stage, she ignited the men in the audience. They whistled and stamped their feet in approval. It was not so much what she did, but how she did it. Annie had that talent. I was mesmerized. I talked Crane into moving with me to another seat closer to the stage. Later, after a Dutch comedy act, she took her second turn. She pranced on stage to a light march, waving a parasol like a rifle. I was close enough to see the light sprinkle of moisture on her forehead and on her upper lip.

She noticed me in the second chorus. She nearly faltered, but quickly moved to the stage opposite. She focused her attention on the audience. I had to let her know that I was in the audience. It was foolhardy. I don't know what I was thinking. Crane and I left the hall before the last act.

"Good program," Steve said.

"I know her," I replied, but he was distracted by the arrival of Bierce. He sat down with us for a late supper.

"I'm having troubles, boys. Women trouble. Got this gal up in Maryland. Widow lady. Rich. Rich enough to marry. Wants me to stay home at night. I'm a nocturnal animal. Got to prowl. But, as I say, she's rich enough to marry.

"Would do it, too, but I haven't figured out what I would do with my one and a half wives in California."

"Wonder if there's anything in the Constitution prohibiting a man from having an Eastern wife and a Western wife?" Crane laughed quietly, enjoying the western wit.

"She doesn't care what I do in the daytime," Bierce said. "But she wants me around at night. It sure plays devil with a reporter's freedom to tomcat around."

"Why don't you bring her along?" Crane asked softly.

"Hell. I can't take her to places I go. I mean, what am

I going to do with her in a parlor house, or one of those gambling hells? She believes that I associate with riffraff, after that she would be fully converted. Unless I give up all that stuff, and stay home nights. At my age it's getting hard to run around all day, romance at night, and still get the copy out."

Crane suggested that Bierce ask Hearst for a young assistant, someone to take care of the job while Ambrose took care of his social life.

"Bierce, I have a serious question. What would it take to see McKinley?"

Bierce swung around in his chair, to face Crane. "What do you mean?" Crane repeated his question.

"You talking money, or what'?"

"No. I mean an interview."

"Well, hell, it doesn't happen. The President by tradition doesn't normally talk to reporters. The last one who did it was Lincoln. Most presidents don't have much to say, anyhow. When he wants something to get out, why, he calls in Senator Hanna, and it's on the street in minutes.

"I would say that if you wanted to see Big Bill you'd have to go through Mark Hanna. Those Ohio ring fellers stick together. Hanna ain't a bad sort. We paint him as some sort of diabolical manipulator. Well, without old Marcus, Big Bill would never have gotten within sniffing distance of that job, and McKinley knows it."

Bierce said he would try to arrange an interview for us through Hanna. The next day, late in the afternoon, Bierce left us a note at the hotel that we had our interview with Hanna scheduled for the following morning.

We entered a big, drafty Senate office and met a massive, tall man with a strangely intelligent face on so large a body. He was as intelligent as he looked. Hanna was generally and rightly considered the political wizard behind the McKinley machine.

Crane came right to the point. "Senator, we want to interview the President." Hanna opened a desk drawer, extradited smoothly: a bottle and three glasses.

"You want to see the President? Hmmm. You know that's unusual. He doesn't give interviews, not like some drummer traveling through Dayton, y'know." Crane said we were looking into the Cuba situation, and wanted the President's thoughts.

"Jim, here, has already spoken to Theodore Roosevelt." Hanna shrugged. "You mean Captain Jingo. Or, the man who wants war by sundown, and annexation by sunrise." Hanna made a sour face. "I understand that a political party has to reward campaign workers, but I've thought that Roosevelt was a little too hair-trigger for this administration. McKinley doesn't want a war. I don't want a war. There's no point to it. Sure, we could maybe grab the island, but what for? Then we'd be responsible for feeding and clothing them. The Jingos don't talk about that—just bullets and hoorays.

"Let me tell you something, boys, Bill was in the Civil War. Seen an awful amount of killing at Antietam. You won't hear Jingo nonsense from him. He knows what war is like."

Hanna said perhaps he could arrange a private interview with McKinley that evening, provided we understood that we couldn't quote the President directly. "I think that your timing is good. Frankly, I don't mind telling you that the Jingos are going too far, and we'll have to pull them aboard the boat soon.

"Gentlemen, you can quote me: this country doesn't need a war. We have just come out of a serious Depression. There are still thousands out of work in the West. It wouldn't be any trouble to recruit many of them for the army, but what for? Have to pay them then, and that means a big appropriation. And that means new taxes.

Congress believes the lower it keeps taxes, the better its chances are for re-election." Hanna boomed with laughter.

As we walked back to the hotel, I pondered what society then considered important. Law, banking, medicine, all these were considered important. I had disappointed my family because I had refused to go into banking. They could not understand why a young fellow like myself would want to tramp around the country for low pay, in a work that led to no tangible rewards they could see. I had argued the point a few times with my father.

Classmates had gone into law, and medicine, but neither held any appeal for me. I did not envy them then, or now. I looked at Steve, and asked him as we walked together if he had ever wanted to do other work.

"Not that I can recall. Always wanted to be a writer. My brother is a newspaper fellow. Runs in the family. I'd like to settle down, though. Make some good money. Hell, don't we all?"

I thought about Dick Davis, older than we were, yet still chasing the elusive news story, for fickle publishers, and an even more fickle public.

"We're just a pair of yellow journalists." Crane smiled.

CHAPTER FIFTEEN

No Picnic Spot

 rane and I pooled our recollections of our interview with McKinley. We decided that what the President said was not all that different from what Hanna, and others in the Administration had said before. We were left with the impression of having talked with a very pleasant man, the kind of fellow who could have been the mayor of Dayton, Ohio, in a reform administration. A man who was a friend of capital and labor. We quickly wrote a joint article and mailed it to New York.

The next day, which began with rain and turned to sleet, convinced us both that we were tired of the muddy city. I sent a telegram to Goddard and he gave us permission to return to New York for the Christmas holidays. The holiday had crept up on me. I was not aware of the calendar any longer.

"Will you go home?" Crane asked

"I don't know. I suppose I should, but frankly, I

don't feel like doing that. Maybe I'll just stay in Manhattan. What'll you do?"

"I'll go up to Port Jervis to see my brother, and my mother. I won't stay long, though. My mother gets to wondering why I didn't follow my father's footsteps in the ministry, and there's no answer for that question. There's little of my life now I can explain to her without hurting her."

On the train to New York Crane said he wished he could return to England right away, as he missed his Cora.

Then, on a wet December 27, with a cold wind whipping down the East River, swaying the telephone wires on poles along Park Row, Hearst gave us our marching orders.

"Davis is coming out of Cuba. I want you two to go in with Sanchez. Meet my yacht in Norfolk, and pick up Davis at Key West. He'll explain how you file copy. Remington is going to stay where he is near Havana. Meet him, and arrange for sketches."

That night we were on the train for Virginia, and the next day we boarded The Cutlass, Hearst's boat. It was a large motor launch, and we made good time beating south toward Key West. I was not comfortable. The sea was not my favorite place. Crane, however, took to the water like a born mariner. He even dressed like one, wearing a pair of white canvas trousers and an open shirt. He didn't shave until we reached Key West, and Dick Davis chided him on his appearance.

It was hot, surprisingly hot, when we arrived in Key West. Summer heat wave hot. The town was a hamlet on a dot in the ocean. The tallest things in the town were the masts on the coal schooners and packets tied at the dock.

The sun baked the place the way it scorched Mulberry Bend in July. Davis met us at the dock. He was dressed in a cool-looking khaki suit, and carrying binoculars and a sidearm. Much has been written about Davis's kit. He practically designed field clothing and equipment for a correspondent. All of it was practical, and the first rule Davis insisted on was: carry what you needed into the field with you. He said it was foolhardy to depend on local supplies. He was right. Davis brought his own bedrolls, netting, clothing, cooking equipment, helmets, watertight packages and canisters, and canned foods.

Davis needed a couple of bearers when he went into the field, but he was able to survive far longer than fools who just jumped into unknown territory, and soon found that their clothing was hot and impractical, and that they couldn't stomach the local diet, and that they couldn't sleep on the ground because of the insects, snakes, and other crawling things.

Scoffers made many jests over the fact that Davis went into the field with dinner clothes, but they failed to note that Davis did not come down with disease, fever, or diarrhea on his expeditions, the way scoffers did.

"Hullo, Jim, Steve. You look like fugitives from 14th Street. Where are your overcoats and boots? Come along. I've booked your rooms in the town's leading hotel."

The hotel turned out to be a batch of small, dank rooms over a saloon. The rooms were stifling in the midday heat. Davis found my wardrobe lacking. "You'll collapse if you wear that woolen stuff," he said, giving me a pair of his khaki trousers. We adjourned to the saloon's covered porch, where we sipped warm beer.

"Well, Dick, what's it like over there?" Crane asked. Davis grinned.

"You fellows are not going to have a nice time. That place is no picnic spot. I'm glad to be out."

"Any trouble?"

"Yes, tons of it. The insurrectos are even suspicious of

us. They're all a weedy group. Are you sure Hearst wants you both over there?"

"I want to go, Dick," I said. Crane just shrugged. "I need the money to get back to England," Steve said.

Davis explained that Sanchez had some business to arrange before he returned to Key West. So, it would be the two of us. Dick gave us the name of a Standard Oil official in Havana who would help us if we needed it. Crane wrote the name and address on the edge of a neckerchief. We waited a few days while the crew refitted the yacht. They much preferred shepherding Hearst and his party around Long Island Sound.

Then a great storm blew up, with heavy rain and high wind for three days. It was my first experience with a tropical storm, and it was worse than anything I had experienced before. We spent the time writing, drinking and reading. Davis, usually the most energetic of men, did not seem to mind the inactivity. He said he had walked too much in Cuba. He gave us tips from his experience for our coming escapade. The night before we sailed a telegram reached us from Hearst in New York. He said that Miss Cisneros was in a Havana jail and we were to free her.

"Now, how the hell are we going to do that without getting put in prison, or killed?" I asked. Davis laughed.

"Don't worry," Steve said, "it'll be a lark." I considered sending Hearst a telegram, resigning from the whole foolhardy enterprise, but I felt I couldn't do that before Dick and Crane. So, on a dark night in early January 1898 we sailed from Key West. The sea was calm, the wind fresh, and my nerves tingling. Before dawn we were off Cuba. The crew put us ashore in a small boat without trouble. We had orders to release a prisoner of a repressive regime. We walked inland, wondering if we would be welcomed, or shot. We headed toward a small town about 20 miles west of Havana. We reached it about midday, hot and dirty from our trek. The town was a church, a cantina, and a batch of unpainted shacks. Some men and children sat near the cantina. We entered it, sat in the rear and Crane ordered us beer in Spanish.

CHAPTER SIXTEEN

Havana, Cuba—January 5, 1898

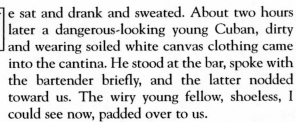e sat and drank and sweated. About two hours later a dangerous-looking young Cuban, dirty and wearing soiled white canvas clothing came into the cantina. He stood at the bar, spoke with the bartender briefly, and the latter nodded toward us. The wiry young fellow, shoeless, I could see now, padded over to us.

"Are you looking for Senor Cisneros?" he asked in heavily accented English. We nodded yes. He was Davis' contact from the earlier trip. As soon as we had reached the hamlet, someone ran with word that two gringos were in town. I did not look too closely at the fellow, but I believe that he carried a pistol. He motioned for us to follow him. For the better part of that afternoon we walked over the hills. I had no idea that Cuba was hilly. There was little shade. We sweated. We emptied our canteens soon, and our guide showed us where we could refill them in a sluggish stream. He did not require as much water as we.

After 5 p.m. the sun began to drop in the sky, and we came to another stream. our guide stopped, and gave a strange bird call, which was answered upstream. Then we were soon surrounded by armed men—insurrectos. They took us to a small shack. There, amid a group of dirty and bearded men, we found Senor Cisneros, resting in the shade of a low tree.

He greeted us coldly.

"I'm afraid that you have come at a terrible time. A group of my best men have been attacked, and slaughtered by one of Weyler's regiments. We are in hiding. There is little I can do for you. Even my daughter is in the hands of the Spaniards."

"Can we get into the city?" Crane asked.

"It would be dangerous. The Spanish are checking everyone. And, if they stop you they might question you, they might put you in one of their camps, or they might shoot you on the roadside." Crane said we had not come to Cuba to hide in the hills. Cisneros shrugged. Over a meager meal later, Cisneros told us his daughter had been arrested at the family home in Havana on suspicion that she was aiding the insurrectos. Senor Cisneros had been working secretly for years in the rebel movement, but once his daughter was arrested he fled to the hills. He said it tore him up inside to leave his daughter in prison, and not be able to do anything for her.

"Senor Hearst wants us to free Evangelina," I said. A surprised Cisneros muttered something in Spanish. He said in English it could not be done. I said we would find a way. Crane chuckled softly.

The following day we set off in a two-wheel wagon with a goat herder taking his flock to market. The herder spoke little English, and we spoke little Spanish. We helped the fellow with his smelly goats. By the time we arrived in the suburbs of Havana, we were grime covered. Crane, with his dark, lank hair, mustache and dark eyes, looked more Cuban than I did.

I hoped that our height would not give us away. We walked through a checkpoint, past a squad of lounging Spanish soldiers at a dusty crossroads. The soldiers, though armed with the latest weapons and good quality uniforms, seemed lazy and preemptory with the Cubans who passed on the road. We walked through without questioning, heads down and shooing the goats. I suspected that the herd smelled too badly for them to want to stop us.

Once in Havana we parted from the herder, and we found ourselves in the wharf area. In a park-like section fronting the harbor, we settled ourselves against some palm trees.

"Well, Steve, what'll we do now? We don't even have a map of the city."

"I guess the smartest thing would be to find someone who does have a map." Crane called to a youth, and wrote a quick note which he gave the boy a coin, and directions to deliver it to the address he had gotten from Davis. Then we sat back to wait. Suddenly I wished that I had a pistol. Crane replied, "And if they catch you with it, they can shoot you as a rebel spy. Sides, we're reporters, not insurrectos."

Within an hour a carriage drew to a stop about 300 yards from us by the sea wall. A man in a white suit alighted and walked toward us. Crane stood and called, "Collins, over here."

The suited figure strolled over and held out his hand. "You gents look like you've walked half the island today. How about a bird and a bottle? Maybe a little cleanup first?"

We followed him down a short street and through a

small doorway set in a stucco wall. We found we were in a rear yard where there was a pump and makeshift washing facilities. "I'll wait for you on the inside," Collins said. We rinsed off most of the dirt and dried ourselves on a dirty rag nailed to the wall.

Inside, we found ourselves in a dark, small restaurant. It had a bar. We gulped chilled beer Collins had waiting for us at a table. "It's all right to speak English. The owner is Swiss, and his wife is English," Collins said, nodding toward the smiling bartender. We introduced ourselves. "Yes, Dick Davis warned me I might have visitors after he left." Collins looked to be about 32. He said he was the Standard Oil salesman in Cuba.

"But, I'm from Boston. Can't wait to get back there. Not part of the Codfish aristocracy, I'm afraid," Collins said with a laugh. "When I was a mere youth, oh, ten or twelve, I worked as an office boy at The Boston Herald. I know newspaper reporters. I've sobered up enough of them."

Ravenous, we ate fried fish and tomatoes. Collins told us that the Spanish authorities had recently clamped down on the populace. At the same time, he said, they told foreigners that they wanted to get off the island. "Can't have it both ways, can they?"

We slept in comfort that night in Collins' villa, a big open house where he had a couple of servants, and plenty of rooms. "I think they're loyal, but no matter. I get visitors all the time," he said. "But I do think you ought to get out of here while the getting is good. The Spanish need me, but you have no such insurance. Weyler is beginning to understand that reporters are as much his problem as insurrectos."

The next morning, while his maids washed our filthy clothing, Crane and I, in robes, and Collins sat on a patio in the sun and had breakfast. Collins gave us the latest about Spanish strength on the island. "They have five regiments, here and there, including one composed of

Cubans. It's a mistake to think that all Cubans want independence. A minority are loyal to Spain, a minority are rebels, and the majority are too hungry, too poor to care."

Collins suggested that we return to our boat as soon as practical. That's when Crane told him we had been sent in to free Miss Cisneros.

"My God," was all Collins said at first. I noticed that Crane seemed worn from the efforts of the last few days. He looked like he hadn't slept the night.

I said, "Mr. Hearst wants the girl out of the prison. We have to get her out. Do you have any ideas?" Collins looked at us, speechless.

"My God, man, that jail is a fortress. You'll get killed trying to get her out. And she'll be killed, too." Collins tried to argue us out of our mission, unsuccessfully. I must admit that I had second, even third thoughts about the assignment. It was one thing to interview someone and write an article. It was another to break into a prison and help someone escape. Again, I realized we were unarmed. The only weapon we had was the $200 worth of gold pieces that Davis had given us before we left Key West.

Later, in clean clothing, we got Collins to take us to the fortress where the girl was being kept. It was an ancient series of high-walled buildings near the harbor. It looked impenetrable. But I noted that its gates and most windows were not barred.

Our stroll through the area did not excite undue interest. The uniformed soldiers only glanced at us with boredom. After our walk we went with Collins to his office on the main commercial street nearby. Collins motioned to one of the Cubans in the office, and they spoke in a soft Spanish in a corner for a few minutes.

"Well, my man says that they are keeping her in one of the buildings, not the cells underground. It's because she's a woman that they have accorded her this privilege. She is guarded, however. So, escape is an impossibility."

"What would it take to bribe a couple of the guards?" Crane asked.

Collins shrugged. He took us into his office, where he dropped wearily into a chair. "You might be able to bribe a few guards, and maybe you could get into her rooms, and maybe you could get her out of the fortress. But what then? Could you get her safely off the island? There's sure to be a big ruckus if she escapes. Weyler will turn the island over looking for her."

"Maybe she could hide in the hills with her father," I suggested. Collins laughed, and pulled at his hair. "Why am I getting involved in all this? Weyler's liable to shoot me too, and the home office won't be too happy about that."

Crane and I argued and cajoled Collins all that day. Finally, in the afternoon, he sent one of his servants with instructions to ask at the Fortress about the girl. The servant was to act as a distraught country relative. She was a convincing actress, and her sobbing, crying act worked. The woman returned to tell Collins what building the girl was in—a small, two-story building where the girl was being held on the top floor under guard.

Collins, fortunately, had an old map of the downtown areas, including the Fortress. The small building was located next to a Fortress wall, and away from the main gate and its sentries. Crane suggested that we could climb the wall, and somehow get into the building and free the girl.

"How?" Collins asked. We had no answer.

For two days Crane and I watched the guards, and their changing of the guard mount. We discovered that the overnight guards usually took their breakfast in a cantina nearby, and the three of us decided to approach one of the sergeants there with our ploy. Collins was skeptical about our plan, but with a shake of his head he agreed to try it. We would be gambling, in a way, with our lives. The approach could result in our arrest, and possibly, execution.

As Crane was the darker fellow, more Cuban looking, it was decided that he would play the principal role. It helped that he could speak a bit of Spanish. The next morning, about eight, after the drum rolls, and clank of rifles, we followed the handful of off-duty guards into the cantina. Collins and Crane began cultivating the sergeant, a thin man with a large nose. Collins engaged him in conversation while Crane sat in the rear of the cantina. Collins bought the sergeant breakfast and a few rum drinks. The sergeant didn't resist. I loitered outside. The next morning we repeated the scene. The third morning, over a mid-morning rum, Collins pried from the sergeant the facts that he had a large family in Spain and it was hard to support it on an army income. Collins suggested quietly that there must be ways for such a man to improve his income. Quiet favors, no doubt. The sergeant laughed. He said that had been possible when he had worked in the storeroom, but it was difficult now just being in charge of stupid guards.

"There may be a way a man could honestly earn $100 in gold without risk," Collins said. I did not overhear the conversation, of course. Collins told me later. The sergeant reacted with interest. Collins went further.

In desperation we had concocted a story that Crane was Miss Cisneros's desperate lover, a man who would pay anything to see his beloved. For $100 in gold the lover expected a few hours with his woman, possibly at night. All the sergeant would have to do, Collins whispered, was to see to it that Crane got into her rooms for a few hours one dark night.

The sergeant laughed, and Collins said he could feel the hangman's rope. Collins took a gold piece from his pocket and dropped it near the sergeant's hand. "You can collect five of these with no work," Collins said. It worked. The man's greed overcame his fear of his superiors. I think the argument succeeded because Collins only spoke of Crane going in, not Miss Cisneros coming out. A few hours dalliance, and who would be the wiser? The sergeant would be the richer. After payment of the first coin, the sergeant explained that the girl was watched during the day by an older woman. The girl was allowed to walk about, but at night she was locked in her room. The sergeant said he could arrange to have his men avoid the area for a few hours.

Collins clinched the deal by telling the man that all he would have to open the girl's door, then lock it after Crane.

That evening we went over the plan, over a bottle of rum. Collins had found a ladder long enough to get us over the wall. It was too long to hide anywhere, so we laughingly decided we would carry it. If anyone stopped us, Collins said, we would tell them we were going serenading. Crane would go over first, meet the sergeant, be admitted to Miss Cisneros' apartment. The Crane would open the second story window and we would use the long ladder from the top of the wall to the window ledge. They would crawl along the ladder to the wall, and from there we would all climb down the ladder.

"My God, we've forgotten something important," Collins yelled after we had gone over the plan for the fourth time.

"What?" we shouted.

"We haven't told the girl that we are coming," Collins shouted.

"Well," Crane drawled. "She ain't going anywhere till we get there. I'll tell her." I took another drink, thinking we'd all be killed. I didn't want to give voice to my fear. Collins said it for us. The rum cheered, but not enough to quell the shudder entirely.

So, about midnight we marched through the silent streets, carrying a long ladder. It was a miracle we weren't stopped.

Collins and Crane went up the ladder first. I held it for them. Then I climbed it and grabbed the top of the wall. It was just wide enough to let a man sit with his legs dangling one on each side. It was uncomfortable, but we lowered the ladder to the other side, and Crane quietly descended. We watched him as he boldly walked to the corner of the building, and then he disappeared in the shadows. Clouds obscured a rather full moon, fortunately for us. We waited. I expected gunfire at any second. I was so terrified I couldn't breathe. I thought the Spaniards would hear me. Collins was impassive.

It was what teemed like a half hour later before we heard the shutters open on the second floor of the building, about 15 feet from where we perched. Then we heard low voices. A woman's voice seemed to soar in anger.

Collins and I lifted the ladder, pulling enough of it over the wall behind us so we could cantilever it onto the window sill across the way. With effort and strain Collins and I managed to get the ladder into the window, and balanced on our end of the wall. About five feet of ladder hung out over the street. We waited.

Soon a figure made its way from the window out onto the ladder, and toward us. It was Crane. When he was close enough to talk quietly, he called my name.

CHAPTER SEVENTEEN

New York—January 13, 1898

e sailed home a few days later, after we waited for further orders from the chief. None came. So, independently, we headed north. We had grown weary of Florida, and Cuba and its problems seemed too much for us. It was hard to think of the rights of a nation and its people when all we were thinking was saving our skin.

Crane wandered away soon after we got to Manhattan. The city smelled and looked differently. I was not used to the pervasive coal smoke which hovered over the town in winter. It was cold, and I shivered for days. My colleagues in the newsroom noticed my Sunday articles, and my sunburn. They said they were jealous. Davis was nowhere around. We found out later that he had gone home to Philadelphia for a visit with his parents.

I found a brief note in my mail box from Chapin. When I saw his signature, I almost tossed it away. It read: "A damn nuisance, name of Reiser, has been pestering me to find out where you are. I told him Cuba, but he won't believe me. You tell him." Typically Chapin.

That morning I wandered around City Hall Park, bored and restless. Nothing seemed to interest me. I was sure that Hearst would have another adventure waiting for me, and Goddard would have the illustrations all planned even before he saw the copy. But I had lost interest.

When I got back to the office I called the Rev. Dr. Reiser, and his daughter answered.

"Why, Mr. Botwright. We had wondered what happened to you. I know my father was interested in talking to you again." She put him on the line.

"Yes, I've been to The World many times, trying to get that troublesome Mr. Chapin to tell me where you had gone."

"Well, for some months I have been in Washington, and then in Cuba for the last couple of days."

"Oh, we must hear about that. You must come for dinner tomorrow, please?"

It was something to do. "Yes, certainly." I knew that without something to keep me busy I would start drinking. I suppose I was just exhausted. But I didn't have any ambition.

The following evening I took a omnibus downtown. Reiser and his daughter lived in a small parsonage next to his church on Grand Street. The area was then mostly east European immigrants, but many Germans remained, the remnants of the first waves of peoples to our shores.

Rev. Reiser opened the door. "Well, well, my boy. You look fine for all your travels. Let me take your coat." I sat and sipped sherry when the clergyman filled his pipe. Hilda came into the parlor, wearing an apron, and smiling. I had never seen her smile before. She was beautiful.

"That newspaper story you wrote last summer has paid

many dividends," she said. "Other church groups in Manhattan and Brooklyn now support us." She smiled, shyly, and returned to the kitchen. I watched her straight back disappear through the swinging door.

Her father said, "She is now working at Bellevue Hospital." Quickly he asked questions which elicited my background, parentage, and schooling.

"Ah, yes, Yale. I attended Hamilton, you know, but Yale, yes, yes." He seemed very pleased.

I asked, tactlessly, about his wife. "She died five years ago. Hilda was our only child. She has stayed to care for me."

The chicken dinner later convinced me that I had been eating badly in various hotels for months. I found that I was famished. I praised Hilda. She blushed.

Over coffee, we spoke of Cuba. "It's a strange place. Many of the natives don't wear shoes. Of course, they speak a different language, and they have different customs, and only a few want the United States to get them free of the Spanish. I wonder if we should do it. Then they might decide they have to get free of us." I spoke on about the island, but my attention was caught by the tall, full-bodied woman in the room. She moved with ease, and I couldn't help but notice how narrow her waist was. When she put the coffee cup near my chair she bent over, and I caught her aroma, like May flowers. This woman was more subtle than, well, Annie. Something was happening.

Reiser excused himself, leaving us together. She looked at me with a straightforward gaze. "Will you go back?"

"That's up to the chief, uh, Mr. Hearst. She looked at her watch, and said, "Mr. Botwright, it's been educational listening to you, but now I must leave to go to work."

"Work?" I asked, puzzled.

"Yes, at Bellevue. I work on the night nursing shift." I said the first thing that popped into my head. "May I escort you there, then?" She smiled, and nodded.

A few minutes later we started off from her doorstep. We walked for two blocks to get a hack. I asked if she encountered any trouble on the streets at night. She laughed. "When I first started, a few men thought I was a streetwalker but they have learned to leave me alone." She waved her walking stick at me.

"Did you ever hit anyone with that?"

"Only once."

As I sat in the cab with this tall, full-bodied blonde with the level gaze and businesslike manner, it struck me she might be an antidote to the low feelings I had been experiencing.

"Would you go to Koster and Bials with me tomorrow night?"

She smiled. "I must work tomorrow night, Mr. Botwright.

You work more than even we reporters, I sighed. She laughed.

We must care for our patients, she added.

And we must care for out publishers, I said. But we can't work all the time. Suddenly it seemed important to me to take this woman to dinner and a performance. I would not give up.

When I look back today I'm glad I didn't. "Then Saturday night. Surely, you don't work on Sunday." She nodded no, and sat quietly. "Well?"

"It would be pleasant," she said, and blushed again. I told her I would pick her up at seven, and we'd have supper afterward. The hack stopped at the hospital, and with a quick goodnight she was out in the street and walking rapidly toward the hospital building. I slumped in my seat. I gave the hackman my address and for the first time in months felt like I had returned home. I got to the drafty Journal office late the next morning. That was the day that Hearst got the famous cable from Remington. I didn't see the cable, just the way Crane and I missed Remington when we were in Havana breaking into a prison. But I heard the story. It became an instant legend. Remington had cabled the chief that his mission in Cuba was hampered because he was not able to find any atrocities to sketch. He told Hearst that all was quiet; there was no war boiling.

"Furnish the pictures, and I'll furnish the war," Hearst replied. I don't know for sure if he actually sent such a message. I find it hard to believe that the Spaniards would allow such a telegram to be delivered. Of course, the chief could have sent it to Key West, where Remington had to return.

Remington was only reporting that the insurrectos were not active. They seemed beaten, hamstrung for lack of arms, supplies and popular support.

That same afternoon Davis showed up in the cityroom, looking dashing in an elegant blue suit, new shoes and one of the new soft collars. "They're more comfortable for daytime wear," he told me. His appearance triggered confusion in the editors' ranks. They thought Dick was still patrolling off Cuba.

"Too quiet down there. And, I tend to get sea sick," he told Goddard with a smile.

Only Davis could flaunt Hearst's directives and get away with it.

Energized by Davis' appearance, I left the office quietly that afternoon and made for Brooks Brothers, where I bought new clothing, shirts, shoes and an overcoat. I had nearly $1,000 in back pay, and I decided to splurge, if only to impress Miss Reiser that I had more to wear than a single set of ragged clothing, like the Yellow Kid. When I realized my intent, I felt much better. That evening I ordered a dozen roses sent to her home.

I spent the next day, Saturday, in the office, looking over printer's proofs of the Davis article—the search of Miss Cisneros. Hearst had decided that the search and rescue would be the perfect one-two punch on consecutive Sundays. Davis was not around. I was dazzled by the Remington drawing. I felt alive and interested in everything for the first time in weeks. I felt like it was spring and not the last week in January 1898.

Hilda was ready when I called, and we set off in a rented carriage. I had decided that any expense was warranted. Hilda wore a plain brown coat over a tan dress, and a tan cartwheel hat. I had arranged for box seats at New York's premiere musical variety house. The program was, as usual, light and very entertaining. I particularly enjoyed a young juggler named Fields who was very humorous in his attempts to keep more than three pins in the air at any time.

Hilda seemed to enjoy the program very much. In the carriage on the way uptown I explained that we would have supper at Jack's. It was on the Westside, in the 40s, and different in most respects from restaurants of the period. You could find all types dining there. It was a newspapermen's hangout, police frequented it, as did lawyers, judges, and even criminals. I had once seen Monk Eastman there one night with a couple of his rowdies, including Lefty Louie, but they were on their best behavior. It was a loud, boisterous place, but suitable to take a respectable woman. It was after ten when we arrived. Jack's was in full operation. The decor was not all fancy. Decor meant nothing at Jack's. The patrons were colorful enough. A waiter I knew recognized me when we arrived, and we were seated at a table for two on a far wall. It was a fine place to sit and watch.

Dick Davis spotted us right away. Richard Harding Davis had the amazing ability of noticing every single person in a crowded room without seeming to do it. There were many he noticed that he wouldn't talk to, and those he ignored.

"Well, James, it's a fine night, and I thought I would compliment you on your new finery, and fine company." He bowed. We shook hands, and I introduced him to Hilda. Dick sat down with us, and chatted.

"I must get back upstairs. The chief is up there with a party of opera singers. He has the most eclectic interests, you know. It's amazing." Davis then turned his full attention on Hilda. With smooth questioning, Davis learned that she was a nurse, and that I had written about her the summer before.

Dick smiled and nodded, and soon excused himself and left our table gracefully.

"I never dreamed that I would meet Richard Davis," Hilda said. She added that young women considered Davis to be their beau ideal. She blushed. "He thinks a great deal of you," she said. I was embarrassed.

"He's a gentleman, who gets along with everyone," I said.

Just then a large party entered the restaurant, distracting us from Davis. The party was made up of girls and young men from one of the musical shows. The women wore shimmering silk dresses of delicate pastel hues, and the young men were all handsome in the new cleancut fashion. Beards and mustaches were considered old-fashioned. Their laughter was like the champagne they ordered.

We stared rudely at them, but they were oblivious of the attention they were getting from the other diners.

"Okay, what'll yez have?" barked the old Irish waiter behind me. He wore a dinner jacket, and a long white apron over his trousers. "Don't waste your time on the menu. Take the roast beef and be glad. Some oyster stew to start." We laughed, and he moved toward the kitchen.

The meal was swiftly served, and it was delicious. Afterward we walked a few blocks downtown, with the carriage and the hired hack driver following us discretely.

"Do you know all those important persons who were in the restaurant," Hilda asked.

"Some on sight, but most of them don't know me."

"No. I would say that many of them know who you are," she said.

I would have walked the length of Broadway that cold night to prolong our parting.

"I must get home. It's nearly midnight. Poppa will expect me at services tomorrow morning."

"What time does he preach?"

"Ten o'clock," she said.

"May I escort you?"

She smiled. "That would be nice." We nestled together in the cab for warmth. I did not put my arm around her, however, and it's one of the things that I've regretted all my life, among many other things.

I was up and finished dressing the next morning by eight. We sat in the front pew. The service was pleasant, and it reminded me that I hadn't been in a church since I last saw my parents.

Rev. Reiser spoke about the need to forgive our enemies. He spoke eloquently and succinctly. I felt that morning like I had no enemies, nor any chances of developing any.

Afterward, outside on the church steps, Reiser beamed at us, and insisted that I stay for Sunday dinner. I accepted gladly. Hilda said quietly, "I've already told Gerda to set another place."

I excused myself to go to a news stand on the next block to buy the Sunday papers. In the Reiser parlor I went through the Journal. The Remington drawing and the abbreviated account of the search of the Cisneros girl took up most of page one. The World didn't have anything to match it. The World was given over to a hodge-podge of accounts of floods in the Ohio River valley, defalcations in the stock houses, and an article speculating on what McKinley would do in the face of Cuban outrages. The Journal had the Cuban outrage.

Hilda saw The Journal on the floor where I had tossed it. She looked at the drawing and read the story. "Do they do such things?" I shrugged. I told her that I hadn't seen it myself, but if Dick Davis had, why, that was good enough for me.

"The Spanish have no shame," she said. "This poor girl. Do you know her?"

"Well, last week I rescued her from a Spanish jail."

Hilda look at me for a moment. "Is she pretty?"

I lowered the page of The World that I had been reading. "Beautiful, just the real stuff," I said, smiling. I thought that Hilda would get the joke. But she just left the room without another word. For the rest of that very pleasant day she looked at me with a strange expression. I couldn't make out what it was, but I definitely had increased my stature in her eyes. The day passed as pleasantly as any I had lived till that point.

We had dinner. Then we sat in the parlor. Mr. Reiser wanted to know about Cuba, and the chance for war.

"There will be war," I blurted. I wondered what had made me make that assertion. Both accepted it as fact, without argument.

At dusk, when I was getting into my coat in the hall later I kissed Hilda. I hadn't planned to do it, it was just that we were standing close together. She smiled, but didn't say anything. I went home without a care, I had no memory of the anger and pain that had ripped at me for months. Hilda was like the new May flowers, all clean and sweet.

Thus lulled, I was not at all prepared for the storm

which roared up the next day. Dick Davis, who had spent the weekend with his parents, returned on a late train, and he picked up a copy of The Sunday Journal at the train station.

He saw the drawing, and the story, and both ignited his temper. A sub-headline indicated that the report had come from correspondent Davis. When I arrived at The Journal office the next morning, a small group of reporters and copyboys were huddled in a corridor near Hearst's office, from which vantage point they could hear Davis yelling at the chief. Davis told me much later that when he had arrived at the paper that morning, waving the offending edition, he had demanded that Hearst immediately put out a correction. The chief, surprised by Dick's reaction, tried to placate him. Willie had to handle the explosive Davis alone. The chief tried everything he could to cool down his star correspondent. Nothing seemed to work.

"It's all wrong. It's false, and it plays into the hands of the Spaniards," Dick yelled. Dick demanded a retraction. Willie refused on the general grounds that the report was essentially correct. The mistake was compounded by the fact that Davis, and he agreed when he had calmed down years later, had not been precise when he reported that Miss Cisneros had been searched.

Dick had failed to explain that the girl was not searched on board the boat by male officials. She had been taken ashore and searched by Spanish matrons, in privacy. But, angered over the picture and report, Dick was twice as inflamed because the chief refused to back down.

After 10 minutes, Davis stormed out of Willie's office, and without a word to anyone, left the building. It looked like Hearst had a major problem on his hands. Richard Harding Davis was a respected journalist who traded on his veracity. He didn't need to lean on Hearst's money, or influence to survive. It did not pay, or make sense, to offend Davis.

For the rest of that day the talk was about what Davis would do. It was obvious that he wouldn't work for Hearst anymore. We didn't have to wait long to find out. Two days later, a letter, written by Dick, appeared in The Herald. It was an admission that the story which had appeared in The Journal was a fraud. Davis, we soon heard, was now working for James Gordon Bennett.

Despite their personal attitudes and opinions about what Hearst was doing to New York journalism in those days, virtually no other publisher in the city would attack the chief, or allow one of his reporters to attack in print another publisher. Then as now, publishers acted as if they were members of the same club. They are. They all had the same interests. Competition in the streets was one thing, but personal attack had long been out of fashion. Except for one-publisher, James Gordon Bennett, a man so erratic he would attack anyone. Fortunately, Bennett wasn't in Manhattan much of the year, preferring Europe. Bennett was not part of the circulation war, or the real war. Bennett was too busy with his own hedonistic life in Paris to care about such things. Among the New York publishers of the time, Bennett was the wild card, a playboy more interested in women and sports than foreign affairs.

CHAPTER EIGHTEEN

Washington

I knocked on Davis' door. He opened it, dressed in a dark maroon dressing gown. "Hello, Jim. Come in." I stood nervously in the hallway.

"Dick, I want to apologize for that article. You see, Hearst had me write it up, even though we, Goddard and I, wanted to ask you a few questions about it. Well, actually, it was Goddard who had the qualms."

"It's all right, Jim. I don't hold you responsible. You just did what you were told to do. Hearst explained that to me. Come on in."

He gave me a drink, and told me that he had taken a job with The Herald. "Dick, I'm considering resigning from The Journal. I didn't like the way Hearst treated you, or the way he treats Steve."

Davis jumped to his feet. "No. No. You mustn't do that. But," he laughed, "I think we must get you out of town before Willie makes you the scapegoat because of all this embarrassment. Willie doesn't like embarrassment. Willie has strange ways of paying back people who cause him embarrassment. Listen, I'm leaving in two days for London. Why don't you come with me?"

Davis said he would show me around. He had me half convinced, when I remembered Hilda.

"You make it sound wonderful, Dick, but there's one reason why I can't leave town now." Davis laughed. "I guessed as much. But, maybe some other time."

He added that Hilda seemed more than enough reason to put by bachelor ways. To change the subject, I asked a question.

"What do you know about Captain Lee, and this English fellow Churchill who says he works for the London Times?"

"Oh, yes, the captain and that reporter with the puffy face. Met Lee at an embassy dinner over there. Awful peachy sort of fellow, you know. Wanted to know what I knew about an awful lot of places and persons. I got the feeling that I was being interviewed. I forget where I met Churchill. He's Lee's pal."

"I think that they're both spies."

Davis laughed. "Of course, Jim. Lee is one, definitely. Churchill, too. Jim, everyone expects military attaches to be spies. That's the point of the job. Churchill,when I first met him, was in uniform, some guardsregiment, I believe. Someone told me that he left the regiment on a sort of military leave of absence, you see, to move around the world for The Times. The British have a lot of the world to patrol, but they generally like to do things quietly.

"Why, if we Americans had to do that kind of work, we'd send in a dozen men where one would do, and eleven of them would be falling over each other, and making a holy nuisance of themselves. Thank God we're not in that business."

Washington, February 16, 1898

I was depressed in Washington. The city was bleak. I knew that my low feeling was caused by my distance from Hilda. Even the companionship of Bierce paled. At 9:40 that night, probably as Bierce and I were arguing over where to spend the rest of the evening, the U.S. Battleship Maine blew up and sunk in Havana harbor, killing 260 sailors and four officers. We knew nothing of this. If I had known of it, it wouldn't have surprised me.

The news came the following dawn, when I was awakened by a telephone call from New York. There being no telephones on the upper floors of the hotel, I was obliged to pad down to the lobby in my robe to listen to a faint-voiced but excited Journal editor tell me that the ship had exploded. I was half asleep.

"The news came in from Key West and Havana, after midnight," he told me. I hadn't even known that the ship had been in Havana. It was there when Crane and I were frolicking with Evangelina at the prison.

"Get all the reaction you can. The chief says this is the story that will make war."

I got dressed quickly, and ate a hasty breakfast in the sickly, gray dawn. I rushed out to find that Washington was not as excited by the disaster as was the New York editor. In fact, Washington was still asleep. The streets were empty. It was seven, early even for the work-bound clerks.

I found a sleepy hackman who took me to Roosevelt's home in Georgetown. I didn't have to pound on his door. A marine guard in uniform opened it at my knock. He showed me to the library where the Dutchman was holding a war council. With him were two officers of our navy, although they weren't in uniform.

Teddy bounded from behind his desk. "You've gotten the news then. Dastardly, dastardly. They will have to do something now. No way to get around it." He practically danced with glee. I took notes and TR didn't seem to mind. He introduced me to one of the men with him, Captain Lucius Nevel. I asked him if he knew the Maine's captain.

"Yes, I know Sigsbee. Fine fellow. This is a tragedy," he said in a clipped Yankee accent. I pressed him for more details about Sigsbee and his career. Nevel answered, after a nod from Roosevelt.

Later that morning we went to TR's crowded office in the War Department. The only real facts we had were that the ship had suffered a fatal blast, her captain had been plucked from the water by the Spanish, and a large loss of life among American sailors was rumored. The Maine, we later learned from cables, burned for four hours before she sank.

About noon, Captain Lee, whom I hadn't seen since he passed me the deLome letter, appeared in civilian dress.

At the time it didn't strike me as odd that Lee seemed to turn up at the momentus time. I took it the way I took everything else during that period—part of the flow of things. British persons were not unusual in New York, where they came on business or to be lionized by the social leaders of the period. To meet a Englishman in Washington did not stir any suspicions I might have had. In fact, I had none. Lee was part of the passing parade, and I didn't question why he, a British officer, was so willing to pass on secrets to a New York reporter he barely knew.

I had a lot of growing up to do. He called me aside. We walked outside together. I waited while he packed his pipe.

"Big trouble, this," Lee said. "We've had cables from our ambassador. He said the ship is down. No one knows how or why. The Spanish disclaim all responsibility. They are blaming the insurrectos. It doesn't look like they deliberately blew up the ship to start a war. The Spanish are very worried about how Americans will react.'

"React?" I said. "Hell, Americans will want to blow up

the entire Spanish fleet. You know that." He nodded, and puffed on his pipe.

I telegraphed my story to New York that afternoon, and it was so long that it cost the amazing sum of $55 to send. I wrote thousands of words.

Later, I ran across Bierce, and he was upset. "This is it, Botwright. I'm leaving. Willie has his war, and he'll want me to lead the attack on the nearest Spaniards. I'm going back to San Francisco." I laughed. At first I thought that he was joking. But Bierce was gone by the end of the week and he didn't notify New York. He just packed and took the train. Bierce wanted nothing to with another war. He told me repeatedly, "This war means the shoemakers and embalmers will get rich. A lot of young fellows will die, and many fools will come out of it with one less arm or leg.

"And, two years after it's over, no one will remember why it started. Have nothing to do with it. Take a cruise. Go to Europe." I never saw Bierce again.

I was very busy for the next three days, filing copy to New York, about Roosevelt's actions as he ordered the American fleet into operation. He hadn't any official orders from the President of these United States, or anyone else. But he did it. He had the ships, and he moved them all over the globe, filling their bunkers with coal and converging on Spanish imperial territories like Cuba, Puerto Rico, and the Philippines.

During the period TR excoriated McKinley for the President's inaction. The President, Roosevelt said solemnly, had collapsed on hearing about the Maine, and could not meet the situation. I could not reach Sen. Hanna to confirm this story, and so I didn't think it was wise to send it to New York, as TR no doubt intended when he told me about it. In my accounts I said that McKinley was "studying the situation."

Each day the New York train brought editions of The World and The Journal, and it seemed that each was vying daily to beat the Spanish on the sea and on land, even though no war had been declared. By the following Thursday, The Journal headlined my story that Roosevelt was convinced that the explosion was no accident.

Hearst put a $50,000 reward notice on the front page of The Journal, for the detection of the outrage. He never had to pay the reward. The World countered by expanding a theory that the Spanish had attached a mine to the Maine's hull. Day by day the newspaper war rolled on, often hanging on big black headlines supported by the flimsiest of information, or no information at all.

I was surprised by it all. The war, it seemed, was being fought between Joe Pulitzer and Willie Hearst. In Washington there was quiet. Roosevelt was making jingo noises, but Hanna, by various political stratagems, had allies hold the warhawks in check for the time being. I returned to New York, where a beaming Hearst greeted me with a $1,000 cash bonus, and slaps on my back.

"Of course, you'll be on our war team," he said happily. Davis, I discovered, was still in England. I had a letter from him awaiting me.

"Jim, the war won't be tomorrow. And, it may never come. But if it does, save me a chair. I'll be back in plenty of time for it. Another war won't make much difference to me.

"This one would be very popular among our readers. But it won't be popular among the brokers and traders, and the bankers. They reflect McKinley's thinking that war now would just be an expensive picnic with little return.

"We could grab a few down at-the-heel territories, which we could probably buy now from the Spaniards."

Dick gave me another piece of advice, one which I took. He suggested that I buy field gear. "Go down to

Brooks and have them fit you for a suit of khaki, make it two or three, get some high boots, and camping gear. Put it on Hearst's bill." The next day I went down to Brooks. I was a bit surprised to see Roosevelt in the store, being fitted for khaki.

"Hello, Botwright," he boomed. "Must get the right rig for the fancy dress ball, eh?"

"I thought you'd be wearing navy blue for the coming battle?"

"Thought about it. Thought about it. But the trouble is I have no experience commanding ships. And that Annapolis crowd has a dim view of civilians in uniform. They don't mind me as assistant secretary of the navy, but they don't want me on one of their boats. And I'll be dog-goned if I'll let em stick me in some shipyard, overseeing clerks buying tar.

"They are good men, mind you, but the navy is a limit-ed partnership, you might say. I don't want to be quoted, of course." He gave me one of those wide grins. I was about to ask him what experience he had in land warfare, but I thought better of it. Irony, I supposed, would be lost on the man. I looked at him: a middle-age husband and father who couldn't wait to go to war. I knew I had no hunger to go to war. I was willing to believe it was as ter-rible as its survivors said it was.

I spent as much time as I could with Hilda. She was my only interest, frankly. The newspapers spoke of war, and the citizens showed the flag that they had tucked away for the 4th of July. There was much shouting and yelling, sounds you'd hear at a close football game.

Hilda and I skated. We walked. As she worked at night we met in the afternoons. I just left the office. Goddard was after me constantly for more Sunday articles, but he also saw something in my face that warned him not to press too hard.

One cold afternoon we sat on the park bench in Madison Square.

"Will they make you go to war?"

I looked at her worried face. "I don't know if they can make me do that. I may have to do it, just to keep my job." I took her hands. "But don't worry. I don't intend to be a hero."

"You silly goose. I know you'll be a hero."

"Tomorrow or the next day I must return to Washington. That's all I care about. Will you come down and see me?"

"I would like to, but papa can't get away."

"Come alone."

"You know I can't, Jim. I must have a chaperon."

"Why?"

She smiled, and touched my face. I kissed her—in public—and I didn't give a damn, not even if the entire 71st regiment marched by, hooting.

The next day Roosevelt and I took the same train to Washington. But we sat in different cars. There was a note from Hanna at my hotel. He wanted to see me. I went to his office the next morning.

"Those idiots mean to stir up a war, and the pressure is building in Congress. Your paper is in large part responsible. Doesn't Hearst realize what war means?" Hanna asked.

I had no reply.

"The Spanish weren't responsible for the Maine. McKinley knows that. It's not logical that the Spanish would blow up the ship then stand by and pick up survivors from the water.

"What would they gain by blowing up the ship? Nothing. The problem we have is that this naval commission we have studying the explosion can't study the Maine, not when it is buried in Havana harbor.

"I want you to write a rational article, explaining these facts. We have nothing to gain by fighting the Spanish, and they have nothing to gain by attacking us," Hanna said.

I rose and walked behind the chair. "Mr. Hanna, what you say may be correct, but Mr. Hearst tells me what to write.

"Well, I'm giving you a statement, dammit, from the President. You can use his name if you have to."

I took out a small note pad, and wrote down his remarks.

They and others went into the daily stories that New York editors demanded. Sometimes they demanded different stories for late editions. It was hard to keep up, but I didn't mind the activity at all. It kept my mind occupied.

Soon the board convened by the Navy Department began its deliberations into what actually had happened aboard the Maine that night. I found out where the board met—an old wooden building near the Smithsonian—and haunted the place. I was the only reporter around for two days. The reason was the other reporters were not inventive enough to find out where the hearing was being conducted. I just drove up to the War Department Building in a hack, and demanded of a civilian guard where it was. He told me. It was not my fault he took me for a possible witness.

The building was drafty, and must have been built during the Civil War. The board met in a large room on the second floor. I was stopped by a marine guard when I entered the first day, but I told him I was there for the hearing, and he too took me for a witness. I calmly walked up the stairs, and found the doors to the room closed. By placing my ear to the wall I was able to distinguish the various mumbles, and piece together a story which I filed quietly that evening.

The guard passed me through the door the next morning, but I knew that I was pressing my luck. This session of the board was to take testimony, and the hallways, both downstairs, and upstairs were filled with men in navy uniforms. I again tried to look like I belonged in their company.

At mid-morning I was lurking near the wall of the room when a civilian climbed the stairs at a bound, and called me.

"Hey, Botwright! What the hell are you doing here?"

It was Collins. His smile was infectious. He wore a business suit, and the only indication that he might have come from the tropics was his tan, which glowed above his stiff collar.

"Are you to testify?" I asked. He nodded.

"Yes. I saw the rescue efforts in the Bay. I didn't actually see the explosion, but I was in a carriage with, uh, a young lady."

"What happened?"

"Well, the ship just blew up. I think it was an accident. The Spanish immediately launched longboats to help with rescue. They were as surprised as anyone. I mean, the Maine was only a few hundred yards from the nearest Spanish ship. I can't believe that the Spanish would have blown up an American ship with their own boats that close. Doesn't make sense. And, afterward, they saved lives." Collins pulled his pocket watch out then, and looked at the time. "I must be getting in there." Just as he spoke, a marine opened the hearing room door and called his name loudly. Collins waved, and walked into the room. The big doors closed swiftly behind him, He was in the room for 40 minutes. Afterward I followed him outside.

He was sober. "I told them what I saw. And what I heard. But I don't know that they believed me. Maybe they want to believe that the Spanish did it."

A tall figure in a navy uniform walked toward us on the steps. The approaching man walked with a slight limp. He had a fresh scar on the left side of his face.

"Well, here's Chief White," Collins said. He waved at a lean, unsmiling sailor dressed in a blue uniform. "I sailed up to Charleston with him. Now, he's the one you have to talk to, he's had an interesting time of it."

Collins introduced me to the silent sailor. We shook hands.

"Chief White, here, was on the Maine. He was blown overboard, and rescued with Captain Sigsbee, weren't you, Chief?"

White nodded.

I could barely believe my good fortune. "What happened?" I asked bluntly. White looked at me coldly. For a moment I thought he would stride silently away.

"My ship blew up. And, that's all I can say about it. Excuse me. I must report inside." He walked stiffly up the stairs and went through the big oak doors to the hearing room.

"I don't think he'll ever recover," Collins said. "It was his ship, you see, and he was the highest rating aboard. Sigsbee may have been the captain, but White was the real master of that poor ship. Now, wherever he goes, he'll be looked on as the chief whose ship sank in Havana harbor. That would be enough to make a man take to drink."

"I think I'll go back upstairs and see what I can learn," I said.

"You mean listen, don't you?" Collins said, with a booming laugh. He made me promise to meet him for dinner that night at the Hotel Willard.

I went back upstairs, and by sneaking into a cloak room, was able to press my ears to the wall, and listen.

Surprisingly, I could hear very well. There was some

byplay among the hearing officers before Chief White was sworn to testify.

He began by telling his name, rank and ship. Actually he didn't have a ship, but no matter. His story was precise, and chronological. He told how the Maine had arrived in Havana two weeks before, and how the visit was supposed to be friendly, except that no shore leave had been allowed. Chief White didn't tell the crusty captains and admirals, but his remarks left the implication that all might have been different if some of the ship's crew had been allowed to visit the town.

"The duty was standard port duty, with regular watches. The only crew that was allowed off the boat was the men who went ashore for some provision or to arrange for a coal delivery." He said only a few carpenters got ashore to buy some planks for repairs, but that's all. There were a few visitors the first week, the captain of the port, a Spanish navy admiral, and a few British officers.

Chief White spoke in a strong monotone, but his story was drama itself. I took down hasty scribbles, and later, put them together for one of the best stories I got out of the war. It was the first word we had about what happened that sultry night in the quiet harbor.

CHAPTER NINETEEN

New Frenzies

ollins had already started on his first drink when I joined him in the Willard barroom.

"Well, was it worth the wait, and sneaking about?" he asked gruffly.

"Yes," I said softly. "Now I know what happened down there."

He tossed back a hefty slug of whiskey. "Well, I wish I knew. Christ, it's a bum situation. I was doing well there. There was a future on that island. The goddam Spanish didn't want war. They know we can beat em, and what's it all for? So that dame's poppa can move into the big house and tell all the peasants what the hell is what. Shit!"

I ordered a drink and while the bartender put it together, I turned to Collins, and asked, "Well, what the hell do you think caused it all?"

He looked into his glass a long moment. "This for Hearst or you, Jim?"

"Me," I said. Collins wasn't worth quoting. No one cared about what he said except me.

"Well," he said, "you have this situation, see, where a Madrid government has this colony, but about 20 percent of the people want independence. About 80 percent don't give a damn, because they're too busy trying to put grub in their stomach. The insurrectos for 20 years have gone to the United States for help, money and maybe guns. Now, what the hell does the United States get out of all of this? Not much, except the pipe dream that maybe it, too can have colonies, just like John Bull.

"And, on the cheap. No big money. Just a little gunpowder, and a few yells, and it'll all fall in our lap, pretty senoritas and all."

He took another draft of his drink. "Now, the Havana government can't fight the rebels in the hills and Uncle Sam, too. The rebels are on their ass. They have no punch. It's all but over. The picture is quite different on our side of the water. Hell, we're big enough to kick ass wherever we want. But, it's bad business. The country is just climbing out of a Depression. But, we haven't had a war since the War Between The States, as they say in Richmond.

"You add that to your man Hearst and that funny Mr. Pulitzer, and the fact that everyone in America reads their newspapers, just for the laughs, and you have trouble. Add on a few loudmouths who seem to wake up each day on the side of bed where they want to kick hell out of someone, and you have a tinderbox."

"You think there'll be war?" I asked mildly.

Collins stared at me, and then laughed. "Christ, let's get some steak and onions. I'm starved." We settled ourselves in the dining room and ordered.

"Of course they'll be war," Collins said a bit more softly, as there were other diners within earshot.

"I can feel it in my bones."

"What'll you do?"

He shrugged. "Well, Standard wants me to go to Mexico. I might do that. You see, I have no family to worry about. Then again, I might stay around New York.

"Maybe I'll enlist for the war. But war is always a sorry mess. More than likely I'll go to Mexico. What are you going to do?" he asked, biting into a large piece of rare steak.

"My job. Chase politicians. And grab paragraphs from them," I said.

"It beats climbing ladders in Havana," he replied. We both laughed, and dug into our meal.

Later that day I ran into Senator Albert Beveridge of Indiana. "What are we waiting for? The United States is a conquering race. We must obey our destiny, and occupy these lands. They will make good markets, when we clean them up."

I wrote another Sunday piece. Hanna was scorned. Beveridge was hailed for his outspokenness. No one asked him where in the world Americans did not then have mercantile interests. The truth was the whole world was the American market. I spoke to some businessmen then in Washington, and they voiced the fear privately that military action would only interfere with their commerce, not support it.

On March 29, after weeks of quiet deliberations, the Presidential Commission reported to McKinley that the Maine was destroyed by a submarine mine which then caused an explosion of the two forward ammunition magazines. The commissioners pinned no blame on individuals, or nations.

Some scientists had suggested that the Maine blew up because leaking gas ignited its coal bunkers.

The Jingoists increased the drum beat, hurling anti-Spanish epithets loosely for publication. Even Roosevelt called the Spaniards "dagos, greasers," or worse. By early April the situation was sliding rapidly toward an international crisis, when Spanish Premier told the U.S. envoy in Madrid that Spain did not want war. The Premier proposed that a Spanish battle cruiser visit New York harbor on a good will trip.

A worse idea could not have been proposed to smooth warhawk feathers. The suggestion ignited Pulitzer and Hearst to new frenzies. The World bloomed with a page one Sunday map, showing the range into Manhattan and Brooklyn of the Spanish ship's guns. The carnage would be high, the paper cried. No one stopped to ask why a friendship mission would end in naval gunfire.

The Journal countered with pictures and words describing a mid-Atlantic clash between the U.S. fleet and Spanish cruisers. The U.S. won the battle in print, of course, sending the Spanish ships to the bottom in less than an hour.

From the look of The Journal, war had been declared months before. The yellow fever was contagious. No one stopped to ask why the rush to war. The respectable anti-war sentiment, outside of a few scattered college faculties, such as at Harvard, was quiet. These people thought the yellow press was disreputable, thus it would not engage in debate with it. The rest of the nation? Well, it followed along. Newspapers echoed the New York press; politicians jumped on the war wagon, flags and bunting appeared on storefronts. The nation was marching. I returned to New York in early April.

"Well, Botwright," Hearst said one day in his office, "it's only a matter of time now. The Congress will push the thing over, and it doesn't matter what that coward in the White House does. I don't understand that man."

"He just doesn't want another war. Told us he saw enough of it at Antietam."

"Aw, he's just another Cleveland. Dressed in Republican clothing. Shouldn't even be mayor of New York, let alone President of the United States."

I couldn't let the remark go by. "Chief, it'd be better if you were President."

Hearst's head snapped back, and he smiled. "Now you've got it, Jim. Now you've got it." Then he laughed.

By April 11 McKinley caved in to the demands. He asked Congress to empower his administration to take final measures. Wan, and apparently beaten down by the Jingoists, McKinley collapsed, and with him went much of the anti-war sentiment.

I attended these matters with only half a heart. History was rolling before my eyes, but my mind and heart were in Manhattan, with Hilda. I didn't care if the Spanish sailed up the Potomac and took Teddy Roosevelt hostage. In fact, that would have solved many problems for all concerned.

After McKinley washed his hands of the matter, Congress waited until April 21 to declare that a state of war existed. It authorized the President to raise 125,000 troops. The Jingoists were in the saddle now. I was unable to leave Washington because of the war fever, and the insatiable demand of the editors for copy—about any-thing related to the war. I saw Roosevelt nearly every day.

"Say, Jim, here's a story for you. I've just been to see the Secretary of War, and he offered me a volunteer regiment to command. I could have my choice. But do you know what I told him? I told him that I would take it only on one condition.

"I told him that I wanted to be posted as second-in-command to a volunteer cavalry regiment. I told him that I wanted him to appoint my friend Leonard Wood the commanding officer of the First Volunteer Cavalry. Wood's a doctor, you know, but he fought in the southwest in the Indian wars. He's Harvard Medical School, y'know."

I nodded, and scribbled. Major Wood and Roosevelt. Some combination, I thought. A doctor and a braggart.

Virtually every day that month Roosevelt was on page one of the Journal. From relative obscurity, TR had become a national figure. It was the constant coverage and he soon gloried in it.

Washington, the city which had been a sleepy Southern town now took on the pace of a New York, or a Chicago, or it tried to. It wasn't easy to end the habits of generations. In truth, Washington was not prepared for war. No more than it was in 1861. Regiments of job seekers flooded the town. I did not have to look far for strange stories of wartime mania.

Democrat William Jennings Bryan, the youthful Presidential candidate in '96, enlisted in the army as a private soldier. The newspapers all over the country picked up the story. Roosevelt and the Republicans were all rushing to be colonels, and the Democrat wanted to be a private. Well, soon strings were pulled in Washington at the War Department.

Soon Bryan was promoted to colonel of the Nebraska militia, commanding a local regiment, which Bryan didn't know, had secret War Department orders never to leave the state.

These stories of political folly were enjoyable to write. Things hadn't changed much since Lincoln's day.

Crane appeared one day, having been sent down by Hearst. He was morose, obviously upset that he couldn't return to England to see Cora. There wasn't much that interested him in Washington. Hearst and Pulitzer had hired six ocean-going tugs to carry correspondents' dispatches. Each publisher had also contributed his yacht to the war effort.

"Willie plans to direct his war from his yacht. Joe is not likely to leave his sound-proofed Manhattan mansion because of his health, and delicate nerves. War is not good for delicate nerves." Crane suddenly laughed. "Christ, Jim, where is this all going to end? It's so absurd."

We laughed over bourbon at the comic opera we were in.

Crane put his glass down and in an instant his face was morose.

"What's the matter?" I asked. He looked at me blankly.

"Just life," he replied.

"What about it?" He looked at me quizzically.

"Did you know my Cora ran a parlor house in Jacksonville?" I was stunned, and didn't know what to say. I said nothing.

"Yes, a sporting house. We met when I was first in Florida in early January last year. Just before the boat sank. Someone said, 'C'mon, let's go over there.' Yes, she ran a parlor house. And there is no way I can introduce her to my family."

I found my tongue. "Why not? They don't have to know anything about her former life. She doesn't run, uh, one now, does she?"

Crane looked at me with desperation in his eyes. "No. She doesn't. But it would kill my mother to learn that I had married a…"

"Well, if it goes that far, then there's no reason why anyone should know. First of all, your mother is in New York State, and you keep telling me Cora is in England. Tell your mother Cora is English. Tell her she's a school-teacher." I was suddenly irritated with the anguish I could see inflicted on my friend. "Why get married in the first place. You've been living together for some time now, why change that? And, maybe you don't give your mother enough credit. Maybe she doesn't care who you marry, as long as you're happy."

"But it wouldn't be acceptable."

"Maybe not, if everyone knew. What do you plan to do,

announce your marriage, and then take a advertisement in The Journal?" I said. I plunged on, "Steve, the question you have to answer is: do you want to get married? Think of all you'll be losing, frantic telegrams to the penny papers from far-away places, among people who want to shoot you, for readers who can't remember for two days how you've risked your life for them." He laughed.

"I met her the first night we went to her hotel. She has blonde hair, cut short. She is not tall. We talked that first night, almost the entire evening. She was impressed that a New York reporter was in Florida to see about the Cuban situation. She knew about the rebels on the island, and what they faced. She knew about a lot of things. She's very intelligent. I was taken with her, and then it became a, a fever, I guess. She said it would end, that I would tire of her, but I haven't. I never will. But I can never introduce her to my mother, or my family. Or Dick Davis." Crane said.

"Hell, Dick would be pleased to meet her. I would too. She's probably better looking and more intelligent than half the women in New York. And, if you're sweet on her, that's enough for us."

Crane took a long pull from his drink. "It's a fever, one that never cools." We had more drinks and cursed that fate that put us so far from our women, and in the path of contrived dangers. A week later he took a train to Florida, to meet the Hearst fleet at Key West.

CHAPTER TWENTY

San Antonio

Almost as if the chief had heard us mock his war, Crane was fired from The Journal before he got to Key West. He immediately wired Pulitzer and was taken aboard The World. It seemed like half of American journalism was forming on Florida.

Davis, of course, was still in London. I got a letter from him in Washington:

Jim,

I understand that my nation is at war. I shall hurry home as soon as possible, so as not to miss the festivities. From what I've seen of war, there will be a period of great confusion, followed by a period of lesser confusion, followed by much blood-letting. I shall hurry, but not so much that I'll miss all that London has to offer in the way of good company, fine food, and compliant women. These latter are most outspoken, and devilishly hard to compare to our national flowers.

I shant bore you with all the details, but let it be said that Davis is reluctant to trade his formal dinner suit for khaki. I do stay awake each night, wondering if Willie Hearst, or Skinny Joe Pulitzer, or Teddy Roosevelt will lead us up the hill against the enemy. No doubt they will be engaged elsewhere, with "important" duties. Enjoy the comfortable life while you can.

RHD

Dick's letters were more cynical than he was. I enjoyed them.

They were about the only things I enjoyed that rainy spring. By May I hadn't seen Hilda for weeks. My letters to her grew desperate. She wrote regularly. At that point I would have burned down Washington for a weekend in Manhattan.

I filed a story about Roosevelt, Wood, and their volunteer regiment. Orders came from New York to go inspect the regiment's training.

I met Roosevelt later that day. We were standing on the sidewalk on the street outside his Georgetown home. I had ridden in his carriage from the War Department. He must have heard something of my frustrated romance.

"Where are you going to train?" I asked.

He laughed. "San Antonio, Texas. Col. Wood says it's the best training ground for cavalry."

"Why, godammit, why do you have to go so far away?"

"Young man, watch your language," he commanded. I apologized. I explained that I would have preferred that he train in any armory in Manhattan. He laughed again.

"Real wars are not fought in armories."

Two weeks later Roosevelt and Wood had left Washington. I boarded the train after them, for the long tedious ride into Texas.

San Antonio, Texas, April 8, 1898

When I got off the train I found San Antonio was a flat, dusty small town with Mexican-style buildings and the unmistakable flavor of the military about it. I checked into a small hotel crammed with women and drummers of every kind. Then I hired a rig to take me to the camp. I scouted around and found Roosevelt not long after my arrival at the dusty spread of parade grounds and tents.

He was sitting on his horse, watching a drill on a hot parade ground.

"Hello, Botwright," he said as I pulled up in my rig. "Come to volunteer for the cavalry?"

"In a way," I replied. "Mr. Hearst wants his readers to know what you're up to out here." Teddy laughed, almost losing his glasses. He looked like a Manhattan lawyer playing cowboy-soldier. "I see that Brooks came through with your uniforms." Roosevelt was dressed neatly in a khaki outfit, buttoned high to his neck. Under his collar he wore a blue and white polka dot kerchief, which became the volunteer cavalry emblem. TR wore high boots and he sat his horse well, testimony to his years as a Dakota rancher.

"By god, this is a great place for training. And the men are performing well. Even Wood says that. He is a marvelous commander, I must say. Never raises his voice. Works like the devil. Even checks to make sure the men change their bedding each week. Pleasure to work with him." Roosevelt beamed.

The enlisted men on horseback cavorted around the parade ground, with much yipping and yelling, like the cowboys many of them were. We had dinner in the hotel that night, Roosevelt and I. He told me about the regiment.

"Wood and I decided to be choosy. We wanted to pick the men for our command. We decided on a formula-one-third real cowboys, one third men who had army experience, and rest from the best circles of Manhattan,

Philadelphia and Boston.

"Now we've got wealthy men from Princeton cleaning stalls as privates and corporals, and taking orders from men who only last year worked on a Montana ranch. The veterans Wood made sergeants. He said they knew the army and its ways.

"Wood is brilliant, you know. I've never seen a man who worked as hard, who walked as softly, and who knew as much about his field." Roosevelt straightened, and beamed just by discussing Wood. It was clear the respect he had for the man. As we finished our meal, a group of enlisted cavalry men entered the dining room with a couple of women who looked like common whores. They set up a cheer for Lt. Col. Teddy, and he stood and bowed. He motioned to the waiter. "Give my men a keg of beer, and put it on my bill." When the soldiers learned of the beer, they sent up another cheer, interrupting all conversation in the room.

"Let's join them for a minute," Roosevelt said.

We walked over to the men; they stood respectfully at TR's approach. "Be seated," he told them. Soon we were all sipping beer. The men wore the khaki uniform. Most all were in their 20s, ruddy from days under the Texas sun, and vibrantly healthy looking. One fellow caught my eye.

"Jim. Jim Botwright. Have you been back to New Haven recently?"

I looked at him carefully for a moment before I recognized a classmate. We shook hands and pounded backs.

"Why aren't you down here with us?" he asked.

"Well, I am down here, with you." He laughed.

I explained that I worked for Hearst, and would be trailing the First Volunteer Cavalry around for some time.

"Oh, it's the real stuff," he said. The fellow's name was Henderson, and I recalled that he was a horseman from Westchester County. His father owned a bank somewhere.

After a bit, Roosevelt and I left the soldiers, and

walked around the square, cool in the night air.

The troopers spread the word through the unit that the colonel had bought them beer. TR became an even bigger hero to the men.

Roosevelt later bragged about what happened to him.

He was reprimanded by Wood for buying beer for enlisted men. The word of the reprimand got around the camp by sundown the next day, in that mysterious army way. I cornered Roosevelt, and he admitted the story was true. It made another light Journal article, one which pleased Hearst enough for him to send a telegram urging more. I spent the next couple of days wandering around the camp, talking with Wood's Wildcats, as they styled themselves. The label Rough Riders came later. I spoke, that is, with those from New York and the eastern seaboard. They, at least, were talkative. The men from the west were as silent as rocks. They did scream and yahoo a lot during drill, but most were unable to frame any but the simplest sentences or grunts when I questioned them.

Once, after campfire lunch, I asked Henderson why he had joined.

"Well, hell, it's good fun. War won't last long. This is a smart outfit. We'll be home as heroes in a few months." He smiled. When I asked about his family, his face clouded.

"Miss the wife. And the kids, too. But, well, she doesn't like horses that much, and most summers they're away in Maine anyway. As for the bank, well, things are usually slow in the summer. no loss. Instead of Newport this year, I'm in Texas."

"You could get killed, you know."

He looked around a moment before answering. "Well, that's true. But I could be killed at home at well."

One morning, while I was filing copy at the telegraph office at the San Antonio train station, I noticed a freight train arrive, loaded with soldiers. They were all black, except for the officers and some of the sergeants. "Ninth cavalry, regulars," the telegrapher said. The men wore hot-looking blue uniforms and carried rifles and packs. They climbed down from the cars, and after a count by the sergeants, they sat in the shade while a new train was slammed together. They sat quietly. Not one wandered away. They smoked pipes, or hand-rolled cigarettes. They looked more like prisoners than regular soldiers. "Where are they from?"

"Some place in Arizona," the telegrapher said. "They're being shipped to Florida. They've been out in the desert, keeping them Apaches under control."

A whistle blew and, without fuss, the silent men climbed aboard the cars. They left as quietly as they had arrived. That night I mentioned the sight to Roosevelt and Col. Wood. Roosevelt showed no interest in troops not in his regiment. Wood, on the other hand, brightened when I spoke of them.

"Yes, ninth and tenth cavalry. Black soldiers. The Indians call them buffalo soldiers. And there is the 25th infantry regiment, all black, except for the officers, of course. They're good soldiers, if properly led. Trouble is most young officers don't want to serve with them. Old officers of the line favor the duty. The War Department has a headache in deciding where to station them. Not many towns want hundreds of armed black men nearby.

Arizona had been the ideal solution to the War Department's problem. Nothing but open spaces, old-time cavalry posts, and troublesome Indians far from anywhere.

"Does the army trust these black men with weapons?"

"Oh, yes," Wood said. "These regiments go back to the Civil War. They fought valiantly then. You see, the army never felt that only Harvard tenderfeet would make good troopers.

"These men have steady work that is respectable. Most

of them support families in the south. They are less trouble than comparable white outfits. Most of their officers are senior line officers, and they have been trained so well that they know what to do without being told. I wish that were the case with our regiment." Roosevelt didn't react at the jibe. Wood and TR had a genuine friendship they brought to the regiment varying qualities. Wood was the planner, the quiet man who knew in advance what to do. Roosevelt brought political connections, a talent for personal leadership, and, of course, newspaper coverage. The troops seemed to know that Teddy puffed up on flattery and cheers. Roosevelt's concern for the troops was genuine.

I didn't understand all the drives which propelled Roosevelt. It puzzled me greatly that this wealthy New Yorker, who could have spent his days peacefully writing legal briefs for the major corporations, left his wife and children to live like a roustabout. I thought it odd that the man's wife would let him do that.

Bad News

ay 5, 1898

> Dear Jim,
> I do miss you. Your letters seem so angry. But our separation is nothing that can be helped now. We were notified at Bellevue by letter that the army needs nurses. The army is offering qualified hospital nurses a contract. Quite handsome salary. For the same work. I plan to inquire about it tomorrow.

The letter frightened me. It was a good thing it was too damnably hot in San Antonio to drink whiskey. I drank only beer. The liquor on the frontier was not top grade. The soldiers called it rotgut, and it led to fights and shootings. The respectable element in the town kept to their homes, where soldiers were rarely invited.

That left the streets and public places to the drifters, grifters, whores and gamblers, and the few correspondents who had come to see the new army train in the dusty town. I kept busy, trying to know the Wood regiment. The men ran around all day, drilling on foot and horseback. Most of them were natural cavalrymen, Wood said. I wondered out loud one day how the army would get all the horses safely to Cuba. Wood looked at me quizzically. "You may have something there," he said.

One night, Wood, Roosevelt and I had a farewell dinner. "Where's Dick Davis?" Roosevelt asked. He was no great fan of Dick's, having engaged in heated arguments with the man over New York politics.

I said, "He's in London, enjoying a whirlwind social life. More active than in San Antonio." Wood smiled.

"But don't worry. Dick will be back in time for the opening round. He hasn't missed a war yet," I added.

"Bully. But you tell him for me that he could do no better than to come along with this regiment when he wants to see the war." I said I'd relay the message. It was Roosevelt's way of asking for press recognition.

That night I drank too much beer, and the next morning I awoke with a brassy headache which lingered on the first of four trains I had to take to make my way to Florida. It rained all the way across the Gulf Coast to Florida. I arrived at Key West out of sorts. I found Sanchez at the hotel. Grinning, he urged me to have a drink with him. We sat in the shade of the porch, drinking warm gin. I was prepared to drain the bottle. I shed my coat and vest.

"Where have you been, senor?"

"Texas. With the troops."

"Oh, I thought you had gone with the navy, like Senor Crane."

"How long have you been here in Key West?"

"Two weeks, or so. I left Havana after the explosion. The Spaniards became very nervous and began taking

Cubans. The dogs panicked. I had trouble keeping my men quiet until the Americans land."

"Where were you when the Maine blew up?"

"In Havana."

"What happened?"

"It blew up." He shrugged.

"Why?"

He shrugged again. "Maybe the Spaniards put a mine on the outside of the hull. Maybe there was too much explosive in the magazines." The mention of explosives reminded me of Hearst's shipment of "candles." "Whatever happened to that dynamite that Hearst had you smuggle into Cuba?"

Sanchez grinned widely. "We used it to blow up a bridge on the main road to Santiago. Some of it we used here and there."

"Where? How did you keep it out of reach of the authorities?"

I reached for the gin bottle.

Sanchez' answer made me drop the bottle. "Why, senor, we kept the dynamite in the explosives magazine of the Maine."

The bottle crashed to the floor. I was stunned. I sputtered some questions. The small, dark man beside me only smiled. He waved them away, as he would flies. He would not elaborate.

The events whirled in my head. Certain facts were known. Roosevelt, the chief war hawk, had been assistant secretary of the Navy. The jingoes wanted war with Spain. Someone had sent the Maine to Havana, on its so-called friendship visit. The ship exploded. What could be a greater push toward a declaration of war?

Hearst bought dynamite, and Sanchez says it was stored aboard the Maine.

In two years of reckless reporting and sensational

headlines in the two major papers in the United states it seemed like success was at hand—the nation would be pushed into war. I had been a witness, even a participant in all of it, but the truth was I was not in control. That was for sure.

Who was?

Was it all planned? Did it all happen accidently? I sat my myself for some time, puzzling over it. Could I write what Sanchez told me? How would I pin it down? Who would publish it? Not Hearst, or Pulitzer, even though he wanted stories that made his competitor look foolish. And, what evidence did I have that there was a conspiracy to push the United States into an unnecessary war? Of course, it was easier to believe that the "candles" were just more explosives in an already overcrowded ship's magazine. The whole combination of events was serving to thrust the sleeping nation into war, like a drunk falling down stairs.

That evening I looked around for Steve Crane, someone to talk about it. Steve was aboard a Navy ship as it patrolled blockaded Cuban ports. He returned to Key West the following evening, sunburned and smiling.

He took a hurried bath and shaved. We sat in the hotel taproom, drinking beer. He wanted to tell me about the Navy.

"They have the best life. Good food, plenty of beer, and even music on the larger ships. That's the way to go to war," Steve said.

I interrupted his adventure to tell him what I had learned. He lit a cigar, and puffed as I spoke.

"What the hell am I going to do, Steve?" I asked. "Can I accuse my publisher of blowing up the Maine on purpose? That would be murder. And, how can I get the story into print?"

"You can't," Crane said, morosely. "Look, a few years ago

I tried to write about how New York police were profiting from prostitutes' income. How they put the arm on the women, and took a share of the proceeds. Roosevelt didn't want to know about it. Didn't want to open the case.

"Some things in this life no one wants to hear about. This story you've heard could be the truth. Maybe not, though. You can't tell with these Cubans. They'll tell you what they want you to believe, I think. The truth is somewhere between. Even if it were true, do you think the public would believe that honest, upright Americans would blow up one of their own ships, just to create a war?

"I don't think so. I don't think Americans would believe that."

Crane shrugged. "The problem, too, is that it's too late now. The ship is at the bottom of Havana harbor, and the dead are dead."

"What the hell am I going to do, Steve?"

He looked at me with his intense eyes, burning from his suntanned face. "Just do your work, and maybe someday we'll find out what this is all about."

I spent the rest of the evening walking on the empty beach. I trudged through the sand until the walking sapped my strength.

CHAPTER TWENTY ONE

Tampa—May 12, 1898

Florida in those days was generally barren of large settlement and cultivation. Inland was all scrub pine, and flat, sandy stretches. It had few cities worthy of the name. It was in truth a backwater, hot, wet and generally unpleasant. In those days most men would not have given you $100 for a thousand square miles of the place.

Tampa was an old town, not at all fashionable. It was a port for goods like turpentine, and cigars, both shipped north. The town had one big Moorish-style hotel, a left over from the 80s, when some boomer had tried to make the port a tourist resort and failed. The town never became an Atlantic City.

Every military and civilian rolling stone on the North American continent moved toward Tampa that month. When I arrived I was told by the gleeful hotel keeper that only a few months earlier a visitor could rent a whole floor in the empty hotel for what he charged me for a suite. The hotel, and the town, became a staging for what I quickly dubbed "the Army of the Bored." To this hot, fly-ridden coastal town came long freight trains bearing tons of military equipment, most of it obsolete, or inadequate, and the thousands of soldiers who had signed up in Indianapolis, Dallas, or Chicago for the exciting adventure. They got little of it there. Instead, they found ragtag camps stuck near the single-line track, in piney woods. They arrived wearing steamy woolen uniforms. They ate whatever their officers could scrounge from the ill-starred quartermaster. The food was usually hardtack, bad beef, coffee and for the lucky, some canned goods. These innocents took the bad conditions in stride, almost as if they knew that they had to expect them when Americans first went to war. They didn't expect, and many didn't survive, the dysentery, and the fever. Daily the sick roll grew, alarmingly.

The confusion seemed almost planned. Wood and Roosevelt arrived with their regiment, about the only one dressed in cooler khaki, but they were horseless. Somewhere in the U.S., between Texas and Florida were the regiment's mounts. The First Volunteers went into action on foot. It was a blessing. After the first weeks the pileup of freight trains at Tampa stretched for miles. They had been sent without regard for the nonexistent facilities. The nation had not mounted such a campaign since the Civil War. Those who knew how to go about it were either in their graves, or long in retirement. Confusion was in the saddle.

Fortunately, the suite I had taken at the hotel was large enough for Crane and Davis, if they appeared. Dick showed up a few days later, without notice.

"Well, what do you think, Jim?" he asked.

I said, "It's a terrible mess." He laughed. "Did you expect otherwise?"

He looked at my gear. "You can beg food and drink

from the army, but you must provide your own plate and utensils. Be sure to boil your water, or drink only coffee. We ought to take crates of cigars with us from this foul place, except that would really be carrying coals to Newcastle."

The other correspondents at the hotel represented newspapers big and small, including even the religious press. They generally were a rowdy bunch, and they shied away from Davis, awed by his reputation and manner. Dick looked like a damn field general. He wore the correct hat for the tropics, a neat khaki jacket, riding trousers, and high boots. When he dined he wore evening clothes. That was enough to stun the locals.

We toured the encampments during the day, watching in wonderment as the army attempted to set up. Dick was not impressed. He thought the commanders were amateurs. He was right. Roosevelt, in a blatant request for coverage, one day suggested that we accompany his regiment into action. Standing with TR in a hot dusty field, Davis said only that he was impressed by the way Wood handled his troops. Wood was the kind of commander who was out with his men, saw their problems first hand, and tried to solve them on the spot.

Roosevelt saw the remark as a compliment of both Wood and himself. Dick found that he had many old friends in the First Volunteers. They were New York clubmen. Dick spoke with Fish, and a slew of tall men with the arrogant look only a lot of money gives. They were not officers, and they seemed proud of that fact. The other reporters watched Dick, and wondered what unit he would choose.

But during this training-confusion Davis played no favorites. We moved from camp to camp, watching with growing distaste as confusion and illness spread. Hundreds came down with fever, many never to leave Tampa except in a coffin. The small hospital was swamped.

The military headquarters was in the hotel, as it was the only building large enough to handle the crush. We met the commanding officer one evening. Major General William Shafter was hard to miss. He was as wide as he was tall. Shafter weighed 300 pounds, and he suffered from a variety of ailments, including gout. He was one of the army's senior officers, reputedly a good field commander. But we thought he was physically more suited to command a depot in Philadelphia than lead a field army.

On June 12, Crane appeared at the hotel, unshaven and wearing scruffy boat clothes. He had been in Cuba, and we were astounded to hear him say, with the marines at Guantanamo for three days while a few companies of marines defended their encampment against strong Spanish counterattack.

Crane had been under fire, and he looked it. He had rings under his eyes, and his hands shook when he tried to tell us what it'd been like.

"It was murderous. War goes on day and night. You never get used to it." Crane took the drinks we pushed on him. After a bath he returned to the hotel bar and took a chair at a back table. He scribbled for hours, trying to capture the routine heroism of marine signalmen who unhesitatingly stood with their backs to Spanish marksmen while they wig-wagged messages to ships offshore. Crane didn't put in his dispatch that he was one of the signalmen. He seemed excited, despite his weariness, from being long in the presence of battle and death.

"Have a look," Steve said, pushing some of his copy pages to me. I read of the marines, in their blue jackets and white trousers, hugging the earth for hours, unable to move except at a crawl, because to stand up straight meant a bullet in the chest or head. The heat, terror and wounded came alive.

"God, Steve, you've written it vividly."

He put his hands over his face. "No one can report it properly. You are so terrified most of the time you can't make notes, and afterward, you can't remember. All I remember now are the yells and oaths of the wounded."

I left him to his nightmares and rejoined Davis, who sat writing his family. He showed me a letter he had written to his sister. "It's a merry war; if there were only some girls here the place would be perfect. The army will have to do a lot of fighting to make itself solid with me. They are a mounted police, but without the horses. We have a sentry here, and he sits in a rocking chair." I laughed.

The truth was that the major portion of the army was still untrained.

Drill was ragged, and military courtesy, except among the regulars, virtually non-existent. Dick was being truthful when he wrote that there were no girls at Tampa. There were women, however. Some were mothers unwilling to let their sons go off to possible death; others were young wives, but the majority were camp followers. These women set up business in any available shack, and soon the medical officers had new diseases to treat.

One morning Dick said at breakfast, "Jim, I have a problem, and I want your advice."

I looked up, surprised.

"President McKinley has written me, offering a captaincy. I don't know what to do."

Somehow I was not surprised. That the President of the United States would write a letter to Dick Davis seemed perfectly natural.

"Dick, you'll make a first-rate officer, if that's what you want to do."

Crane nodded agreement.

"That's the problem. I don't know if I want to do it."

"Dick, there are drawbacks. If you accept, you could find

yourself out in the pines in some volunteer outfit which may never get to fight, and you'll have to stomach it. You'll be under military rules. I don't think you should do it."

Crane agreed. "You can make your own vantage point as a reporter," he said.

Dick thanked us for our advice, but he didn't indicate how he would decide. I thought, but did not say, the offer might be an attempt to remove a most potent critic with a wide audience. For the truth was that Dick was growing more depressed by the state of the army. He thought it was demoralizing to stay in Tampa, as little he saw in the field was correct.

The uniforms were wrong, for example, winter issue for tropical conditions. Equipment sat and rotted in freight cars on siding. Quartermaster troops tried to bring order out of chaos.

One afternoon, Dick and I hiked a hot seven miles to a Michigan encampment. The men had just unloaded a shipment of cheap felt hats before we arrived. They were sporting them. They provided protection against the sun. But it showered that afternoon, as it did most days, and the hats seemed to melt off the troopers' heads. The hats were flimsy, and this depressed Davis.

"They are cheap hats, no good for this work. Someone made good money on this government contract, and someone else passed on this kind of shoddy. So, the men go into battle without good hats in this sun. It's criminal, Jim."

Soon it was common knowledge that Davis had passed up a commission. One afternoon, a group of loafers, men from the Chicago and New Orleans papers, were discussing the offer at the hotel bar, their favorite location. The consensus was that Davis was a coward for refusing the commission.

I was about to say something, loudly, when Crane, who

had been writing at his rear table, stood suddenly and marched to the bar where he confronted the loudest critic, a braggart from The Chicago Tribune.

"And, what about you, colonel? Have I heard that you have volunteered for the Rough Riders? Or the quartermaster?" Crane's outburst, unusual for the usually silent reporter, embarrassed the other men into changing the subject.

The climate, and the inaction, all conspired to raise tempers at Tampa. Neither Crane nor Davis were present for what I later called my battle of Tampa. Dick had taken the tug down to Key West to do a article about navy life aboard a battle cruiser. Crane had just disappeared.

That afternoon I had run across Sanchez in the lobby. He had come and gone since I had arrived. I presumed that he was slipping into Cuba by boat at night. That afternoon he was with two other men, Cubans, obviously insurrectos.

They were scruffy looking, I concede. Sanchez said they had just come out of Cuba, so naturally I was interested in interviewing them. It was a natural story. Cuba had been cut off from the rest of the world as far as Americans papers were concerned. At the start of the war, the Cubans stopped all traffic to the States, and all cable traffic went to Jamaica. There were a few newspapermen left on the island, men for British, Spanish and French papers. Often New York knew more about what was going on in Havana than we did.

I took Sanchez and his companions into the bar, and we began our conversation when a pack of drunken reporters saw us and began making loud remarks about "Greasers" in the hotel.

"Hey, Botwright," a Chicago reporter yelled at me, "why do you spend your time with dagos? They the only ones'll drink with yez?" Other similar comments were shouted. I walked the length of the bar and quietly explained that I was trying to do an interview, and would they please shut up. The Chicago braggart shoved me, and then the fisticuffs began. I guess now that we were all in the mood for a fistfight. I can't say that I enjoyed it. It was one against three. I sat one man down hard with a right to the jaw. I was knocked against the bar.

Within a minute I had given a few good punches and taken as many. My coat jacket was ripped, and I found myself on the floor, a common barroom brawler. The Battle of Tampa came to an end when the bartender, a ginger ancient with a polished pate, raised an old revolver and ordered us all off his premises. My attackers looked boozily down the barrel and decided they would migrate elsewhere.

"Why didn't you help me?" I yelled at Sanchez. He smiled, and shrugged.

Davis heard about the fight two days later, after he had returned from a stint aboard a navy ship. He was upset. He thought there were too many so-called reporters in Tampa, the count was above 200, and too many of them were low-life. In the dining room that night he looked around before he sat down and said, "Gentlemen, my colleague Botwright was assaulted in this hotel recently. If any other incident occurs, the miscreants will answer to me." Davis meant he would take on opponents singly or in tandem.

The rowdy reporters looked at him respectfully. Davis had the build and muscle of a heavyweight. No one challenged him. But I was hurt more by Sanchez' attitude. Suddenly, I was made aware that there was no real affection between the Americans and the Cuban rebels.

June 15, 1898
Dear Jim,
I have such good news. Today I signed a contract with the army, to be a nurse in one of its hospitals. I don't know

where yet. I feel so proud of myself. Now I feel like I'm participating in the big effort. I can't let you have the war all to yourself. The army doctor said we would have to go to Washington next week, for some training. Not in nursing, but in the army. I look forward to that. I know all about nursing, but I don't know anything about the army. I pray that we will meet soon. Perhaps I'll be sent to the camp in Florida? That would be such good luck. I do enjoy your letters from Tampa, but you sound so critical of the effort. Are you ill? I do wish you would see a doctor, and see if you are well. You must take care of yourself. I told father about my decision to sign up as a army contract nurse, and he supports me entirely. He said he was as proud as if I was a son going off to war. I do miss you, James. Perhaps I'm doing this so we can be closer. I counted last night, and do you know we've been apart for two months now.

The letter was an icicle in my heart. She had joined the confused monster known as the army. God knows what they would do to her. The way the army operated it would likely send her to Seattle. I would never see her. I found Crane, and together we finished a bottle. He mourned his absent Cora. "And, this is where I met her, in Florida. And now she's in London, and I'm here. Goddam!"

Davis listened to us for a moment, and then said sternly that we sounded and acted like a couple of miserable greenhorns. "Jim, if you miss her that much, take the train to New York. And, you, Steve, you can get a boat to England easily." We looked at him drunkenly, and then at each other.

The steamy days passed in drink and frustration. Whores all but invaded the hotel. We even had a few women who claimed that they were reporters, from papers in Cincinnati. One accosted Davis one morning in the lobby. "Mr. Davis, you must take us around, and show us the army camps."

He begged their pardon, and left them standing in the middle of the room. Dick had not been rude, but the competitive edge in him could barely tolerate men, and women journalists were unthinkable.

"How could I take them to a camp?" he asked at dinner.

"Those men out there walk around half naked all day, in this heat. Most haven't seen a woman since they left home.

"One can't be rude, but I'm not being paid to teach a couple of ladies a job they couldn't perform well anyhow."

"Your mother was a writer," Crane said softly.

"Yes, she was," Davis said, "but she wasn't a correspondent in the field, a special like us. She would be the first to see the folderol in women coming here to be reporters. This is war, this is the army, this is confusion, and it's not for women." He closed the conversation by pouring the wine.

Davis may have had the largest, and possibly the only wine stock in Tampa during that time. He had it, and other foodstuffs, shipped to him from Delmonico's. How he managed to have it arrive in one piece, and collectible was beyond us, but we gladly drank the wine. His example kept us from following the example of the other reporters by spending our days and nights in whiskey.

The lady reporters were not the only ones to invade the hotel. Women came from New Orleans, and other southern towns. Some were very attractive, and they only served as aching reminders to me how far I was from Hilda. One was a startling red-haired woman. She said she was a musical "entertainer" resting between troupes. She set her cap for Davis early on. We learned that she was from Alabama, and she said her name was Alice. I never learned her last name. Alice was not opera-company material. She had a fair church-choir voice, but it had been a long time since she had sung in a loft. She had very pale skin, shrewd vivid blue eyes, and a full figure. What caught my eye was that she didn't seem to wear the corsets standard for women of the day. So when she moved or walked, she was an entertaining sight.

The hotel management put up with these women as long as they were discrete. And the women were. They acted better than common harlots, and were discriminating in their clientele. They acted as if they were on vacation, rather than on a business trip.

Alice one night approached our table at dinner, and began singing. Davis had been talking about the terrible conditions under which stokers worked on navy ships.

In a languid southern accent, she asked, "Would Richard Harding Davis offer a lady a chair?" She was wearing a lavender dress, lightweight and almost transparent. Davis turned to her in surprise. He stood with a bow, and held her chair. Crane and I were stunned.

"Would you care for some wine?" Dick asked. She took a glass, and soon was deep in conversation with Davis. We could not tell what he thought of her intrusion. His politeness required him to be the gentleman. Alice, for her part, stared at him as is his words held the secrets of the universe. Maybe they did, to her. Crane and I quickly excused ourselves.

"Looks like Dick has himself a red-hot stove he can warm himself on if he wants," Crane quipped as we walked through the lobby. Davis did not sleep in our suite that night, nor the next. Apparently he had been brought to ground by the redhead. Crane was correct in calling her a stove. When she looked at Dick she almost glowed. We, of course, said nothing of the affair. Davis was always absolutely discrete in his romances. He treated women of the underworld the same way he treated ladies.

At great frustration I managed to stay away from the

prostitutes, though many of them at the hotel were attractive, and attentive to the journalists. They must have thought that we could easily afford them. The way that many of the reporters acted, spending money freely in the bar, and in restaurants, the women were acting on good evidence.

A new diversion appeared one morning. A group of foreign military attaches from Washington. They wore a motley of uniforms, most of them suitable to the tropical climate. Captain Henry Lee of Her Majesty's Guards was the group's unofficial leader.

"Well, hello, Botwright," he said loudly in the lobby. "Been reading your articles in The Journal. Good stuff. He turned to his companions, a dour French major who said little, a small, nervous Prussian who spoke excellent English, and a real surprise, a small Japanese naval lieutenant. He wore a light cotton white suit which never seemed to soil.

"We've come to see your little war," Lee said with a laugh. Lee and I had to intercede with the hotel manager when he first refused to let the Japanese fellow have a room. We even showed him the officer's diplomatic passport to no avail. But what worked was when I told the manager that his refusal to give the Japanese a bed would make page-one stories around the world. I was bluffing. No editor would have cared, and no reporter would have been fool enough to file such a story. Afterward Lee thanked me.

"You saved us a bit of trouble, old chap. Ticklish thing. You never know how far such snubs would go. I say, where is Mr. Davis?"

Mr. Davis and his paramour had not ventured out of her room for a day, except for some meals. But I wasn't about to tell Lee that. "He's around," I said.

Dick did join us in the dining room that evening, in

his usual dinner clothes. Lee wore a formal uniform. The two were a sight. We pulled two tables together, and Crane and I joined Lee, Dick and the other attaches.

"Would you be so good as to arrange for us to visit the camps?" Lee asked Dick. There was no problem. Visitors were welcomed openly—there were so few of them. The next day I overheard Lee explaining to Roosevelt what he could expect in the field.

"Colonel, your regiment is about the only one here which is dressed for the job. And your men have Krag rifles. They're the equal of the Mauser." Wood had issued Krags to his men. Other units still had the Springfield rifles from the 1870s.

"The Mauser is a singularly efficient rifle. It fires a devilishly long-range, high-speed bullet very accurately. But, I say, your artillery won't do. You can't go into the field, firing black smoke charges. Give away your positions on the first firing mission.

"And, I would suggest that you buy your men some hammocks. You don't want them sleeping on the ground. Too dangerous, scorpions and spiders, y'know." The usually volatile Roosevelt stood in the sun for the better part of an afternoon while Lee criticized his men's equipage.

At the end, TR said brightly, "Well, hell, Captain, we aren't going to be over there long." Lee smiled politely, and saluted. Later that evening,at dinner, he said he was dismayed by the innocence and arrogance displayed by American officers.

Lee said, "It is somewhat sickening to see these men sacrificed as surely they will be." Davis nodded gravely.

Crane tried to change the subject. "Well, Dick, what perch have you picked out for the war?" Dick finished a bite of his steak.

"I think I'll stick with Teddy, and Wood. I've met more

Harvard men there than in any other unit." Dick was joking, but the remark set off Crane. He had become upset when his New York editors demanded more news of socialites and clubmen in the 71st New York militia.

"Why should we give a fine damn about them? We're always writing about Reginald Marmaduke Maurice Sturdevant, Princeton'92, when it's the Private Nolans, the regulars who carry the burden."

Davis laughed. "Steve, I wrote about those who interest me, and if they interest editors, fine. Now, if you'll excuse me, I have an appointment with a carriage." Dick marched across the dining room with straight back precision.

"Damn fine fellow," Lee said to no one in particular. "I hear he's got himself a bit of fine woman here, too." Neither Crane nor I replied.

To our surprise, Dick left the next morning early for another hasty trip with the navy. She found me in the hotel corridor outside our suite. In many ways she reminded me of another dangerous woman.

She smiled. "I need your help, Mr. Botwright. Do you know where Mr. Davis has gone?" I told her that I didn't.

"He comes and goes, sometimes unexpectedly, as his paper demands."

"But he didn't bother to tell me," she pouted.

"Is there any reason he should?"

She gave me a blazing look and flounced away. I suspected that perhaps Dick had tired of his redhead, and sought a way of ending it.

I tried to keep busy, and out of the bar. That afternoon I got a telegram to report to Mr. Hearst's yacht at Key West. I took a tug south, and at sundown, I climbed aboard the chief's elegant home-at-sea. There was a strange-looking boat tied up at the next dock. A servant told me it was Hearst's floating print shop. The chief was going to publish a newspaper at sea off Cuba for the troops.

I was ushered into the chief's cabin, a spacious suite on the main deck. The chief was effusive. "Well, Mr. Botwright, you look fit enough to go to war," Hearst said in his tenor voice. The rigors of Florida had trimmed me down to under 150 pounds, and I was brown from the constant sun. "What'll you have to drink? Beer." The chief gave the steward the order.

Jim, you've been doing fine work, fine work." Privately, I thought that Crane and Davis had been beating me for the last few weeks. Crane with his combat coverage of the marines, and Davis with his articles about army preparedness. Hearst, obviously didn't care about marine skirmishes, or bad news of quartermaster problems.

Hearst said, "I'm going to take this boat over, along with the tug for carrying messages, and maybe the printing boat. It's my own idea." Hearst beamed. "I decided in New York that we'll print up a military edition of the Journal. It'll cost a lot of money, but hell, this is war.

"As I'm making the assignments now," the chief said pleasantly as I sipped my beer, "I wonder if you'd mind going back to Washington." I nearly spilled the beer.

"Chief, I'd prefer to follow the army. I believe that all the action has moved from Washington. This war will be short, if only because we can't sustain a long campaign." The chief frowned. I had treaded on patriotic ground, and criticism was not welcome.

"Don't you think we can win, Botwright?"

I rubbed my face. "Chief, our troops are excited enough for a short successful campaign in Cuba, provided that they don't run into heavy opposition. The Spaniards..."

"I don't want to hear about the Spaniards," Hearst said softly.

"Well, I presume we shall capture Havana, and it should be over in a month. If it goes longer, we'll have trouble," I said.

"Trouble?"

"Yes, chief. Illness, fever, Spanish bullets. But I think it'll be short." A range of emotion from irritation to laughter crossed his face. "I should hope so. I do want to be home in time for the Fall music-hall season on the Bowery.

"All right, Jim. I want you to go in with the troops. Creelman is here with me. He'll go in, too." Creelman was one of Hearst's favorite correspondents.

"Wherever we land, we'll have a tug offshore to pick up copy. If I can arrange I'll have messengers go ashore with you. The trick will be to get the copy off the island and to a cable-head before the opposition. I may extend a special telegraph line to Key West. Here, let me show you."

Hearst began to draw a rough map of southern Florida, to show what he meant. I heard a rustle to my right, and noticed a figure entering our cabin from another door. I looked up distracted. The surprise was so great I stood with the beer bottle still in my hand. I was unsure whether to yell or run. Her hair was done up in a pig-tail fashion, like a schoolgirl. She was wearing a sailor's costume, with short sleeves and a skirt which ended just below her bare knees.

Hearst looked up at us from the table. "Oh, Botwright, I believe you know Miss Hampton." She nodded, and smiled. But only with her mouth. Her icy blue eyes held my stunned gaze.

"The chef has asked what you prefer for dinner, dear." He looked at me sheepishly, and then at her.

"The fish would be fine, with a bit of vegetable. And, of course, the pinot blanc." She nodded and left us. I was transfixed in surprise. Hearst seemed not at all embarrassed by the interruption. I was on the brink of blurting out what was on my swirling mind, but a caution made me hold my tongue.

"You'll stay for dinner, too," Hearst said.

"Chief, I told Sanchez I would look for him in town. I would like to stay, but he said he might have some important news from Cuba." The lie came easily. I headed for the nearest bar, where I found Remington lounging with a small Englishman he introduced as Jimmy Hare, a photographer for The Journal. I asked them about Hearst's companion.

"Nice bit of fluff, eh?" Remington said. "The chief likes his comforts when he goes to war. He met her in Boston, or New York, I forget. She was in some shabby music hall. Willie does like his playthings." Annie had become the latest in a long line of playthings. But did Hearst have any idea of the danger he was in? Or, myself, for that matter?

I tossed all night, trying to figure a way of removing the danger to us all. There seemed no solution to it.

CHAPTER TWENTY TWO

Bang!

I went back to Tampa early the next day. Hearst had said that he would soon join us there before the troops left. It was expected anytime. I sought out Dick Davis. He had just returned from another hot trip to the camps.

I told him about meeting Annie with Hearst. His eyes grew wide.

"Well, pal, it looks like we both have women we should be shed of. If she did what you say she did, then she's extremely unpredictable. Maniacs are not reasonable.

"We owe it to Hearst to warn him before he becomes the next victim." Dick lay back on the bed. "Let me think about all this a minute." Two minutes later he was snoring.

I let him sleep, and went downstairs to walk the veranda, pacing back and forth, too nervous to sit in one of the large rocking chairs. What to do? My publisher may have caused the Maine explosion. He was now with a murderess. How would I extricate myself from the mess.

I could just leave. Go back to New York, or Pittsfield, and forget it all. Except I would never forget, and I would never forgive myself for not staying. That much I knew.

I could approach Hearst. Would he hear me out before he fired me? Who knew? A few hours later I woke Dick.

"I think I have a solution," he said quietly.

"What?" I nearly screamed. He looked at me and smiled. "My solution is that I will go to Hearst and explain it all to him. He's not a fool. He'll know the danger he's in. He shouldn't be carousing with a woman down here at all. Bad form, definitely."

"Good," I said, relieved that Davis would do something.

"The only problem I have," Dick added, "is I can't leave this room without falling into the clutches of that red-headed woman again. She's too much temptation, my friend."

"Throw her out a window," I yelled. "This is a matter of life and death."

Dick Davis fell back on the bed, laughing. He was too much the gentleman to use crude methods to remove himself of a nuisance. I had no such qualms.

"Do you have a pistol, Dick?" I asked.

He nodded and pointed to his Gladstone bag by the window. "A .44 pistol, loaded except the next chamber, why?"

"I want to go armed."

Davis swung off the bed. "All right. I can't believe you could bring yourself to shoot a woman, though. I know I couldn't do it."

I had no reply to that. I unpacked the pistol, a clean blue-metal weapon with a scent of light oil. From now on I would go armed, especially at night, her favorite killing time. It would be like her to excuse herself from Hearst upstairs, and come down to knock lightly on my door.

I would open the door, unsuspecting.

Bang!

A bullet to the face. Maybe two. She would have to be sure. Suspects? Dozens, all kinds. Who would suspect a pretty woman? Another newspaper reporter shot over cards, a whore, or what-have-you. Nothing for the authorities to get excited over. Not a personage of substance. Oh, Hearst might get a few headlines out of the killing, maybe even insinuate that Spanish agents, or Pulitzer's minions had done the deed.

Hearst arrived from the yacht with her the next day. He took the last suite, the most expensive in the hotel. It wasn't the coolest, however, as it was up under the eaves. He sent a note around, saying that he would like to have us all come to dinner; Davis, Crane and anyone else I thought should be there.

Hearst and Davis were the only two in the entire hotel dining room dressed for dinner. The others wore jackets, but no ties, and some went without jackets.

Hearst shook hands formally all around, and softly asked a waiter for champagne. She stood next to him, in a shimmering lavender dress. Despite the heat of the evening, she wore cream-colored gloves. A soft breeze blew through the open floor to ceiling veranda windows. It was a warm, moist breeze, but it chilled me.

I didn't look at her. The others did, however. Crane seemed enchanted with Annie. He stared at her openly.

"As the representative of The World," Steve said, "I insist that this lady sit by me." Hearst beamed. Annie seemed to study the handsome Crane. He smiled at her. Steve was not well, but the sun and his boyish air had conspired to conceal his weariness. He engaged Annie in conversation, and soon she was laughing. I couldn't tell what they talked of. The table was large enough for us all to have our own conversations.

Hearst rapped his water glass with a knife, and held up his champagne glass to say that the coming adventure would make us all famous. Dick Davis didn't take the compliment silently.

"Maybe so," Dick said, "but this war will not be a cake-walk. The Spanish are well armed, and in good numbers on that island. Our troops, well, I hate to say it, but they are not well armed, or trained.

"If we could wait a year to form a proper army, or find proper generals we would be better off."

"Now this Shafter," Dick continued, "he looks like he belongs in a hospital. The man is ill. He has gout. He can't move. The volunteers and the regulars don't even wear the same uniform, or shoot the same rifles. And, no one knows for sure how the volunteers will perform under fire."

"They'll do excellently," Hearst replied softly.

"Just as they did at Bull Run," Davis said.

Captain Lee had overheard the conversation, and he walked up to our table. "I think that the most amazing thing your army has is its captivating spirit. Why, you can't help but feel it. I went out to General Wheeler's headquarters today. Well, you know, I'm used to a head-quarters with a dozen tents to house the staff, y'know?

"Well, I rode out there. And there was one tent. Three horses, and this old graybeard sitting in the shade of a pine tree. The old man was wearing riding pants, sus-penders, and an open shirt. I asked him where I could find the general.

'You found him,' he said. Amazing!"

"General Wheeler told me he had last fought with the Army of Northern Virginia as a cavalryman, and that he was one of those who thought that Bobby Lee could have held out for another year." Hearst laughed.

"Well, the general seemed to enjoy the confusion in the camp. I asked where his troops were. He said, 'Last I saw of them they was out roundin' up some mounts."

"He told me they had packed the men and horses on different trains, and now they were in different states. I asked him about the invasion. Don't know where it'll be or when. No point in wastin' time worryin' about it,' he said."

We all laughed at Lee's account. It was correct. Our army was slap-dash. You could not take it seriously. It didn't take itself seriously.

Crane stirred then. "Yet, I never saw braver men than the marines before Guantanamo. You know how it is. You can't even see the man who is trying to kill you. They shoot these Mausers a half mile away, and there is a little popping noise above your head. If you can hear it you're all right. But, around you men are dropping. The Spanish soldier is not as easy as you would imagine. He will fight, and what's more, there are Cuban troops with him. We forget that many Cubans support the Spanish government. They will not be happy with a gringo invasion.

"What surprised me was the powerlessness you feel. One night we were pinned to the ground by rifle fire. A doctor was killed near me. I was afraid to go to his side. He was a friend. We had talked all that afternoon. He was painfully wounded, and he yelled in agony. But I could not go to his side for fear I would be killed." Crane gulped some wine.

Davis cleared his throat. "Gentlemen, I have no doubt that the American soldier will fight valiantly. The problem is that the officers are narrow, slipshod men who don't know what war is."

Hearst frowned. He didn't like such criticism. "But don't you believe that we'll prevail over the Spaniards? They can't stand up to Americans, surely."

Crane spoke up. "Chief, the Spaniards did not run from the marines. They shot men dead. They fired at them from trenches. We could not see them. Pop, pop, and the man next to you was dead. This war is not going to be a picnic."

Hearst was becoming visibly uncomfortable. I tried to lighten the mood.

"This war will have to wait until the confusion at the docks here at Tampa gets untangled. I've never seen as many boats in one place, all going no where."

We drank a lot during that dinner. Annie, I could see, was smiling, but she spoke only to Crane, softly. I relaxed. There was no way she could shoot me at table, before company. After dessert, Hearst excused himself. I followed him.

He headed for the creaky elevator.

"Call of nature," he said when he saw me next to him.

"I need to talk privately, chief," I mumbled.

"Okay. Come up with me." We ascended in the elevator to the top floor. Hearst spent about ten minutes in the bathroom. I stared out the window, at the hazy town.

Soon Hearst entered the room, minus his dinner jacket. He pulled a long cigar from a box, and lit it. I was searching for a way to begin. Direct, I told myself. He deserved the facts.

"Chief, I have a couple of things to discuss. First, you recall the shipment of candles you sent to Sanchez?" He nodded.

"Well, Sanchez stored the dynamite aboard the Maine somehow, and it may have destroyed the ship." The chief puffed away.

"What?" he asked in his soft, musical voice.

"Sanchez told me that he had hidden the dynamite aboard the ship. He made it sound like you knew"

Hearst shifted in his chair, but said nothing.

"Sanchez didn't come right out and say it, but he let me think that the explosion was planned and you knew about it."

"What?" he asked again.

I took a deep breath. "I believe Sanchez when he says he put the dynamite aboard that ship. The point is it was your dynamite.

"Well, what of it, Mr. Botwright?" It was the first time he had used my last name since the first time we had met.

"Chief, someone is saying that you were a party to the Maine explosion, and that it wasn't an act of war by the Spanish."

"That's a hell of a story, Mr. Botwright," Hearst said.

"Yes, it is. And, it would be a great story for Mr. Pulitzer's World, wouldn't it?"

Hearst stood. For the first time since we met he seemed angry, and I realized how large a man he was, taller than I was, and heavier.

"The other thing I have to tell you is this. Annie Hampton is a killer. She's killed two men, that I know about. Fitzpatrick, and her lawyer, Lawlor. You could be next."

"Damn you," Hearst said, moving quickly to me. I saw the arm swing before the left caught me on the forehead.

I fell to my left, crashing into a small table. I scrambled to my feet as he came at me. I decided that I had to defend myself. I put up my arms, trying to block my head from his blows. He grabbed me by the shirtfront, and propelled me the length of the room, to the door. He opened it, and pushed me out.

"No one insults me this way, Mr. Botwright. I don't know what your game is, but blackmail won't work. Consider yourself out of my employment." The door slammed. It was only the start of what turned out to be a black night.

I found Dick Davis in the lobby, speaking with an army officer. I interrupted rudely and told Dick that I needed to speak with him. He saw the look on my face, and excused himself.

We walked outside, on the hotel's grounds. I paced nervously. My senses were alert.

"I've told Hearst about Annie, and about the dynamite, Dick."

"Some combination," he said puffing a cigar. I explained quickly what had happened in Hearst's suite. Dick was silent as we marched under the palms.

"What am I going to do, Dick?"

He puffed silently. "You're fired. You have insulted your publisher. You've accused him of blowing up the Maine, and living with a murderess likely to kill again if she doesn't get her way."

He laughed. "Then you get into a fistfight with the chief, I would say that you've managed to put a nail in each corner of your coffin."

"What am I going to do?" I asked again. He stopped and grasped my arm.

"You can take the first train home. Forget about all this. You could try to convince the chief, or, you could let me try. I believe that he respects me." Dick shrugged. "He should, too."

Quickly Davis outlined his plan. I would have to get out of the hotel. Go to one of the camps, perhaps with Wood's regiment. That wouldn't raise suspicions, and I would be safe there, from Hearst and from her.

"Or," Davis said, thinking out loud, "you could go with the Navy on a patrol. While I try to clean up the mess here. God only knows how I'm going to do it."

Dick wrote a name on a piece of paper. "Take this to the Navy tug down at the pier, and tell them you are replacing me for the patrol. I have carte-blanche with the Navy, so it won't raise any suspicions

I turned to return to the hotel for a bag. I saw her come out of the lighted door. Crane followed her.

Davis took my arm. "No, don't go back. Just get down to the dock."

I nodded, and hurried off. Davis told me later that a few moments afterward Crane approached. "Dick, that you?" he asked in the dark.

"Yes, Steve. Is Miss Hampton with you?"

"No, " Crane said morosely. "She went to get a carriage. She said she wants to take a moonlight ride—alone. No room for two, I'm afraid."

CHAPTER TWENTY THREE

Buzzing Insect

I lost my way at least twice on my way to the pier area, The streets were badly lit. I heard a clip-clop of a small carriage. I paid it no mind.

Once at the pier I couldn't find the Navy tug. Davis had neglected to tell me how to find it. It was a quarter-moon night, and all shadows. The ships were black, most shuttered as their crews were ashore.

I marched to the end of the pier, and could not make out a Navy tug. I was walking back toward a warehouse on the quay when I saw the figure. A chill went down my spine. It was a woman, I could tell, and somehow I knew it was Annie.

I felt the heaviness of the holstered pistol on my side. Could I shoot in self-defense? How could I explain the killing of a woman under any circumstances.

I stopped, and looked toward the edge of the pier. It was about six feet away. I could sense more than see her approach me.

Her voice was cutting. She was not loud, but I made out every word.

"He would believe you, Jim, I can't let that happen. This is the best thing that's ever happened to me. I have a chance now. He might not believe you right away, but he'd know. And, then it'd be too late. So."

I moved nervously. Did she know I was armed. What would she do if I pulled out the 44?

I couldn't see her weapon, but I knew for certainty that she had one, and it was pointed at me. And in a moment it would send me kicking into eternity. There could be no appeal.

I recalled what Davis said about maniacs.

"Too many people know now, Annie," I croaked.

"Who?" she hissed.

"A detective in New York, and a few people down here," I muttered. I couldn't mention names. They'd be victims, too.

As silently as I could I shuffled toward the edge of the pier. She must have felt what I was going to do, for as I jumped, I felt a hot buzzing insect brush my shoulder. I tumbled off the pier into the dark water. As I sank I heard two more explosions above me. I sank further, wondering idly how long I could hold my breath. Then I wondered if I was already dead.

My arm brushed something hard. I reached out reflexively and grabbed. It was an iron spike in one of the pier supports. I held on for life.

I have no idea how long I held on, but it soon became a matter of pain. I let out the breath I had taken before hitting the water. I had to surface. I pulled myself around the piling and slowly climbed it. It seemed forever. All was black. All I could feel was the pain. All I could see was black.

CHAPTER TWENTY FOUR

Shared Impressions

The trip to the surface took 40 minutes, it seemed. Finally, I broke into air, through the scummy, oily water. I gasped, and I could hear the hammer pounding of my chest, heart, in my ears. Enough to wake all of Tampa, I thought.

"I'm dead meat," I thought. May have even muttered it. But looking up, I saw that I was under the pier, protected from further bullets by the planks.

I clung to the piling for what must have been a half hour. Then I heard some voices. Male. I called for help.

Two sailors fished me out of the water. I had found the crew of the tug.

"How did you manage to get under there?" one sailor wanted to know.

"I was looking for the tug, and I tripped. Can't swim, you know."

The second sailor laughed. "Neither can I," he

said. They took me aboard, showed me where to change my clothes, gave me some cotton duck pants and an old shirt to put on. At first light they cast off, and we headed for Key West, and the battle-cruisers.

I climbed a ladder to the battlecruiser nervously from the swaying tug. It felt good to be on a more stable platform than the smaller vessel. It had been a pleasant voyage southward to Key West, and with every mile I felt more secure.

A marine in blue coat and white duck trousers saluted me as I stepped aboard the North Carolina. A young navy officer escorted me to the captain's quarters, where I was introduced to Captain Raymond Newberry. He was a spare man dressed in a smoking jacket, open collar, and what looked like bedroom slippers. He was smoking a pipe, and offered me a drink of whiskey. I readily accepted. Drink was allowed aboard U.S. Navy ships in those days. It wasn't till before the Great War that all liquor was banned. When I knew the navy, the officers drank whiskey and the other ranks drank beer or rum.

"Well, how is Mr. Davis?" Newberry asked.

"Fine, fine," I said heartily. "He couldn't make this trip, so he asked me to cover for him," I half-lied.

"But Mr. Davis is employed by The Herald, and you're with The New York Journal," the officer said.

I realized suddenly that the captain was no one's fool. "Yes," I said, "but when only one of us can go on an assignment, well, we share impressions."

It struck me hard then that I was a reporter without a newspaper. I had been fired. Mr. Hearst would not accept my copy any longer.

A youthful ensign named Halsey showed me a tiny cabin I would share with him. He was good humored about its size, and in a Texas-drawl he described the ship to me as we walked over its steel-plated decks and cramped quarters.

Halsey showed me the engine room, and the hell where the Black Gang worked, hurling coal into flaming furnaces. The heat smote us like the large black shovels the men used.

Above decks, Halsey took me to the officer's wardroom, a cramped kind of dining room, where a black steward brought us coffee.

"Well, where will the ship sail?" I asked.

The ensign made a circular motion with his hand. "Just around, some more. Like we've been doing these weeks. We steam off Havana, chase from one rock to another, and chase a few tramp steamers away from the harbor, and maybe if we feel good, why we have some gunnery practice." About two hours later I was on the bridge as the ship hauled anchor, made steam, and moved out into the stream.

I stood out of the way mostly, and watched as the sailors moved about their business. Each man had his job, and duty post. Not much was said, and conversation was limited. The rumble of the engines was felt and heard even on the bridge. From the height of the bridge I felt the commanding feeling of being a ship's captain.

My problems seemed to evaporate in the ship's wake.

By mid-afternoon the battlecruiser was off Havana, though there wasn't much to see. They told me we were about ten miles off the harbor.

"Sometimes we get close enough so you can see the castle," Halsey told me. We were having the dinner meal, and I found my appetite was great. Salt air. Afterward the gentle swell and roll of the ship rocked me to sleep. I slept 12 hours, and awoke refreshed.

Damn it all to hell, I thought as I sat down to breakfast. Damn it all to hell! Damn Hearst. Most particularly damn Annie! Damn them all. Damn Cuba. Damn the war!

I must have muttered the latter, for some officers

nearby looked up and smiled. I smiled back.

I spent the day on the open decks, interviewing everyone who would speak to me. I made so many notes that I had to borrow stationery from Halsey.

About 3 p.m. a lookout spotted a steamship off our port bow, making for Havana. It appeared to be a new ship. An officer on the bridge hastily thumbed through a commercial vessel log, seeking identification of the ship. The lookout reported the ship showed no flag.

"Looks British," Captain Newberry growled. "Make ready-the forward gun turret." A sailor called the order into a pipe, and soon I saw the massive metal turret swing.

"Signal them to move off," Newberry said. Within a few moments two sailors were using wig-wag flags in a kind of shorthand to tell the steamer to veer away. Nothing happened.

"Prepare to fire across her bow, one shot," the captain said.

I expected the shot swiftly. It took at least a minute, or two to translate itself down to the turret gang, where sailors sweated and heaved powder charges into the cannon's breach, after they manhandled the 12-inch shell. I had seen the size and danger of a ship's magazine, and the fear the sailors lived with. Any spark and all the powder would combust, killing them all and sinking the ship.

The barrel of the huge rifle moved a bit before the shot was fired. We felt the recoil on the bridge even before we heard the boom.

We saw the shell arch into the sky. I was amazed that it seemed to be moving so slowly. It landed with a explosive splash about 100 yards in front of the steamer's bow. The steamer seemed to go dead in the water.

Quickly the lookout reported that the ship was showing the British ensign, and wig-wag flags.

"Damn him," Captain Newberry said, lowering his binoculars. Newberry turned to me.

"Happens all the time. Usually they try to sneak in at night. This fellow was desirous to discover if we meant business. Probably a load of horse blankets. But a hell of a row if we were to sink one of Vicky's boats."

Not much happened after that. A day later we turned toward Key West. I got the feeling that Captain Newberry and the other officers chafed at the absence of real battle. All the warlike action was taking place on the Orient Station, where an obscure naval officer named Dewey, I later learned, had saved the New York newspapers from making up too many stories to keep three million readers in a state of perpetual excitement.

I was relaxed from the sea tour, but nervous about returning to Florida.

"Maybe we'll have some fun when the Spaniards come out of Havana," Halsey said. "But I feel they'll come out and make a run for home. They don't want to fight, that's for sure."

We shook hands on the dock, and I walked out of the Navy station without luggage, the way I had arrived. I stopped at the hotel and inquired whether Mr. Hearst had returned. Jimmy Hare was at the bar, as if he owned it.

"No, Jim, he's still up at Tampa with that dory. I guess he likes it up there." I must have sighed, with relief, or concern, I didn't know what.

"Looking for the chief?" Hare asked. I nodded, unable and unwilling to provide more explanation.

I took a mug of beer and sat in the back of the taproom, and thought about my situation. I had enough money in Tampa to get back to New York. I could return to Pittsfield. If I went to New York I could probably get another job, perhaps on The Herald. Maybe I could ask Mr. Chapin for a position. He might be willing to take me back, if only to show the folly of going to work for Hearst.

Whatever happens, I decided, I would have to return to Tampa, at least temporarily, to get enough money to continue my journey. I didn't feel like telegraphing Dick Davis, or Crane, as I didn't know where they would be.

Someone might recall I worked for Hearst, and the message would be delivered to him—and to her.

The hot, stuffy train moved slowly northward. I was in no hurry. I sat and wondered how I could stay alive once I got to Tampa.

CHAPTER TWENTY FIVE

Jeopardy

I swung off the car with no enthusiasm. I was in luck. There was a sergeant I recognized from Wood's regiment. He was waiting to pick up a case of navy pistols. I begged a ride out to Wood's camp. The sergeant was so used to seeing one or another of us around that he didn't think the request unusual.

As we rolled through the sun-baked streets of Tampa I shuddered with fear that I would be seen. An hour later I relaxed.

"Well, Botwright, you're back!" Roosevelt barked when he spotted me. He wanted to know where I had been? "With the Navy," I said. That took the wind out of Captain Bully. He obviously knew that the navy was at war, while he and his men sweltered in the pines.

I asked him if I could send a message to Dick Davis, or Crane.

"Of course. I'll carry it for you, if you like. I'm on my way to headquarters at the hotel. They'll be there, too,

I imagine," he said. I hastily scribbled a note to Dick or Steve, announcing that I was back, and asking either or both come fetch me.

Davis showed that evening, just as I was sitting down to some camp stew and a metal cup of coffee. The navy had better grub, I had told all Wood's rangers within earshot. They just laughed.

Davis arrived in a rig, which contained my luggage, and some money.

Dick seemed weary. We shook hands, and he had some coffee. "Well, I think I've fixed it for you," he said.

"What do you mean?" I asked.

"I went to Willie, and talked some sense," Davis said. "He listened."

"Well, what did he say?" I asked. Davis slumped into a camp chair, and after a long sip of coffee he explained how he had faced Hearst the morning after I was nearly shot to death and how he thought the meeting went and what Hearst said and felt.

"Botwright couldn't figure out a way to tell you about this. He figured that you'd take him for a jilted suitor, or worse, one trying to interfere in your, ah, affairs. But we feel that you should know the truth," Davis said straightforwardly.

Hearst, seated in a wicker chair in his hotel bedroom, watched Davis closely. He knew he had been hearing the truth. It was impossible not to believe the man. What a story it would make for the paper, he thought, gleefully. Botwright had known then that she was a murderess. She had really killed Fitzpatrick and Lawlor, too. My god, who would be next? he wondered.

He recalled the straight figure, the narrow waist, the blonde hair, the blue eyes, and the laughter. Above all the laughter, and the openness in bed. It would be ticklish, but he thought he would be able to handle it.

Davis wanted to add something, "Chief, we were worried that you were serious about this girl. Even if you, ah, aren't serious, you're in jeopardy. She has killed, we believe, without regret, and the same could happen to you. Botwright was also worried that you might, ah, marry her, without realizing..." Hearst dismissed the idea with a wave of his long arm.

"Dick, tell Botwright thanks. I'll not forget it."

Davis left the room. Hearst walked onto the upper story veranda outside the room. He sat for an hour, until she arrived from a shopping expedition. She was flushed and damp in the heat. He asked her to sit with him a moment. He poured her a glass of lemonade, and smiled at her.

"Darling, I've been thinking. I don't think it would be safe for you to go with me to the war zone. The yacht is unarmed, and the Spanish have a great fleet. If anything were to happen to you, I'd never forgive myself."

"You're sweet."

He smiled. "So, I think it would be better if you stayed here in Tampa, or returned to New York until the war is over. No telling what'll happen. But I don't want to risk your life. I'm thinking of the future." She smiled, and patted his arm. She went into the bedroom, and took off her dress. Hearst turned his head so that he could see her lush body as she toweled perspiration from her shoulders, breasts and legs.

No need to give her reason to panic, Hearst thought. If she believes we have a future together she is less likely to panic. And, she is an accommodating woman. I might as well enjoy her while it lasts. Hearst sipped at the lemonade.

Davis told it like one of his short stories. It made sense.

CHAPTER TWENTY SIX

Ice Cream

hat did he say?"

"Relax, Jim," Davis smiled, "he understands. He'll take care of her."

I unscrewed a bottle of whiskey I had bought from a sergeant. "This calls for one hell of a drink." I believe I stayed drunk for at least a half-day. Dick sobered me up, and we visited Shafter's field headquarters in an old tobacco barn outside Tampa. We saw confusion. Dick kept asking when and where.

"Santiago," a bald staff officer told us.

"But that's on the other side of the island from Havana? Why not capture Havana and be done with it?"

"The navy says that the Spanish fleet is at Santiago. They want us to land near there, and scare the fleet into open water."

"It's a hell of a note when the navy uses the army."

While we talked war strategy, a solid-looking tall lieutenant walked into the office, and he looked angry.

"Good morning, major. I'm Lt. John Pershing, acting quartermaster of the 10th Cavalry.

"My men have no blankets, no horses, and only the ammunition they carried here," Pershing said forcefully.

"We have to borrow coffee and canned food from the other units. The 10th, sir, is regular army. These procedures are against regulations." He cracked his gloves against a table top. He looked as if he wanted to crack them against someone's head.

The major rubbed his face. "Lieutenant, all the regiments are sorely missing most everything. We are trying to make do. The railroad just parked the supply cars on the mainline, and spurs, miles from anywhere. The cars are not marked, and after we open them we have no place to store the goods. Send you men out to the cars and have them take what they need."

"Sir, this is not military at all."

The major sighed. "Listen, son, six months ago I was a happy lawyer in Washington. I never dreamed that we'd all be spending the Summer here in Florida, in all this confusion. The army never dreamed it. Where were you six months ago?"

Pershing smiled. "I was stationed at West Point." General Shafter waddled into the room. "Pershing! You back again?" he bellowed. Pershing came to attention. "Yes, sir."

"Well, there's nothing new for you. I don't know where the damn tropical uniforms are stored. Or even if they've been shipped. You'll just have to wait."

"Yes, sir, but it's a hardship on the men to ask them to wear wool shirts and trousers." Shafter waved his arm in dismissal. The tall man glared at the fat general for a minute and turned on his heel and left the room. I followed him from the building.

"It's a damn shame, all this confusion," Pershing muttered. Outside of Col. Wood, Pershing was about the only officer I had met in Tampa who was concerned about his men.

Those last few days at Tampa are now a blur. I recall that Davis, after a day in the field, would soak for an hour in a hot tub. The hotter the better, he said. "You will soon have acres of dirt pounded into your skin. You'll feel that you never were clean. You will not realize that you smell. You'll look on a hot bath as the ultimate in luxury."

Crane smiled. "I missed ice cream the most. At Guantanamo there was some liquor. But I didn't want any. I wanted ice cream. There wasn't any. Toward the end I would have sold my soul for a dish. I guess each man finds the one thing he wants. It must be the constant terror, lack of sleep and decent food which does it."

One afternoon Dick and I stopped by the hotel, and I was stunned to see her in the lobby. I stood paralyzed on the ground-floor veranda. Hearst had not sent her away. What could he be thinking of? I quickly told Dick I would wait in the back garden while he conducted his business. I found a small group of reporters there, relaxing in chairs under the palms.

Jimmy Hare was there with another man, a tall, thin man, and they both were adjusting a box on a tripod.

"What is it?" I asked.

"A cinema machine," Hare chirped. "Say hello to Harry Hemment. The chief wants him to make moving pictures of the war. He's the best in the business. Sit down over there, while Harry and I get this thing working." The contraption looked like a large camera box, with a lens opening, and a crank on the side. I took a sip from the bottle the reporters passed around. Crane and Davis came by. Dick watched with interest as Hemment and Hare fiddled with the camera. Finally, they had us all sit together on a bench, after we put the bottle out of sight, and then he told us to stand and walk around. The opportunity to cavort was too strong, and we pushed each other. Hare also raised his portable box camera and took shot after shot in the afternoon light.

Years later Hare told me that when Hemment shipped the film north for development, it was ruined. The heat had destroyed the chemicals. Hemment, he added, never went to war. The man developed yellow fever in Florida, and was shipped home to die. Jimmy Hare gave me a print of the still photos he made that day, and I still have it, showing myself with a drunken leer, a sober Davis, and a sleepy-looking Crane. We all looked young and healthy enough to live forever.

CHAPTER TWENTY SEVEN

Sea Sick

June 10, 1898

Dear Jim,
We are learning about the army, and it is so boring. I thought it would be exciting. We live in a sort of boardinghouse, the dozen of us, and we report each morning to an old building, where we sit in an airless room and listen to an old army officer explain the forms we'll have to fill out. There are more forms than I would have thought possible. Papa is coming to visit tomorrow. He couldn't stand being alone, and decided he would come down for the weekend.

The navy has a small hospital here, but would you believe that the army has none? I'm learning something new every day. I wish you were near.

June 12, 1898
Dearest Hilda,
We will have to invade Cuba, and no one knows how that will go. The American army has not had

experience in such maneuvers. Except for the Mexican war, its great battles have been fought on American soil. And now we have the same men in command. It is safe to say they don't know what they are doing, but all make a great show of displaying grand confidence.

I miss you so much that I ache. I will try to stay out of harm's way.

The exchange of letters did not help. The momentary delight in receiving one was replaced by the ache of separation. On the early morning of June 14 we got the order to board ships. The mad scramble was on. Much has been written since about it. Roosevelt and Wood had to commandeer coal cars to move their men to dockside. They literally had to steal a ship assigned to another regiment. The confusion was supreme. The army had never moved in invasion force before. No one knew how to do it. After much sweat the soldiers found themselves packed into a collection of rotting tramp steamers that the government had collected. We didn't move. The navy refused to budge.

"Why the Sam Hill don't we get going? We can't sit here in the bay all week, and wait for the Spanish to come to us." Roosevelt was so angry that he paced the deck, talking to himself. Davis leaned against a rail and puffed on his pipe.

We learned that the navy had stood fast because it had an intelligence report that said the Spanish fleet was coming out of Havana to form on Key West. A day later the navy learned that the report was false. The Spanish fleet was bottled, and so were we. Davis smiled at our predicament. "God takes care of drunkards, sailors, and the United States army," he said.

As soon as we entered the Gulf I became sea sick. The old boat rolled and tossed with a distressing motion. The voyage was a nightmare for days. I couldn't eat, and could barely swallow the rum that Davis pressed on me.

On the other hand, Crane survived the voyage in the best of shape. He always seemed healthier at sea. On June 22, our flotilla formed off Daiquiri and Siboney, coastal villages outside Santiago, places where Davis had visited during earlier explorations of Cuba. It didn't look like the Cubans or the Spanish army were expecting us. Our ships pulled into the rickety docks, and began unloading. The landing was uncontested. It would have been a disaster if the Spanish had put up breastworks and had cannon in the hills above the docks. We surprised them. We surprised ourselves.

The unloading was as chaotic as the loading. Mules fell overboard in the haste to get off the ships men and supplies toppled from ships into the water. Some drowned even before touching Cuban soil. And the cursing was heard everywhere. Soldiers who waded into the shore from small boats lowered from the steamers found themselves foundering in the surf, weighted down with bullet-pouches, bedrolls and other gear. Only after the first detachments had moved into the villages did I leave our steamer. I could barely walk, so weak was I from the sea sickness. The sun hammered at my head. Davis, prepared for everything in a pith helmet, went off to look for Roosevelt and Wood.

"What regiment do you want to follow?" Crane asked.

"How about the 10th cavalry?" I asked. We didn't have any problem finding the black men. Many were struggling through the surf on Daiquiri beach, trying to unload their equipment. They still wore the blue wool uniforms. I asked a sergeant where the commanding officer was. He looked me up and down before replying, "Sir, the major, he's back of the hill." We went over the hill, and there we found the headquarters encampment—a few small tents in the shade of a few low pine trees. I saw Lt. Pershing, and called to him. He took us to a short, white-haired Major Stevens T.

Norvall, the regimental commander, who looked too old for field service. The age differences in the army were confusing. Thirty-two-year-old colonels led volunteer regiments, while 60-year-old majors commanded regular army units, assisted by 45-year-old captains,

"I've no time to chat with reporters," Norvall told us.

"We would like to stay with your unit during the coming battles," I said.

He looked at us sternly. "This is regular army, mister, we have no provision for pressmen. Stay with General Shafter."

And with that we were dismissed. Crane and I looked at each other and smiled. Pershing said he had to go see about water supplies. Water in Cuba was a big problem. Soldiers drank from streams, and the few wells. The water was not very pure, and we knew it. I drank only boiled coffee.

On our way back to the dock we watched some black soldiers dig a privy. Their shovels opened the soft, sandy soil quickly. They sang as they dug, swinging their arms to the chorus. They had shed their awful wool shirts.

The Spaniards were not in evidence. A few ragged looking Cubans wandered in, begging for food. They looked very shabby, and some said they were insurrectos. They looked like starving dogs. And, they did not raise much in the way of sympathy from the soldiers.

I had a bad night's sleep that first night ashore. It was a sleep ruined by the erratic shooting of nervous pickets. The army grumpily awoke at dawn and nervously looked around. Then, it ate a hasty breakfast, and wondered what it should do next.

Crane and I stayed around the Daiquiri dock, where we watched a tiny man in khaki negotiate with navy officers and a parade of army officers. The little man wore a slouch hat, cavalry boots, and on his shoulder straps the brass star of brigadier general. We walked up to the little man and introduced ourselves.

"Joe Wheeler," he said in a soft, Southern accent. Wheeler looked old enough to be in a old-folks home. But here the former Virginia congressman, through some alchemy of the War Department, had a field command in wartime. Crane and I were not impressed. We thought Wheeler would soon topple from the heat. In fact, battle brought "Fighting Joe" to life. His eyes glittered, and even his short, white beard seemed to bristle. Wheeler was a born scrapper, and his first order of the day was to move inland.

"Let's not sit around here on our asses, waiting for the Spanish to find us, let's go find him." By 8 a.m. Wheeler had scouts moving cautiously down the main road toward Santiago, about 15 miles away. By that time General Shafter had come ashore, but he seemed more intent on getting his personal carriage off a steamer than leading his army. Wheeler filled the breech, walking as often as he rode among the units which made up his cavalry brigade. They were cavalry only in name. The soldiers had no horses. They were left behind in Georgia or Florida. Only a few of the officers had mounts. And we quickly saw that horses weren't suitable for the narrow roads, and tangled undergrowth.

The terrain was rough, dotted with low bushes and pine trees and vines. The hills made marching difficult. The roads were primitive. Wood's troops had machetes, and they were indispensable for cutting through the heavy ground cover. After that first day on the trek, the First Volunteers took to calling themselves "Wood's Weary Walkers." I do not recall the name "Rough Riders" being used at all, primarily because the men were not riding.

The black troopers who moved alongside Wood's men did their marching in silence, with none of the joshing and skylarking common to the militia units.

CHAPTER TWENTY EIGHT

Whup Em

rane and I trod behind the scouts. It was hot and dusty. So we were all covered with grime. Some troopers collapsed from sun stroke because of their hot clothing. I was thankful for my khaki. Crane hummed music-hall favorites and his spirits seemed to lift the closer we came to the point of action.

Crane's eyes blazed as the threat of combat loomed. He was breathing heavily. I noticed it, but he denied my comments that he was having trouble. I didn't know it but Steve was suffering from the tuberculosis which later killed him. He seemed fearless, and had no nervousness about peering over the next rise in hopes of spotting the enemy. We had not seen the enemy, and had no idea what he looked like. All I could envision were the lazy, sloppy-looking soldiers at the crossroads during our previous trip. We were, it seemed, chasing ghosts, and involved in some kind of tedious club outing.

By noon the soldiers were swearing, at their packs, and the army mules, which wanted either to race ahead of their handlers, or lag well behind. Had the Spanish concentrated artillery on those roads they could have struck our forces a crushing blow.

I knew there were about 200,000 Spanish and Cuban troops on the island. We were less than 20,000. Terrible odds. Finally, the sun's hot hammer went down. The officers called a halt. We fell into makeshift camps by the side of the road. Weary pickets were sent out to serve as a screen.

General Wheeler appeared in our midst as we settled to the ground. He pulled out a folding spyglass, and searched the ridge about two miles to our front. He grunted. Then he turned to his staff, a beefy major, and a rumpled sergeant.

"Send out runners to all the regiments for a commander's call." We watched while Wheeler quietly drew a rough map with a short pencil on a piece of yellow paper he rested on one leg.

I contributed a bit of coffee to a trooper's pot, and we had a cup within a few minutes. It tasted like the best you could find in New York. The regimental officers, from the 1st, 10th, and 1st Volunteers straggled up to Wheeler at dusk. They sat on the ground without military formality.

Wood and Roosevelt brought a couple of portable, folding chairs. I was amazed. I could not believe that some man or animal had to carry them up and down the ridges. Roosevelt sat on one chair, crossed his legs and waited. Wood, characteristically, gave the second chair to Major Norvall, who in turn gave it to General Wheeler. He sat, crossed his legs, reached into his jacket, and found a pipe.

"Gents, we have to our front a fortified building. It's up the road a piece. I think tomorrow we gonna have to hit that place. Can't have them sitting up there and watching us. They could throw a lot of artillery down on us if we try to walk around them." Wheeler then passed his scrap map around.

"So, gents, tomorrow morning, after breakfast, we'll go up there and take that place. We'll attack in three columns to the front. First Volunteers over on the left, the 10th in the middle, and the 1st Regulars on the right. Suit you folks?" I looked around at my first battle council, amazed that it would be this informal and matter of fact. General Wheeler sat quietly and puffed on his pipe. "We'll keep it simple. Some of you might have trouble climbing that hill in front of us." Crane was seated next to me. He was hunched over his notebook, scribbling furiously. He accidently kicked over his coffee cup. I picked it up, ambled over to the pot, and refilled it for him. He smiled at me, his eyes bright over the beginnings of a pirate's beard.

Davis appeared, walking in front of a mule and its skinner. The animal was toting Davis' kit—two large trunks and two suitcases. Dick found a large tree nearby and told the skinner to unpack there. Dick wandered over to the circle of officers.

"Say, Davis, you're just in time for the attack."

"Am I? Hope it's not before dinner." The others laughed, including Wheeler.

"With General Wheeler in charge we're liable to be attacking by candlelight."

"Not likely, Davis. Not likely. We'd only shoot each other up that way. I shall presume that our valiant Spanish foe value their sleep as we do."

Davis grunted and sat down on the ground. "General, how much ammunition should we issue?" Wood asked.

"As much as they can carry. Have them fill their canteens tonight. Maybe they could boil the water first."

Wheeler looked at the gray outline of the ridge in the

distance. "Can't stop them from having fires tonight. The greasers know we're here anyways. The trick is to hit them hard tomorrow, and push them back."

Wood smiled. "Will General Shafter be coming to the lines tomorrow?"

"Don't know," Wheeler said. "Last thing he told me was to find the Spanish and whup em." Davis stretched out on the ground, and took a snooze while the officers chatted for an hour, excited by the adventure they were in, and then they drifted nervously back to their commands. Here and there in the glade, troopers cooked beans and coffee over fires, and chewed their hardtack as night quickly spread over the country. It occurred to me that I was not lonely, or homesick as would be expected. Nor was I longing for Hilda. It sounds odd, but the sheer effort to get some dinner, and wonder about the morrow's events, pushed everything else out of my head. It was also weariness. The trek was debilitating. Davis didn't even bother with dinner. He padded over to his bedroll and climbed in.

Years have gone by, but I still contemplate what she was doing then. The bits and pieces I learned later went this way:

Annie felt the first weakness the day after Hearst left. The farewell was businesslike, she thought. He just packed, pecked her cheek and climbed into the waiting carriage to take him to the yacht. She would've gone with him. She was not frightened by war. She was not frightened by anything. She knew something was wrong with her, however, after the first wave of dizziness, and the nausea.

She collapsed on the lobby stairs later that hot afternoon. She had gone downstairs to ask for more ice water. She felt the weakness and dropped to the stairs. Before she blacked out she saw the red-haired woman rush toward her. When she awoke she was in her room, and the red-haired woman was standing over her bed.

"How do you feel, honey?"

Annie nodded.

"We've called for a doctor. I don't know one in this town. They tell me they've all been busy out at the army camp, the fever and all. You may have to go to the hospital." Annie shook her head emphatically

"Oh, it's all right. I don't think you have fever. It's too bad that Mr. Hearst left you here. Is there any way we can reach him?"

Annie ignored the question. She knew that this florid woman knew she was Hearst's mistress. She might even have guessed her background. Women in the life found it easy to recognize others. The woman looked at her, and smiled. "I think I know what's ailing you, honey. You're gonna have a baby." The woman smiled.

Annie turned away. This could not happen now. It would spoil everything. Hearst would not tolerate that kind of blackmail. She would get some money, and orders to have another abortion. It would finish all her plans and she would have to start over.

The doctor came that evening. He looked her over, with the red-haired woman acting as nurse. He seemed intrigued by her. He called her Alice and she flirted with him. Annie watched them both, and decided that Alice was a woman unable to resist any man.

As Alice cleaned up the room, the smiling, bald doctor leaned over the bed and said., "Ma'am, you don't have the fever, thank God, and unless I miss my guess, you're in the family way."

She managed a weak smile. After he left, dawdling at the door with Alice, she called the woman to her bedside.

"Do you know where I can get rid of it here?" Alice showed the surprise in her eyes. She sat down. "Honey, you're talking like someone in the life. Don't you want this baby?"

The next day Alice found the name of a black woman in Tampa who was a midwife, and also capable of "fixing" social embarrassments for the gentry.

Three days later Annie lay on the kitchen table in a shack in the black section. The shades were drawn, and the old black woman and her younger assistant worked by candlelight. Everything went smoothly, except at the end when they couldn't stop the bleeding. Annie passed out. They took her unconscious in a wagon to the hospital and left her on the steps.

CHAPTER TWENTY NINE

A Different Wind

"Botwright is showing one of the symptoms of battle nerves," Steve Crane said to Col. Wood. Both were seated on the damp ground, with a tin plate on their knees.

"Yes," Col. Wood said, "He's hungry." Wood smiled. I laughed out loud. I had been spooning the beans. They tasted good.

Wood turned to Steve. "Crane you've been through this before. I've read your stories with the marines. You and I, and Wheeler, we know what it'll be like tomorrow, and in the coming days. These innocents," he waved to include me, "will have to learn the hard way."

Crane nodded in agreement. "There isn't much we could do to educate them. You have to live it," Steve said softly.

Wood shrugged. "Well, son, we could've trained these men better. We're a weak brigade. There's some infantry coming ashore, but the

Spanish have the men to make a real fight of it and I pray that their heart is not in it. Then, maybe, we'll get off easy. Otherwise." He spooned more greasy beans into his mouth.

Crane tried to change the subject. "How is it, colonel, that you're a doctor, and you can lead men into battle, where you know that some of them will be wounded, and killed?"

Wood shook the food remnants onto the ground. "Good question. I could refuse to answer. The truth is that I decided that doctoring wasn't for me. I decided that after I was a doctor, unfortunately. I much more enjoyed mounting up and taking a troop out after Geronimo. That's what got to me. Maybe if I hadn't've gone into the army as a contract surgeon, I wouldn't've known. I would still be in the Boston hospital wards, wondering why I was unhappy.

"Who's unhappy?"

We hadn't noticed Roosevelt's appearance behind us. He knelt by Wood. "This is no time for unhappiness. Tomorrow we go into battle."

Crane laughed. "Are you happy, Crane?" Roosevelt asked.

"When I'm writing. But war seems a high price to pay just to have something to write about. There doesn't seem anything else with the same excitement. War seems to be getting very popular," Steve said.

"Yes," Roosevelt boomed, "you and Davis and Botwright here will have enough wars to keep you busy."

Wood shifted his body nervously. "Maybe this one could have been put on the back burner for awhile. Look at our situation," Wood said. "Most of these regulars have never seen, or been part of a brigade in one place before. They wouldn't know what to do with a division, much less an army. But they'll learn. The hard way." Wood pushed himself to his feet. "Excuse me. I'll go check the men, Teddy."

Wood walked into the shadows as we watched silently.

I wondered if we'd all be dead this time tomorrow night.

Crane poured Roosevelt a cup of coffee from the pot hung over the fire.

"There's one thing that still bothers me, colonel," I said, perhaps too loudly.

Roosevelt looked at me, his spectacles reflecting the firelight.

"Why was the Maine in Havana harbor?" I asked.

Roosevelt sipped at his hot coffee. "Well, Mr. Botwright, there's no secret about that. The Maine was sent down here to show the flag. A goodwill visit."

I snapped the question. "Did you send the ship?" Crane stretched out on the ground, as if to sleep.

"The ship was ordered off station by the admiral of the Atlantic fleet," Roosevelt said.

"Why?" I persisted.

"Oh, for God's sake, Botwright, I've just told you." It was the first time I had ever heard Roosevelt use an oath, however mild.

"Yes, you have," I said. "But it seems odd to me that a capital ship of the United States Navy would be sent to a nation that many in government wanted war with," I ended lamely.

Roosevelt's laugh was explosive. "Happens all the time, Botwright. You see, war plans need all kinds of information." He rose, shaking dirt from his trousers. "I'm afraid that's all I can tell you. You see, it's government business."

"Just what I expected," Crane said from the darkness. I watched the middle-aged Roosevelt march from the campfire, a wealthy lawyer-politician who was risking his life in this adventure. For what? Tomorrow his wife could be a widow, and his children fatherless. There were many things I didn't understand that night, nor to this day.

I awoke before dawn, shaking from the chill. Unwashed, and unshaven, I waited for the others to stir. The soldiers lay on the ground like so many corpses. I looked over at Crane and his pale skin above the stubble looked unhealthy. I waited nervously for what promised to be an exciting day, a day different from all the others I had lived. Soon birds chattered, men stretched, and a few set fires burning for coffee. I gulped some, with a bit of stubborn, stale bread. Crane and I splashed water on our faces from a small stream before the troops turned it into a muddy slough.

"Well, Jim, which way should we go?"

"You make it sound like we have a choice?" Crane laughed.

We decided in apathy to follow the main road with the 10th. Davis heated some water in a pot, and actually shaved himself. After collecting all our gear, and counting heads, it was about 8 a.m. before the advance units moved out on the road. It was actually a narrow country path, suitable for a donkey cart. The troopers walked in a rolling gait with loaded rifles at the ready. Some rid themselves of gear, and soon the roadside was strewn with heavy shirts, blankets and other bulky items.

We swung into the line with General Wheeler. I half expected that he would say something about the waste. He barely noticed it. Twenty minutes later we heard rifle fire ahead.

Crane always maintained that the U.S. rifles went "prut" as the bullet went overhead. And the Spanish Mausers went "pop." They sounded alike to me. It quickly got hot.

A messenger ran up to General Wheeler and said that 1st Cavalry skirmishers had run against entrenched Spanish soldiers. No one knew the name of the lonely place. I learned much later that it was called Las Guasimas. There was the ridge, and an old sugar warehouse, and it commanded the ridge and it was an ideal defensive spot. The Spanish had decided they wouldn't attack, but they would defend. The general sat by the roadside and scrawled pencil messages to the three regimental commanders. We heard rifle fire on the left. That meant that Wood's men had been spotted. They had reached a small hill directly in front of the ridge. You could see tiny figures—Spanish riflemen shooting at the Americans.

Immediately to our front was the column of the black troopers from the 10th. They ran into heavy rifle and Maxim machine gun fire when they emerged from a jungle grove. The road swerved to the right to skirt the steep ridge. The black troopers fired from the tree line, kneeling to get a better uphill angle.

The old white-haired General Wheeler moved to the front line, waving his arm and pointing. "Let's go, boys; we're gonna go up that hill as fast as we can." About 20 men responded, running out into the sloping, open field. Wheeler watched, and swung his hat from his head as the men charged the ridge. We could see a few of the small dots—Spanish soldiers—running the other way from the trenches. "That's it, boys," Wheeler yelled. "now we've got the goddam Yankees on the run."

Wheeler almost jumped out of his uniform with excitement. I had to laugh at the general's outburst. He really said it. The old warrior really had only one enemy, and these Spanish were surrogates.

Steve and I kept up with the sweating, advancing troops. Their shouts and the prut-pop of the rifles made a steady noise. We moved out of the tree line, and onto a grassy area, an open valley before the ridge. Crane moved over to his left, heading for Wood's regiment. We could hear heavy firing, but could see little through the trees.

Men began falling around us. The enemy trench a few hundred feet above us had not been emptied by the fleeing Spanish. I stood in the clearing, upright, and watched raptly as the troopers struggled up the ridge. No one ran that day. They walked bent over, as if heading into a hurricane wind. It was a wind of hot, whistling lead. If you heard it, you were safe.

I didn't hear or even feel the slug which tore into my side. I felt a soft, spreading burn. I was conscious, but I can't recall what I thought at that moment. I toppled over onto my back, face to the blue sky. No feeling. No panic. No strength. I could not move. The hot metal insects with their sweet sting buzzed over me, but I was uncaring. I quickly went into shock. I was half-awake but uncaring. Sometimes I could hear, but not see, and other times I could see, but not hear the crashing of rifles, and yelling around me.

Men began falling around me. The trench above still contained long-range death.

I must have lain on that field for hours before Crane found me, he thought at first, dead. Corpses were scattered in the meadow like so many rag dolls. Crane found some stretcher bearers, and they moved me back off the battlefield to a shady collection point for wounded under a tree. A harassed army doctor looked at me, Crane said later, and shook his head. Fortunately, I was not awake to see it.

CHAPTER THIRTY

Pale and Sweating

I t was months later, in England, over a glass of rich port, that Crane told me about that afternoon. He had come across me in the high grass.

"You were pale and sweating but you seemed to be alive, with the promise to stay that way for a bit. Your breathing was weak, though. I was afraid you'd die before I could get help. I must be honest and say that I had a feeling that you'd die anyway, either in Key West, or Tampa. I paid some army litter bearers to carry you the five miles to the dock at Daiquiri. I saw a group of black stevedores unloading cargo, and near them a tall figure in a white suit. There was a smaller man with him. It was Hare and Hearst."

Crane said, "I ran the length of the pier. I yelled, 'Mr. Hearst, your man Botwright is seriously wounded. May die. Got one in the stomach, We're trying to figure out what to do with him. Dick and I.'"

"Well, Hearst looked at me, and said, "Do with him? Hell, Crane, let's get him to a doctor.'"

"The army doctors say that they're too busy. One told me that Botwright's wound is too serious."

"Well, Hearst spun around to Hare. 'Get the mate, Jimmy. Tell him to get the yacht ready. We'll put Botwright on it, and send him back to Florida immediately. Hop to it,' he said.

"You were slung aboard the chief's boat, and razzle-dazzle, you were on your way to Florida," Crane said, sipping his wine. 'She'll make good time to Tampa,' Hearst told me," Crane said.

Steve was exhausted that night he told me the full story of that hot, painful day, wan from the struggle of supporting a household and trying to write. But he could still laugh, a warm, soft chuckle that was truly good-natured.

"The chief then turned to me, and said, 'Now, Mr. Crane, if you'll excuse me, I must get back to the war.' "I watched him march down the pier, and toward his carriage. I decided that I would find Dick Davis, and hope that he had managed to pack some whiskey in his luggage. It was hot that day, but I suddenly needed a drink."

"Who wrote the battle account that appeared in The Journal?" I asked. Crane twisted in his chair. He looked embarrassed.

"I knew that you'd ask, sometime," he said.

"It was a good piece, Steve, but it should've had your name on it."

Crane smiled, and reached for the wine bottle. I don't recall arriving at the hospital. The doctor told me later that I had surgery immediately. The doctors took the slug out of my gut, and sewed me up as best they could.

I must have slept for days, unconscious because of the amount of opium they had given me. When I did awake- it was to a downpour. Rain slashed the windows, and the bed was clammy.

I ached, and it was agony to move. A short, balding doctor came to see me in my private room upstairs, where they kept all the surgery patients. There weren't many of them, as the majority of those in the hospital were ill with fever.

He checked my sutures, and neatly snipped them, and washed my stomach with alcohol. It stung wildly, but it also was cool.

"When can I get up?" I groaned. The doctor smiled. "As soon as you can walk," he said.

The next day I staggered from the bed and made it to a chair by the window. It had stopped raining, but the sky was overcast, matching my spirits. The hospital, I noticed, was quiet. I looked down at the court yard, and noticed the burial detail. Three soldiers were digging, under the direction of a corporal. Nearby six bodies lay under sheets on the ground.

The soldiers worked steadily, silently, their shovels biting into the sandy soil. They dropped the bodies into the shallow graves without much ceremony. I couldn't tell whether the bodies were men or women. Not that it made much difference. The men seemed in a rush to complete the job.

A day later I made it down the curving staircase to the main floor. There I found the doctor in his small office. There had been two doctors in the hospital, and three nurses. But one doctor and the nurses had died of the fever. In the kitchen I found an old black man, Amos Rawls, who was about the only help in the place.

For two days I helped the doctor care for the dozens down with fever. Many died, and the soldiers buried them swiftly. Many of the fever victims were in tents in the rear yard. I had Amos light cresote torches and without knowing it until much later, we inadvertently kept the disease-carrying mosquitos away.

My mind was on the nursing work. I forgot about the war, Hearst and Annie. That was a mistake.

One evening, feeling strong enough, I dressed and packed the canvas bag that had come out of Cuba with me, belted my holstered pistol on my waist, and came down to find the doctor. He was not in the sick ward. I shuffled into the kitchen, and called to Rawls, who was cooking.

"Where's the doctor?" Amos looked at me. "He's sleepin' in the front, I think."

"Be right back. I want to ask him something." I padded through the kitchen door and down the long dark corridor to the front part of the building. The doctors used one of the front rooms there for eating and sleeping. I saw the door open half way, but no light showing. I pushed the door and there was a figure in the room with its back to me. It registered that it was a woman. At first I thought it was one of the nurses, then I noticed the glint of her hair. Blonde. Annie.

I must have gasped, for she turned, moving her right arm upward. I knew what was in it. Without a word I leaped for her arm, while at the same time I swung at her with all my might. My right connected with her jaw, and she collapsed. Fortunately, she didn't pull the trigger. The pistol clattered to the floor as she sagged to follow it. I grabbed her around the waist and pulled her backward through the door. I put her on a sofa nearby, and was wondering what to do next, when the doctor appeared, sleepy-eyed, in the doorway.

"That you, Botwright. What's going on? He lighted a gas lamp, and walked over to the sofa.

"So, she's back."

"You know her?" I almost shouted.

He looked at me. "Yes, she was a patient here until the other day. She went back to the hotel. Did she just come in?"

"She was a patient here?" I asked. He nodded. "Well, I warned her that she would feel weak from the ah, operation." He rubbed his face. "God, I'm tired. Let me wash, and I'll see to her." He walked back toward the kitchen, down the darkened hall. I looked at the unconscious figure on the sofa, her hair in disarray, spilling down her shoulder. I followed the doctor, numb. In the kitchen he splashed some water on his face at the sink, and I stood watching him. I wondered what, if anything, I should tell him. And how much he would believe.

"This woman out there, you say that she was patient in this hospital?"

"Yes, she was. I, uh, can't tell you about it, though. But she was here. She wanted to leave too soon. That must explain why she came back. I didn't hear the bell. She must've let herself in." He dried his face and hands. I followed him down the corridor. He stopped and lighted a few of the corridor lamps. She was not on the sofa. The doctor looked up the staircase, thinking perhaps she had gone to the upper floor. I opened the front door and saw the figure by the gate. She turned on the path. I saw the arm come up, bearing the heavy pistol. The first shot splintered the door frame. I just stood there, numb.

I reached into my holster for the pistol and drew it. The second shot she fired struck the flesh of my left arm like a hot iron.

The force of the impact nearly spun me around. I could see the doctor crouched in the doorway, uncertain what to do. I faced her again. She had her pistol pointed at me and I could see a wisp of smoke curling upward from the barrel in the hot, still evening air. I sighted down my right arm, pulled the trigger, and saw her collapse. I turned away, and stumbled back into the building. The doctor helped me into his room. He ripped my shirt away from the wound. It burned fiercely.

The doctor gave me a narcotic, and I became unconscious.

CHAPTER THIRTY ONE

Deep Sleep

I t was nearly midday before I awakened, and the pain in my arm throbbed. It was wrapped tightly. The doctor stood at the foot of the bed. He looked terrible.

"Fortunately, it's only a flesh wound. Should heal fast." I couldn't speak. I motioned to the water pitcher. He poured me a glass. I sipped it carefully.

"Do you have any whiskey?" The doctor left the room and returned with a bottle. He poured a large drink into the glass. It burned, but I managed to get it all down.

"Did she get away?"

"She's dead," the doctor said softly. I was not surprised.

"I didn't mean to kill her," I said.

"You didn't," he said. "She died of blood poisoning. That's what I put on the death certificate."

I was stunned. I pulled myself off the bed, and padded to the open window, through which a slight breeze was blowing.

"You missed her. She must have collapsed from the strain. She was ill. I warned her. She died during the night. There was nothing I could do," the doctor said.

I saw the old black man digging in the yard. There were two figures wrapped in blankets nearby. "We're burying her—with the others," the doctor said.

"You say I didn't shoot her?" I turned to the doctor. He looked haggard.

"When she came here she had lost a lot of blood," the doctor said. "She had an abortion, somewhere in town."

He didn't look happy, his worn face was creased by fatigue. "This time she was alone. Before, when I first examined her, she was with a large red-haired woman at the hotel. I saw that she had a pistol in her bag. I asked why and she said she was bothered by some of the soldiers and needed protection. I didn't think anything of it then." He stood with his back to the sunshine flooding the small room, as if recalling the scene in another room off the same hall.

"I told her that from the looks of her, ah, it wasn't her first, ah, abortion. She told me that it was none of my business.

The doctor sighed. "I told her she ought to stay another few days. She said she had to get to New York, and that she had decided to move back to the hotel.

"Then she said that I must not tell anyone what had happened to her, under any circumstances. I told her that my oath kept my patients privacy, but she didn't seem satisfied with that."

The doctor had become a witness. No wonder she showed up with a pistol. "So I shot and killed her, from the doorway," 1 said.

"No. She died of a hemorrhage. You can go check, if you want." He leaned against the wall. He seemed close to collapse.

So was I. I staggered back to the bed. He helped me

into it. There was no possible way I could get downstairs and check the corpse. I didn't want to see that body again, ever. I would have to take the doctor's word for it.

"I think I knew something was wrong when I first treated her. Why did she come here again yesterday?"

"To kill you," I muttered. The doctor stood silently by the bed, and absorbed what I told him.

"Well," he said after a few moments. "There's not much I could have done against that. I suppose your appearance in the room interrupted her?"

I nodded.

"Well, she's dead. I don't see the sense of going to the authorities about it now," he added. I nodded again, and drifted off into a deep opium sleep.

When I awoke, about three hours later, there was a vaguely grinning and familiar figure by the bed. I could not at first place the face. Then the hat gave him away. Only a New York detective would wear his hat in a hospital room.

Detective Rooney looked tired, as if he had traveled hundreds of miles with little sleep.

"They tell me that you're the war hero now," he said in a lilting brogue.

My head felt stuffed. My tongue was thick. I reached around to a glass of water on the bedside table. It was warm and flat. I would have given a year's pay for a cold glass of beer.

"I could use a schooner of draft," I croaked. Detective Rooney laughed.

He pulled up a chair and sat. He stared at me, his eyes showing amusement.

"The doctor here," he waved toward the door, "tells me that you two have closed my case for me."

I wondered what in hell he had been talking about.

"What?" I asked brilliantly.

"Hampton. Dead. Case closed."

"Why are you here?" I asked.

"Well," he said, unbuttoning his wool suit coat. "I would have been here sooner, after I got Mr. Davis' telegram. But, with one thing and another It wasn't easy to convince the Department that I should come to Florida. I had another case in Manhattan, and when that was finished, why Tammany decided that, yes, the Lawlor murder required my checking out all the leads."

"Dick Davis telegraphed you about Annie?" I asked.

"Indeed he did. Told us about her presence, and her alleged assault on a friend of his. You wouldn't know who that would be, would you?" He smiled wider.

"She tried to kill me. Shot at me on a pier. I fell into the water."

"Well, then. She didn't pump a bullet into you, eh? Left that to the Spaniards?"

I could not tell if he was mocking me, or just making conversation. I did not much care. I was beyond caring. I was alive.

"Yeah. The Spaniards shot me. I don't know which one, and I'll never find out now. Doesn't make a difference. She's dead. Doctor says she died of a hemorrhage."

"Yeah. That's what he told me."

"She shot at me, dammit. Hit me, too. Here in the arm. That's why I can't move." I studied Rooney a long minute.

"What the hell do you want?" I asked.

He stood. His face sobered. "Nothing, pally. You've taken care of my business. She's dead. Your pal Dick Davis thought I could come down here and catch her in the act of shooting her next lover, or some other victim. Doesn't work that way. We always show up after the body is cold. Not much fun, I'm afraid.

"The Department will jump all over me for the expense of this trip, but what the hell? Tammany will love it when I tell them that she's where she belongs. I may embellish the report a bit, say, how about I tell them she was put in the ground by a stalwart Democrat who knew she was up to no good."

"Go to hell, Rooney," I said.

"I thought I was already here, as hot as it is," he said softly.

"Let me give you a bit of advice, pally, " Rooney added. "When you get back to New York, a war hero and all, stick with the good girls, huh? The other kind are no good," he said in a growl.

At the door he stopped, turned, and in a voice that was more sincere than in our former bantering conversation, he said,

"I would have been here sooner. Maybe it would have helped. Maybe I would have frightened her off. But the damn war has the railroads in a holy mess. Not even Tammany could get me south of Richmond." He laughed. "I guess Richmond is about as far as Tammany influence goes. Take care of yourself, pally."

CHAPTER THIRTY TWO

Goddam War

I t was September when we got back. I was not aware of the month or the day. I was confused. War had been declared in April, after months of drum rolls, which I helped direct. May and June were given to the so-called training of the army. By late June the New York papers were calling for invasion. In July we went into Cuba, and by August, when I was in the hospital, it was all over. August was a blur, except what I've reported here. The war was over practically after it had begun, and that was a miracle.

The stench of death was creeping up the American continent from the war zone, and it was something the American public had not smelled since the gore of 1865. It was not something that could have been continued indefinitely. The headlong rush to war, which I acknowledge my part, was like a drunk falling downstairs. I used that analogy later on when someone would mention the war. Not many did, afterward.

Richard Davis came back to New York with his profile pointed toward Europe. Crane returned to face more professional problems. Even Roosevelt admitted in the public prints that the army could not have withstood a prolonged campaign in Cuba, because of rotten food and illness.

For in truth, a burning burden I will always carry with me, was that fewer men died of Spanish bullets than they did of the fever. Pine boxes carried the victims back to Minnesota, and Buffalo, and Sacramento, and no one spoke up to ask why. A few had in the beginning, but they were roundly shouted down in the newspapers, and made to look unpatriotic.

I was soon hustled into Hearst's office, where the Chief sat with his feet on his desk, reading newspaper clippings, and with newspaper pages strewn over the floor.

"Botwright," he yelped, and jumped to his feet. I felt a twinge of pain in my stomach, and arm. I sat down in the nearest chair.

"I've come for my pay," I said through the pain, Hearst, meanwhile, was practically dancing around the room with joy. He yelled through his door for the paymaster. "What happened to you? We thought you had died in Florida."

"Mr. Hearst, do you want to know what happened? I'll tell you what happened. I almost got killed in your goddam war." The room went silent.

"Yes," I yelled. "Your goddam war. I was shot. Then they put me in a hospital in Tampa, where everyone was dying of Yellow Fever. Then your mistress tried to shoot me to death, like she has done to all her other lovers. You were lucky to escape with your skin.

"I have seen enough death to last me a lifetime." It poured out of me, the confusion, the foolishness, the death under palms, and the staring at freshly-dug graves where pitiful corpses were dropped into the red earth holes without as much as a prayer.

Hearst sat back and listened to my tirade without a word. The paymaster entered the office. The Chief waved him to a chair. I finished, worn and embarrassed. Willie looked at me mournfully.

"You must write all this for Sunday," Hearst said, with a nod toward Goddard's department. "And, as for afterward, what do you want to do?"

I misunderstood the question.

"I want to get married, and get out of this asylum for as long as I can."

Hearst slammed the desk. "You shall have it. By God, sir, you shall have it. How much do I owe Mr. Botwright?" he roared at the nervous paymaster. The paymaster said about $1,500.

"Double it, and see that Mr. Botwright gets it in cash Or a check, as, he wants." The paymaster scrambled out of the office. The sudden windfall didn't surprise me. Hearst was open fisted to a fault. He stood, and extended his hand. "Mr. Botwright, I've done you a disservice. For a moment, an angry moment, I thought you were disloyal. I know now that you were acting out of the highest loyalty that a publisher and editor could ask. I count myself fortunate to know you, sir."

I was embarrassed. I couldn't very well not shake hands. I took his, and winced as he gave it hearty shakes.

Hearst beamed. Then his face clouded.

"There is the matter of the dynamite, too. You didn't really believe that I was capable of exploding an American warship, did you?" Hearst asked.

"Mr. Hearst all I knew then was the evidence and statements told me."

"Well, you can rest assured that I am nothing if not

an American," Mr. Hearst whispered emotionally. He didn't deny it was his dynamite.

"I had no knowledge of what they did with the dynamite. The Maine, I believe, was sunk with underwater torpedoes. Spanish torpedoes, Mr. Botwright," he said emphatically.

That day I was a hero at The Journal. Two days later I finished the article for Sunday about the Tampa hospital, and took it around to Goddard.

"This is the stuff, Jim," he said. He had it illustrated with a large drawing of a hospital ward showing patients writhing in pain. Of course, it wasn't actually like that. The article was not complimentary to the War Department. I pointed out the mistakes, poor planning and the death and suffering.

The army released Hilda a few days later. Her father and I met her at the Grand Central Station. She was thinner. The war had taken its toll everywhere. It angered me, but the joy of seeing her pushed all other thoughts out of mind.

I escorted them home, and before I left, I asked Rev. Reiser if I could call on him in two days "on a matter of Hilda's future." He smiled, and nodded.

That Saturday evening I arrived at 8 p.m., and found that Hilda had prepared a large dinner. I offered a toast to all our health.

"Tell us about the war," Hilda asked. I wondered if she really wanted to hear about it. I put my fork down, and told them about the mess in Florida before the invasion, and what I had seen on the island. I spoke of my wound. Hilda became alarmed. I quickly glossed over the incident, explaining that it was a minor wound.

Rev. Reiser asked the pointed question, "Have they discovered yet what sank the Maine?"

"No," I said. "But I think the Cuban insurrectos sank

the ship on purpose, using dynamite that was supplied them." The clergyman was stunned. "Surely that can't be true," he said.

"We'll never know until the ship is raised," I said. I never understood why it took nearly ten years to bring the hulk out of the harbor mud. When they did, the wreckage showed that the hull was rent by an interior blast. The steel plates were bent outward. But, by that time it was old news.

That evening I interrupted the dessert to ask Rev. Reiser for his daughter's hand. He smiled at us.

"It's up to her," he said, adding, that it was opinion for some time that we were headed for the altar. Hilda reddened and remained silent.

"I guess I'm out of luck, then, because Hilda hasn't said anything," I quipped.

"I have a lot to say," she said, "but I'm pleased to accept your offer."

We spent the remainder of the evening in the quiet of the house, talking about the war, the newspapers, and the country.

"Will you leave the newspaper now?" Rev. Reiser asked.

"No," Hilda said. "He will stay and do good. Nothing is accomplished by leaving." And, that's the way it happened.

Up to the wedding ceremony she repeatedly made me tell her about my wound. On our wedding trip, however, I was caught between my remarks and the clear fact that I had two wounds on my body.

We were in a Philadelphia hotel room, and I was forced into a decision—to lie, or to tell her the truth. Or a measure of the truth. I wondered for a moment what would be gained by telling the truth.

Could I tell my wife that a beautiful woman had shot me in the arm, and that she had tried to kill me before? Could I tell her that I had raised my pistol and shot at that woman? Or that the woman had subsequently died, of hemorrhage, the doctor said.

"No, my dear, This wound I got in a hunting accident in the Berkshires many years ago, when I was still in school."

"How is it you haven't spoken of it before?" she asked perceptively.

I mumbled an answer. Annie would stay dead.

We returned to a snowy New York. It was almost 1899 and everyone was excited about the coming new century.

"They'll be so many good things, " Hilda said. "And so many sicknesses will be cured. So many miracles."

But not much had changed in the short time since I had returned from Cuba.

I felt like I had come back from the dead. Death had kissed me in Cuba, and death had surrounded me in the Florida hospital. When I thought of Annie, and I did often, I decided that I had been wrong in the way I had treated her. I should have told the police what I knew. I should have shot her with a pistol when I first saw her with Hearst in Florida, and claimed that it was an accident. That's what I told myself.

Then I told myself the truth—that I had let her escape. There was no way around it. She had tried to kill me once, and I didn't do anything about it. I felt better when I recalled what the doctor had said—that she died of blood poisoning. He had told me about the abortion, and that explained everything.

The world spun a few times, and it was all over. No one wanted to hear anymore about the war. It was swiftly forgotten. The Dutchman came home to Long Island, where he landed with the Volunteers in August. Within a few months Roosevelt was running for governor of New York State, the most popular figure in America, and on every campaign platform he used uniformed Rough Riders. But that was the extent of public interest in a war that no one wanted to hear about. Crane pushed and got a publisher to get up an edition of his expanded stories from Cuba. It was excellent, but it didn't sell. Dick Davis looked around the world for his next war. He knew he had to keep on the move.

"Let's roam," Davis said to me one night.

"No, Dick. I've decided that I like New York too much." I said it with conviction. I had changed.

The war was over. A peace treaty was about to be signed. Hearst was not upset by my criticism. Post-war criticism, I have learned, is more acceptable than carping before the first gun is fired. The hospital story caused another sensation. Too many families had suffered loss in the short, merry little war. Two congressional committees were formed to investigate the conduct of the military medical department. I went to Washington to appear before one before my wedding. It wasn't a satisfying experience to testify. I left the committees with long lists of witnesses each could call, but they never did.

We traveled for six months in Europe. It was a working trip. Every week or so I sent Goddard a piece about a city, or a country. We spent a week in England with Crane, and although I was happy to see him again, it was not a pleasant time. He and his Cora lived in a strange little house in a London suburb.

I didn't care for the place, and told Steve that he belonged in New York. I argued with him over it. But I didn't convince him. He was ill and we all knew it. Crane looked ill, but that didn't stop him from drinking too much. Cora told me privately that they needed money. I gave her some, with orders not to tell Steve.

"Get away from Hearst," Steve told me one night after dinner. "You'll waste all your energy on his work, and you'll have none for your own work. That life is only for the young and innocent. I don't intend to go to any more wars.

Dick Davis can have a monopoly on that industry. I haven't got a lot of time, and I want to make the most of it."

A year later Steve died of tuberculosis. It was a week afterward before I got the news. There was nothing I could do then. Crane had become a popular author, hailed by the very newspapers and editors who had scoffed at him when he was alive.

CHAPTER THIRTY THREE

Washington—June 22, 1906

The White House looked little changed from the visit Crane and I had made on McKinley years before. Dick Davis and I had drinks in a large ballroom. with a gathering of about a hundred men. Some wore old and faded khaki. Most were in dinner clothes, which Dick and I wore. One man wore a blue polka-dot kerchief around his neck, and I noticed that the President, now fatter than in his warrior days, was handing out the scarfs to the socialites in the group around him. I had noticed few if any genuine cowboys in the crowd. Those Rough Riders were no doubt working now in Oregon logging camps, or riding the range in Wyoming, and had little wherewithal to make the long train ride to Washington.

The Dutchman bounded up to Dick, hand outstretched. "Evening, Mr. President," Davis said. I nodded.

"Glad you could come. Why, you two are about

the only honorary Rough Riders in the world. An honor."
Teddy hung the white-spotted blue scarfs around our necks.

"Don't you wish you were back on Kettle Hill?" he
boomed. A circle of ex-volunteers surrounded us.

"Not really," I said.

"What?" Roosevelt yelped.

"I was shot and nearly killed on that ridge in Las
Guasimas, and before it rains my scar itches. I hated
every minute of it. It was an idiotic war." Dick laughed. I
was serious.

Roosevelt puffed out with irritation. "What the hell are
you saying, Botwright? It was a bully war. It was the best
war we ever fought."

"Mr. President, I said, "it was a stupid, unnecessary war
in which I almost got killed. I'm sorry now I had anything
to do with it." There was some angry muttering from the
socialites around me. I didn't care.

TR looked at me closely through his pince-nez. His
small pig's eyes enlarged by the lenses. He grew red.

"Why, damm you. Many good men died on those hills,"
Roosevelt sputtered. I raised my glass.

"And I'll drink an honest toast to the memory of
those good men who died there. But, the war was unnecessary." The mumbled "hear-hear" and the clink of the
glasses drowned out my last remark. Roosevelt, usually
the most composed of men looked perplexed. He was not
experienced in dealing face to face with another view.
He turned from us, and barked, "Well, boys, let's go eat."
He marched off, leading the hungry crowd into the state
dining room.

Dick clamped his strong left arm through my right.

"You'll never convince him," he said softly. "Teddy
believes it was all a lark. You've just angered him." The
remainder of the dinner was a blur to me. I drank too
much wine, but I managed to remain silent during the

after dinner speeches which hailed Warrior Teddy and his fallen comrades.

Afterward, in the light of a crackling hangover, I realized that I had told off the two men—Hearst and Roosevelt, whom I most blamed for the war, and it had meant nothing.

Hearst wasn't at all bothered by my anger, and Roosevelt wouldn't listen. The war was history, and no one cared. Few wanted to remember it. The national memory made the war fade faster than normal.

"I know the reason," I told Davis on the train back to New York. "The country senses that it was an unfair war, a made-up war, and the public is ashamed of what happened. Men died for land we could have bought at distress prices from the Spanish. It was all so unnecessary, and that's why the war has faded. We have become an imperial nation, just like England, but no one wants to admit it. We have our colonies now. Cuba, where the nationalists are still seething, and Puerto Rico, which no one seems to know what to do with, and the Philippines, where we have told the people they'd better love us, or they won't get their freedom in about fifty years."

Dick didn't disagree. He nodded. "Can't stop history," he said.

Epilogue

Chapin of The Evening World was convicted in 1919 of murdering his wife in their hotel suite. Chapin was sentenced to life in Sing Sing Prison, where he became a model prisoner, making flowers grow in barren prison yards.

Joe Pulitzer gave up the newspaper war with Hearst after the Spanish-American War. Hearst was clearly the winner, and both men had been drained of millions. Pulitzer turned his papers back to more respectable journalism. He died in 1911. His New York papers died in 1931.

Willie Hearst became a national publisher and lived in California until his death in 1951. He became a legend, but for reasons not of his making. He was a failed Presidential aspirant.

Steve Crane returned to England, and his woman, Cora. He wrote hurriedly of his war experiences to make expenses. But soon he died of tuberculosis. A stone marks his grave in New Jersey. Scholars rank him the first of the 20th Century's new wave of writers.

Ambrose Bierce returned to work for Hearst in San

Francisco. He disappeared in Mexico in 1914, where he went to cover the revolution.

Henry Lee became a Guards colonel, and died on the Western Front in 1918, shortly before the end of the war.

Winston Churchill became First Lord of the Admiralty, and repeatedly, the Prime Minister of Great Britain.

Evangelina Cisneros returned to Havana after the American occupation. She married a Cuban lawyer, had three sons, and died a grandmother seven times over in 1935.

Manual Sanchez was appointed an official in the new Cuban government in 1899. He was shot in 1916 when another revolution ousted the government.

Theodore Roosevelt returned from the war to become in short order, governor of New York, Vice President of the United States, and President. In 1917 Roosevelt tried to raise his own army division to take to France. President Woodrow Wilson refused the suggestion, on the advice of General Pershing. Roosevelt died in 1919, the most popular politician of his generation. Pershing returned that year a war hero.

Leonard Wood became a general, governor of Cuba, and The Philippines, and when he tried to become a combat unit commander in World War I he came no closer than Kansas to France. General Pershing didn't want Wood in his command.

Frank Collins rose to be a vice president in the Standard Oil Co., and he had eight children, one of whom became a U.S. senator. He retired to Palm Beach, Florida, in 1926, and died there in 1930.

Richard Harding Davis gained more public acclaim for his coverage of the Boer War, the Russo-Japanese War, and finally, the Great War of 1914. He married, and after some years, was divorced. He remarried, a stage comedy actress, and the couple had a daughter.

Davis wrote some of the best war reportage in the Great War, and by 1916 he was convinced that the United States was unprepared for its eventual role in the war. He, in late middle age, embarked on a training programs for college youths. That year, incensed at a political remark made by a labor agitator, he collapsed and died at his home in Mount Kisco, N.Y.

James C. Botwright wrote Davis' obituary for the New York Journal. It ran to 16 pages, and Mr. Botwright wrote that, "Whether for a Broadway opening, or a disagreeable, dirty little war, Mr. Davis was always correctly dressed as befits the gentleman he was." Mr. Botwright became Sunday editor of The Journal, and in 1919 left the paper to produce motion pictures in California. He returned to Pittsfield, Mass., in 1930, where he established a weekly newspaper. He died in 1949. Mrs. Hilda Botwright died there in 1953.

Annie Hampton's remains were accidently overlooked when officials reburied fever victims in 1902 in Tampa. The hospital was expanded, and used until 1995, when construction began for a medical center on the site. An earthmover exposed part of a skeleton, and the authorities became involved, and the local newspaper picked up the story. The medical examiner performed a detailed study of the bones, and the paper had a second-day story when the pathologist announced he believed that the partial skeleton was that of a woman and that the victim had shot once in the head. It has been an open homicide case ever since.

YELLOW FEVER was designed by Christina Scott, Tom Suzuki, Inc., Falls Church, Virginia. Cover design is also by Christina Scott. The book was printed by Lightning Print Inc., La Vergne, Tennessee.

The text is set 11 on 13 Goudy.